REUNION

DI KATE FLETCHER BOOK 4

HELEYNE HAMMERSLEY

Print ISBN 978-1-913419-34-9

ALSO BY HELEYNE HAMMERSLEY

...for Graeme

PROLOGUE

Dusty looked up as the door opened, allowing the bright light from the floodlit car park to pierce the pub's gloomy interior. She'd been among the first to arrive and had worked hard to avoid getting too caught up in the conversations of people that she barely remembered and had nothing in common with. She was here for only one reason – to see the other two. The announcement on the local newspaper's website had seemed like fate.

She'd not been back to Thorpe since she'd left for university in 1995 and, even before that, she'd not spoken to Lucky and Ned for seven years. Not since they'd left Sheffield Road Junior School in 1988 and gone their separate ways – Lucky to the Catholic school, Ned to Thorpe Comp and herself to the ex-grammar school in the next town which offered the best chance of the decent A-level results which would be her ticket out of South Yorkshire.

At first she'd missed her two best friends, but she'd promised her parents that she'd work hard and not let them down, so she'd thrown herself into her studies.

Her mum and dad were pleased with her and they thought

1

she was happy. They'd never found out about the razor blades that she kept wrapped in tissue in the hollow base of her bed. They never knew about the time she'd got so drunk that her friends had panicked and called an ambulance – only to send it away after she became hysterical when one of the crew had tried to loosen her top to allow her to breathe more easily.

It hadn't been easy, coming back, and she knew that facing the other two was going to take all the strength that she could muster, but it was something that had to be done. Their meeting again was as inevitable as if they'd sliced open their palms and sworn on each other's blood.

The person coming through the door wasn't familiar. It could have been any one of the boys that had teased her all the way through her early years at school for her gangly limbs and unruly dark hair, but it wasn't Ned or Lucky. They'd come, though. She knew it as certainly as she knew her own name. It was time.

1

'Mrs Tsappis?'

Kate was vaguely aware of a voice calling from reception as she stuffed her packed lunch into her walking bag. She and Nick had a full day's walk planned on the Langdale fells and she was lost in thought, wondering if she'd ordered enough food from reception the previous evening.

'Mrs Tsappis?'

The name suddenly registered, and Kate turned to Nick who was checking the straps on his rucksack, a look of mock-innocence barely concealing his grin.

Kate marched back to the reception desk. 'Yes?' she demanded, unable to conceal the irritation in her voice.

'Your hat.' The woman held out Kate's insulated beanie.

Kate managed a smile and grabbed the errant garment with a mumble of appreciation.

'What the hell was that?' she asked Nick as they approached the car park. He'd insisted that they drive up to Cumbria from Doncaster in his Mercedes after months of complaints about having to fold himself in half to get into Kate's Mini.

'What?'

'The woman on reception calling me Mrs Tsappis. What was that all about?'

'She must have assumed that we're married,' Nick said. 'The room's booked in my name so it's an obvious mistake to make.'

Kate wasn't convinced. There was something in Nick's expression suggesting that he'd either done nothing to disabuse the receptionist of her error or that he'd actually encouraged the assumption that Kate was his wife.

'What should I have done? I could have booked in both our names I suppose but that seems a bit long-winded. Or maybe I should have announced us with a calling card. Doctor Tsappis and Detective Inspector Fletcher.'

Now Kate knew that he wasn't serious. One of the things she liked about Nick, apart from his dark good looks, was his inability to take himself seriously for too long. They'd been seeing each other for nearly a year – ever since Kate had met him on a previous case – and she was yet to tire of his daft sense of humour.

'You never call yourself *doctor*. I thought it was a mark of your seniority that you use mister. I never really got that though. Surely it's a demotion.' She opened the rear door of the car and threw her rucksack onto the back seat. She wasn't even sure why she minded; except that she wasn't ready to change her name again. Once was enough and she'd never even thought about going back to her maiden name after she'd finally divorced Garry five years earlier.

Slipping into the passenger seat, she clipped on her seat belt and grabbed Nick's upper thigh, enjoying the firm feel of the muscles. 'You never know, I might surprise you one day and actually answer to Mrs Tsappis.'

Nick shook his head as he turned the key in the ignition. 'It'll never happen. It'll be Detective Inspector Tsappis.'

'Hey!' Kate rebuked him by squeezing more tightly. 'That'll be Detective *Chief* Inspector Tsappis.'

The windscreen wipers seemed to be making better progress against the drizzle as Nick turned onto the road which led deep into Langdale and, as they passed through Elterwater, a muted scraping against the glass announced that the rain had completely stopped.

Kate gazed out at the landscape noting familiar landmarks from her past life in Cumbria. The cloud was lifting slightly as they meandered through Chapel Stile and it had left cotton wool-like clumps nestled in the bracken-brown corries and gullies of the mountains. Kate had been the first to admit that the end of November probably wasn't the best time of year in the Lakes but, as usual, it had been difficult to tear herself away from work and from the effects of a recent case on some members of her team.

Two of her DCs, Hollis and Cooper, had been deeply affected in different ways; Cooper was still trying to shrug off the memories of an assault that had put her in hospital and Hollis was grappling with psychological issues related to the return of his biological mother. Kate felt for them both and had done everything she could think of to integrate them back into the job as smoothly as possible.

Now, with a brutal murderer awaiting trial and an unusually light case load, she was glad that she'd booked some leave and had no regrets about taking her first trip with Nick. Even if it was to the Lakes in November.

'It's stunning,' Nick breathed, lowering his head and leaning forward so that he could get a better view of the mountains that were starting to dominate the skyline as they travelled deeper into the valley.

Kate had to agree. Autumn had been exceptionally wet in Cumbria – not as bad as the 2009 floods or Storm Desmond in 2015 – but the Windermere ferry had been cancelled due to high water levels and there were reports of minor flooding on some roads. The becks, cascading down from their sources high above the road, were full and furious.

'This it?' Nick asked, slowing down so that he could read the roadside signs.

'Yep. Turn right into the car park. We head up that path there,' she said, pointing to a scar of erosion beside Stickle Beck. 'Sunset is at fourish so we should have enough time to get back before dark.'

Nick pulled into a space close to the start of the path and they spent a few minutes tightening laces and checking the contents of their rucksacks before finally heading off up the path aiming for their first break at Stickle Tarn.

It had been a great day. After the early mist and drizzle the cloud had gradually parted until, by late morning, they'd been walking in full sunlight. As they trudged wearily back towards the Old Dungeon Ghyll Hotel, Kate noticed, with some satisfaction, that Nick seemed to be as tired as she felt. Those snatched hours in the gym at Doncaster Central Police Headquarters had paid off after all if she'd managed to match his fitness.

Just as they approached the first gate across the valley track, Kate noticed two walkers ahead of them on the path. They'd stopped and seemed to be looking at something off to their left, slightly up the hillside. Curiosity piqued, Kate picked up her pace to see what had caught their attention.

They were an elderly couple, probably in their mid-seventies. The man had a thick shock of grey hair exploding from beneath his dark red woollen hat which had a home-made look to it. He was much taller than his companion and seemed to be concerned about her as he wrapped an arm round her shoulders, oblivious to Kate and Nick's approach. His wife was petite, and Kate couldn't see much of her face as it was buried in her husband's shoulder. In the gathering dusk it was hard to make out where one person began and the other ended as their matching blue waterproof jackets seemed to meld together.

'Everything all right?' Kate asked.

The woman's face turned towards her, pale and frightened. 'Not really...' she began.

'Up there,' the husband took over. 'We were just on our way back to the car park and Eileen saw something moving up on the hillside. Turned out to be a few Herdwicks mooching about but they set off a bit of a gravel slide and that's when we saw him.'

Kate followed the direction of the man's outstretched finger and could make out something red about fifty yards up the slope.

'Him?'

'Alec went to investigate,' the woman said. 'He told me to wait here and I'm glad he did.'

'It's a body,' the man confirmed. 'Looks like a walker had a fall. Rain probably washed him down the gully and the sheep must've disturbed the body when they went across.'

'You say it's a male?' Kate asked.

'Looks like it. I think I could make out a beard. I didn't want to get too close and it looks like he might have been out there for a while. One of the hands looks like it's a bit decomposed.'

His wife flinched slightly at his choice of adjective.

'Obviously we were going to call the police but there's no

signal here. We'd just decided that we'd both go back to the Old Dungeon Ghyll when you two turned up.'

He looked hopefully from Kate to Nick, obviously seeking guidance. 'I didn't want to leave the body there in case somebody else came along and got a shock but there didn't seem to be anything else that we could do.'

The man was starting to ramble, his eyes glassy, cheeks a hectic red. Kate recognised the first signs of shock setting in and realised that she needed to get these people out of the cold and get a hot drink inside them. She cast another look up towards the body. Even in the fading light, the patch of red was obvious and might attract the attention of other passers-by. The man was right – no need to inflict that on anybody else.

She turned to Nick who had been standing slightly behind her during the exchange. He'd allowed her to take charge, she realised, and hadn't interrupted as the man had told his story.

'This is Nick,' she told the couple. 'He's a doctor. He's going to walk with you back to the hotel. When you get there, have a hot drink or a stiff whisky, whichever you prefer. Nick's going to ring the police and they'll want to talk to you both. Where are you staying?'

The man explained that they were at a cottage in Elterwater, but their car was parked in the car park next to the hotel.

'That's fine,' Kate reassured him. 'Just wait for the police. If you don't feel up to driving, I'm sure they can arrange a lift back to your cottage.'

The woman, who introduced herself as Eileen Caldwell, seemed to have gained control of her emotions now that she could see that there was a plan in place. She stepped away from her husband and looked at Kate. 'You're going to stay here by yourself?' she said, concern evident in the lines of her frown.

'I'm going to have a look at the body,' Kate explained. 'It'll be dark soon and the police are going to need as much information as possible. If I can get a good look while there's still some light, I might be able to help.'

'Is that wise, dear?' the woman asked. 'From what Alec said, it's not a pleasant sight.'

'I'm a police officer,' Kate said. 'I appreciate your concern, but I honestly know what I'm doing.'

'She's a detective inspector,' Nick said, and Kate was surprised by the note of pride in his voice. 'Trust me, she's seen much worse.'

Apparently convinced, the couple allowed Nick to shepherd them along the track. Kate waited until they were out of sight before rummaging in her bag for a head torch and setting off across the hillside. The going was trickier than it had looked from below. Dead bracken threatened to trip her up every few steps and, hidden beneath the brown fronds, rocks and stones promised a turned ankle if she put her foot in the wrong place. As she drew level with the body, she glanced up at the gully above. A dark slash into the mountain, it looked like the entrance to a Tolkienesque underworld, the stream it contained set deep within its walls.

She could see just above her where the sheep had disturbed a bank of scree causing the mini avalanche of stones which must have released the body and allowed it to travel down to its current resting place, lodged next to a huge moss-covered boulder. Kate switched on her torch and tried to make out details. From the waterproof leggings and Gore-Tex jacket it was difficult to determine gender although the bulk contained inside the weather-proof clothing strongly suggested a male.

Kate scanned the torch along one outstretched arm looking for the detail that the elderly man, Alec, had shared with his wife; the decomposed hand. She was no pathologist, but it might suggest roughly how long the body had been lying on the fells. The clothing would have protected his legs and torso and she presumed that his feet were encased in boots, but the hands and face would have been a huge temptation to rodents and crows.

In the light of her torch she could see fingers, stretched out as though he'd been trying to haul himself out of the gully and, as Alec had suggested, they were a greenish colour. She adjusted the beam of her torch to get a closer look and realised that he'd been mistaken. The green wasn't decomposition, it was a glove. The body wasn't necessarily as decayed as she'd been led to believe.

She shifted position, trying to angle the torch towards where the face should be, looking for the beard that had been suggested, but the beam cast shadows and it was hard to make out exactly what she was seeing. She slipped and stumbled as she clambered round the restraining boulder for a better view. Finally, she managed to train the light on a mop of dark hair and, as described, a thick black beard. A man then.

Kate angled the torch beam away, thinking about heading back down to the track, but something about the face caught her attention as the shadows shifted. She took a step closer, her brain struggling to make sense of what she was seeing. It couldn't be. It must be a trick of the light. She tried a different angle and suddenly she saw the face clearly.

Had she known this man?

JULY 1988

The Three Amigos sat on the low brick wall that bounded two sides of the school field and surveyed their kingdom. Eleven years old, they felt like they knew everything and could do anything. Strikingly different in appearance, like a sepia colour scale – Dusty very dark, Ned with his mid-brown mullet and Lucky's blond hair so fair it was almost translucent in the sunlight – they'd bonded over a love for the cinema and a shared disdain for the other students.

The trio had already eaten their sandwiches, swapping jam for salmon paste and corned beef as was their custom, and now they were discussing the greatest event of their school career so far. The early summer sun had already baked the winter mud patches and dust plumed in the warm air as games of football and tiggy raged in different corners of the school grounds. The wall gave them a vantage point from which they could see across the field and the playground, and into the tall window of the school staffroom. Most of the time they liked to watch the teachers and try to guess what they were talking about, but they had much more pressing matters to discuss in the limited time that they had before lessons started again.

'Do you think everybody in our class will go?' Dusty asked the other two.

'I bet Jamesy doesn't,' Lucky responded. 'His mummy won't let him.' Ned snorted derisorily. Aaron James's attachment to his mother was legendary at Sheffield Road and the bullying that the lad had been forced to endure had been low level but relentless for the past three years – ever since his mum had stormed onto the school field one sports day and demanded that he stop running so fast in case it made him wheezy.

The amigos hadn't really joined in with the taunting though – not after the initial hilarity of nicknaming him 'Wheezy'. It wasn't really their thing. They liked to think of themselves as being above the general hubbub of school life and, even before they'd seen the film which had given rise to their nicknames, they'd preferred each other's company to that of any of the other kids at school.

'Will your mam be able to pay for you?' Lucky asked Ned. Dusty frowned at him and shook her head sharply, warning him not to remind their friend about his fatherless status and his mother's lack of funds. Fiercely protective of each other, they were loyal enough to be able to talk about anything, but Dusty didn't believe that meant that they necessarily *should* discuss each other's problems unless invited.

'Doesn't matter,' Ned said. 'Mr Whitaker said that there was a special school fund to help kids whose parents don't have much money. School might pay for me and I can just ask my mam for a bit of spending money.'

The other two nodded, accepting Ned's matter-of-fact approach to charity in the same way that they accepted Lucky's Catholic faith and Dusty's gender.

'I don't think we'll need much spending money,' Dusty said. 'The campsite's in the middle of nowhere. There won't be shops and stuff.'

'We might be able to sneak off though and find some.'

Dusty laughed at their naivety. 'It's Derbyshire. There's nothing there but grass and sheep. The shops'll all be miles away from where we're staying.'

They sat for a while contemplating the idea of camping in a field in the wilds of a county that none of them had visited before even though it formed a border with South Yorkshire only a few miles outside Sheffield.

Mr Whitaker had announced the planned trip in the fourth-year assembly, and it had taken him a couple of minutes to get the students to settle down, such was the excitement. He hadn't given them any specifics but the promise of a few days off school as a fitting end to their time at Sheffield Road Juniors was enough to fire the imagination of every child in the school hall.

'You ever been camping?' Lucky asked.

Ned shook his head but Dusty was keen to share her knowledge. 'We rented next door's caravan at Bridlington for a week last six-week-holidays. It wasn't camping but we were on a campsite and had to use the toilets with everybody else.'

'That's not the same,' Lucky said. 'I went on a Catholic camp with the church two years ago with our Ian. It was brill. We shared this little tent and slept on my nan's airbed. Our Ian kept farting all night though. I thought we were going to take off and float round the campsite like a hovercraft.'

The other two collapsed in a fit of giggles, Ned making farting noises between gasps of laughter.

'I hope I don't have to share with anybody farty,' Dusty said.

'No. You can share with us,' Lucky said, and then realised his mistake. Dusty's gender wasn't an issue for the two boys but they were aware, as they got older, that it was an issue for other people. During their last year of juniors there had been a lot of talk amongst the other kids of boyfriends and girlfriends and Dusty had been the butt of a few snide comments from other girls. Not that she shared much of this with the other two – it would only highlight the difference.

'She won't be allowed,' Ned said. 'She'll have to share with one of the other lasses.'

The three contemplated this injustice in silence for a few minutes.

Dusty dismissed the topic. 'Well, it'll only be the nights and we'll all be asleep anyway.'

'I'm not going to sleep,' Lucky said. 'I'm going to sneak out at night and have a wander round.'

'What for?' Dusty wanted to know.

'Dunno. Just to see what it's like.'

'And then you'll get shit-scared and come running back to the tent,' Ned said with a laugh. Lucky gave him a big grin of acknowledgement. He wasn't the bravest of the three by any stretch of the imagination. He wasn't even the second bravest.

They spent the remainder of the lunch hour lost in their plans for the camping trip and the tricks that they were going to play on the teachers. By the time the bell rang for lessons, they felt ready to conquer the world.

The camping trip was important for another, less exciting reason. None of the three wanted to acknowledge it but it would mark the end of their time together. They'd been in the same class since their last year of infants but that would all change after the summer holidays. Lucky was going to the Catholic secondary school, Dusty to the ex-grammar in Rotherham and Ned was destined for Thorpe Comp. Though they were sworn amigos for ever, each secretly understood that new schools would mean new friends and new allegiances. They didn't live in the same part of Thorpe and each knew that the likelihood of them maintaining their friendship was slim. But they still kept up the pretence and, often, they managed to believe it.

Only Dusty heaved a regretful sigh as they made their way back into the school building. She knew that her two friends felt much the same as she did about their imminent separation but, being boys, they weren't going to talk about it unless she forced them into some sort of confrontation with their feelings.

2

K ate decided to stay with the body rather than return to the track, watching as the figures of Nick and the Caldwells disappeared into the dark shadows of a patch of trees. She wasn't sentimental. She had no sense of keeping the dead man company, but she didn't want to risk anybody else clambering up to see what the red splash on the hillside might be. Not only would they be in for a shock, they could potentially contaminate the scene. Switching off her torch, she waited in the gathering gloom, trying not to think about the possible identity of the dead walker. She needn't have worried. It seemed that all the other hikers had beaten her and Nick to the valley floor and nobody passed below her along the path.

When Kate saw the lights of a vehicle approaching, she switched her head torch back on and used the flickering beam to lead the way back down the hillside where she met with two uniformed officers from Cumbria Constabulary. One was obviously more senior, the sergeant's stripes on his shoulder confirming his rank. His stubbled chin and bloodshot eyes suggested that he was coming to the end of a long shift and wouldn't have appreciated being called out on what could potentially be an all-night vigil.

'Not your patch,' he grumbled, totally unimpressed, as she'd flashed her South Yorkshire Police ID. He continued to gripe about the weather and the lack of light as he shrugged himself into a high-vis jacket and grabbed a torch from the glove compartment of the vehicle. His companion was standing on the sill of the passenger door from where he reached up to the roof bars and angled one of the powerful spotlamps up the hillside.

'He's over there,' Kate said, using her torch to indicate the jagged black line of the gully, the light forming eerie shadows amongst the rocks and bracken. 'Be careful, the ground's a bit rough.'

The second, younger officer gave her a smirk which suggested that rough ground was nothing to a hardy Cumbrian police officer. Kate bristled at his attitude, but she knew that pulling rank wouldn't do her any good here.

'Best get over to the hotel,' he said. 'Get warm, have a drink.'

Tempting as it was to stay, Kate knew that he was right. She couldn't do anything to help; in fact, she'd be more of a hindrance, especially if she told the officers that she had a possible ID for the body. And was she really sure? She hadn't seen him for nearly three years after all. It could just be somebody that looked like him. Most men seemed to have beards these days, especially amongst the hill-walking fraternity. Better to wait and see if her first impressions had been correct rather than starting a wild goose chase if she was wrong.

Kate shouldered her rucksack and set off along the track, trying to make sense of what she'd seen. Or what she thought she'd seen.

'You okay?' Nick asked as soon as Kate had finished reassuring the Caldwells and had left them in the care of two female PCSOs who had obviously been dispatched to the pub to help with the witnesses.

'Fine,' she replied, feeling anything but. She still couldn't shake the image of that bearded face staring up at her with sightless eyes and the full lips almost hidden by thick dark facial hair.

'You don't seem fine,' Nick said. 'I'd have thought that something like this wouldn't be too awful for you, but you look like you've seen a ghost – if you don't mind the awful cliché. Is it that you're off duty and relaxed?'

His concern was touching, especially as he wanted to find a reason for her reaction rather than assuming that she must be a crap police officer if she got shaken up by the sight of a dead body. She had to tell him what was really bothering her.

Casting a glance towards the Caldwells to make sure that they weren't close enough to hear, Kate lowered her voice and said, 'I think I knew him.'

'Who?' Nick looked baffled and surveyed the lounge as if some old acquaintance of Kate's had walked through the door.

'The body. It looks like a DC I worked with here in Cumbria. We weren't in the same team but we both worked out of Kendal Police Station.'

'Are you sure?'

Kate shook her head. 'No. But it looked a lot like him. He was a keen hill walker so it's not unlikely that he was up in the Langdales.'

'That's why you're so shaken up? Was he a friend?'

'He was a colleague who I got on really well with,' Kate said, trying to evade the question, but she could see that Nick wasn't convinced. 'When things were really shitty between me and

Garry I used to talk to Chris. We'd sometimes meet up in the canteen after a shift and have a natter.'

Kate suddenly became aware of the silence in the bar. It seemed like all the air had been sucked out of the space and she and Nick were left in a vacuum. She'd never spoken to anybody about her relationship with Chris Gilruth. She'd barely admitted to herself that it *was* a relationship before she'd been offered a promotion and a transfer to South Yorkshire.

They hadn't kept in touch. Chris was married and Kate knew how it felt to be the one waiting at home for a man who would rather spend time with somebody else; anybody else. They'd kissed a couple of times. That was it. But there had been an intimacy to their talks which could have very easily led them to bed and to potential disaster in terms of their working relationship and to Chris's marriage.

'So, when did you last hear from him?' Nick asked.

'We last spoke a couple of days before I left Cumbria. A chat over coffee in the canteen. There was no point in us keeping in touch – he was a new dad with a busy job and I wanted to establish myself in my role in Doncaster. If I'm completely honest, I haven't thought about him much since I moved.'

'Well, you have had a hunky oncologist to occupy your thoughts,' Nick said with a grin. 'But are you sure it's him?'

Kate shrugged. Was she sure? It had been difficult to tell in the beam of her torch. Every time she'd focused on one part of his face the rest was in darkness. It was like looking at all the separate pieces of a jigsaw and trying to get a sense of what the finished puzzle might look like without the box as a guide.

'I can't be certain,' she admitted.

'Yes, but dark hair and a beard, that could be anybody. It's not like it's an unusual look.'

Nick was right. It could have been anybody but, as Kate

downed her second whisky in an attempt to get warm, she was becoming more convinced that she hadn't been mistaken. And, if it was Chris, what was she supposed to feel? It seemed like such a waste of a life, falling off a mountain and being left to rot in a gully. If the sheep hadn't disturbed the scree, how long might it have been before some poor soul had made the grisly discovery?

Kate was surprised to find herself close to tears. Chris had been younger than her by nearly ten years and now, remembering him, he seemed so vibrant, so full of life.

'DI Fletcher?'

Kate turned, about to snap at the interruption to her thoughts, and found one of the PCSOs standing behind her. She was about the same age as Kate, blonde hair cut into a short bob and she'd removed her hat, holding it to her chest as though for protection.

'I'm sorry to bother you but I need to take down your details. Both of you,' she said with a glance at Nick. 'It's just procedure but, if we need to follow up on anything, somebody will be in touch.'

Kate reached into the pocket on her trouser leg and removed her mobile phone. She opened her contact card and held it out to the woman who placed her hat on the bar and removed a notebook from her breast pocket. She scribbled down Kate's mobile and work numbers and turned to Nick who was holding out a business card. She took it, noted down the details and passed it back.

'Thanks for your help today,' she said, her voice formal. 'The Caldwells were lucky to run into you both. I hope you can still enjoy your evening.' She grabbed her hat and, placing it firmly on her head, walked away towards the door.

'Shouldn't she have clicked her heels together?' Nick whispered.

Kate smiled. She'd been surprised by the officious departure, but it was understandable. Kate was a superior officer, albeit in another force, and the woman clearly wanted to be seen as having done a good job. 'I think she was just being thorough,' she said.

Nick took a last gulp of his coffee and checked his watch. 'Still got to walk back to the car,' he said. 'And it's bloody dark out there.'

It was less than a mile of road walking back to where they'd parked but it felt like much further after Kate's head torch finally flickered and died and they had to rely on Nick's phone. Kate was irrationally overcome with relief when she saw the solid lines of Nick's Merc nestled amongst the car park's trees.

3
_____

Calvin Russell loved his job. He enjoyed the responsibility and the trust placed in him to ensure that clients got exactly what they wanted; and he did try his best to ensure that every client was happy when they left. Calvin knew that it wasn't a career though; there wasn't much scope to progress to the upper echelons of Doncaster Storage Solutions as the *upper echelons* meant Mr Hibberts, who owned the warehouse, and Calvin couldn't ever see himself owning much more than his old Kawasaki ER500 motorbike and his Xbox. But it was a secure income and he was allowed to make some decisions for himself.

He was in that position now. A few days ago, he'd noticed an unpleasant smell coming from one of the storage units and he was beginning to think that he'd need to look inside. It was a unit hired by one of the cash-only customers, which made Calvin a little wary of interfering. Mr Hibberts had a few clients who paid upfront, in cash, on the understanding that a blind eye was turned when they deposited or collected their belongings. Calvin suspected that they might be storing stolen goods or possibly even drugs – he'd seen something similar in a news report on television – but Mr Hibberts had been clear that it was none of Calvin's business and that he should just take the cash.

The man who had paid for the unit which was currently causing a problem hadn't been one of the 'usuals', but he'd had the cash for a six-month rental so Calvin had simply shown him one of the smaller units and, when the client was satisfied that the storage space was big enough, taken his details and given him a key and a receipt for his cash. As far as Calvin was aware, after depositing a number of bags and boxes, the client hadn't been back. He still had three months before he had to pay for more time or remove his goods, but the smell was getting worse and Calvin felt compelled to intervene. He'd rung Mr Hibberts who had simply told him to do what he thought was best, so Calvin had dug out the master key and decided to investigate.

Now, stooping down to unlock the roller door, Calvin was beginning to regret his earlier zealousness. The smell was definitely stronger than it had been the previous day and it got worse as he eased the door upwards a few inches. His first thought had been that somebody had been storing some old clothes and they'd been put away dirty and damp and had started to get musty and mouldy. But then the smell had intensified and was more like spilt milk or yoghurt that had been left in the fridge too long. He reared back as the door rattled upwards in its tracks, allowing the foul odour to fully engulf his senses. It wasn't milk or dirty clothes – he'd smelt this before. His older brother had worked at the maggot farm near Thorpe and his overalls had been impregnated with a similar stench. This was the smell of rotting meat; of something dead.

Calvin's hand went to the phone in the breast pocket of his shirt. He needed to report this. But who to? Mr Hibberts wouldn't be very pleased if Calvin had the police crawling all over the facility because somebody had left their dead dog in a poorly secured box. If he rang Mr Hibberts he was fairly sure what the boss would tell him to do – find the source of the smell and get rid of it. If there was a mess, contact the person who'd rented the unit and get them to pay.

Lowering his hand, Calvin made a decision. He'd see what was causing the smell and then contact either Mr Hibberts or the client. No point in jumping the gun – it might just be a mouse or a rat that had found its way inside and then died. Calvin shuddered. He hated rodents and he knew that he was kidding himself – one of the reasons he'd been happy to work here for so long was the lack of vermin. Mr Hibberts was scrupulous about the hygiene of the place and checked every month without fail that Calvin had cleared out the rat traps in the outer corridors. That was one job that Calvin hated. It gave him what his grandma used to call *the heebie-jeebies* because he had to pick up the metal containers and check for dead mice and rats. It wasn't the dead ones that worried Calvin, but he dreaded finding one that was still alive and pissed off with whoever had tried to kill it. Oddly though, and to his great relief, he'd never found a dead rodent in any of the traps. Which made him think that it was unlikely to be a decaying mouse or rat causing the stink.

Calvin stepped back into the corridor and took a deep breath of relatively clean-smelling air, holding it in his lungs before crossing the threshold into the storage area. There was no going back now. If he had to ring Mr Hibberts, at least he could say that he'd done his job properly.

The space was quite empty compared to some that Calvin had helped to pack and unpack, which surprised him as it was one of their smaller units. There was a rolled-up carpet, a mattress propped against one wall and something that looked like a tent, poorly packed in its stuff sack. Against the wall off to his right, plastic boxes in a range of sizes and colours were stacked up neatly, all fitting together like that Tetris computer game that he'd played as a teenager.

Calvin's eyes were drawn to the carpet. He'd once found a complete dog skeleton in a rolled-up hearth rug abandoned on the disused railway near his father's house. This carpet was loosely rolled and could easily have disguised a dead pet. He took two steps closer and gave it a tap with his foot. Dust rose up, motes caught in the light from the corridor, but the smell didn't get any worse. Another tap and the carpet unrolled slightly, the foam backing flaking and cracking as the fibres straightened.

'Come on,' Calvin said to himself, trying to summon up the resolve to investigate properly. 'It's just a bloody carpet.'

Bending down he pushed the bulky tube until he could see that there was nothing hidden in the middle and nothing between the layers, lurking like an unpleasant Swiss roll.

The smell seemed to be getting worse but that could just have been his imagination. Calvin seemed to remember though that your senses got used to smells quickly and that often a bad smell could seem to improve or even go away. That wasn't happening though and, as he turned to the plastic boxes, he struggled not to gag as a wave of rot washed over him. It had to be in the boxes.

Hands trembling, Calvin reached out for the nearest box. Orange plastic obscured the contents as he shook it like a child trying to guess what was in a Christmas parcel. Nothing. It felt empty. Calvin peeled off the lid and peered inside. There was nothing there. Who would store an empty box? It made no sense. He tried another from the top layer. Empty again. Baffled, he picked up a larger box from the next row down. This one wasn't empty. He felt something shift with a wet thud as he tilted the box from side to side, but the dark blue lid meant that he'd have to look inside to be certain what the box contained.

The smell instantly intensified as he peeled back the plastic, but he still couldn't make out what he'd discovered. It looked like a chunk of bone surrounded by something jelly-like. Was it the dead dog of his imagination? It seemed unlikely as there was no fur. He tried another box, still struggling to contain his gag reflex. This one was bigger, a square box about twelve inches by twelve and, as it was slightly less opaque and white in colour, he could make out a shape inside it. He tilted it to one side and the shape changed, part of it obscured by a dark wave. Another tilt and Calvin dropped it with a squawk of fright and disgust. He threw up on his shoes, doubling over as he heaved up his break-fast. His gaze fixed on the object concealed in the box. He had no doubt that it was a human head and that one of the eyes was staring back at him.

4

'Good holiday?' Hollis asked as he struggled to pull the protective overalls up his tall, thin frame.

'Not bad,' Kate said. She was glad he'd asked; glad that their relationship seemed to be getting back to what it had been before he'd almost left the force due to family complications. Kate knew it had taken every ounce of Hollis's strength and character to walk back into Doncaster Central and face his colleagues. He'd felt let down and abandoned and Kate wouldn't have blamed him for walking away from the job, but it seemed Dan Hollis was made of sterner stuff and she respected him all the more for his determination and dedication.

'Not bad? A few days away from this in glorious countryside with the man of your dreams?' He was grappling with the hood which seemed determined to thwart Hollis's every attempt to cover his impeccably cut blond hair.

'Dan, it's November. It was cold and wet.'

'But at least it wasn't here. Doing this.' He gestured towards the police tape across the entrance to the storage unit.

'Oddly, it wasn't far off,' Kate responded, trying to blank out the memory of the familiar face on the darkening hillside. She'd not told her colleagues about the grim discovery during her walk; she didn't want to discuss it with anybody, at least until the identity had been confirmed. She'd asked the SIO on the case to keep her informed – as a professional courtesy – and he'd grumpily taken her business card with a vague promise to be in touch. She wasn't holding out much hope, understanding very well the pressures of a busy investigation, but at least he'd given her his contact details.

Hollis laughed, obviously thinking that she was making a joke about how grim the far north of England could be at this time of year and Kate didn't enlighten him. Instead she zipped up her own protective clothing and waited while Hollis lifted the police tape high enough for them both to duck under.

Kate had noticed the smell as soon as they'd entered the building and hadn't been surprised to see every opening window gaping as wide as possible and the doors at the far end of the corridor propped open to allow cold air through from the grimy concrete courtyard at the back of the building. Inside the unit, though, these measures didn't seem to have made much difference.

A team of SOCOs were gathered around a collection of plastic boxes of assorted colours and sizes. Yellow crime scene markers indicated that the contents of other boxes had already been investigated and recorded.

'Dismembered body,' one of them said, turning to face her. 'Not too badly decayed – probably due to the airtight storage boxes and low temperatures,' he said, pointing a purple-gloved finger towards the closest container. The lid had been removed and laid on a polythene sheet, dark smudges of fingerprint powder informing Kate that it had already been inspected. She took a step forward until she could see inside the box and immediately recoiled. It contained the lower part of a human arm which appeared to have been neatly severed at the elbow.

Another glance told her that the hand bore a single gold ring on the third finger and that it was a left hand. Married then. Somebody might be missing this person – if that somebody wasn't the one who'd done the dismembering.

'Is it all here?' Kate asked. 'The whole body?'

'Appears to be. It's a woman. Looks to be quite elderly. The torso's wrapped in some sort of nightgown. Have a look. The head's in a separate box but the face is quite decayed.'

He pointed to a pair of larger boxes further inside the storage unit, but Kate declined the offer. She'd seen what she needed to see and would wait for the post-mortem.

'Thanks, I'll pass,' she said, and the man gave her a knowing smile. She wasn't one of those detectives who felt the need to view gory crime scenes just to establish her 'hard' credentials and to prove that she had a stomach as strong as those of her male colleagues.

Hollis was scanning the small room, seemingly oblivious to the stench of decay and the foul remains.

'We need to find out who rented this space,' he said. 'And who has access.'

'Already on it,' Kate told him. 'You stay here and see what else turns up. I'll see where Matt's got to.'

DC Matt Barratt had been the first one on the scene and Kate knew that he'd have followed her instructions to the letter. She'd asked him to secure the scene and wait for the SOCOs. He'd also been tasked with keeping tabs on Calvin Russell who'd called in his grisly find, after throwing up all over himself.

Kate headed back to reception near the main entrance, hoping that she'd correctly memorised the route through the maze of corridors. Pushing open a door behind the main desk, Kate found Barratt and Calvin Russell deep in conversation. Russell glanced up at her as she pulled up a chair and sat next to him, fear and distrust clear in his widely spaced blue eyes. Even sitting down, Kate could see that Russell was short. He looked to be in his mid-twenties and was wearing dark blue work trousers and a white polo shirt under a black zip-up fleece. His dark hair was cut close to his skull, reminding Kate of the 'realistic' hair on her cousin's Action Man doll from the nineteen seventies. Something about his expression suggested that Russell didn't fully understand what was happening.

'Are you the boss?' he asked, his voice little more than a whisper.

'I'm the senior investigating officer, Detective Inspector Kate Fletcher.' She held out her hand. The man looked at it and then back at her face as if unsure how he was supposed to respond. Then, slowly, he reached out for the briefest of handshakes before pulling his arm back as though he'd been stung.

'I understand you were the one who found the remains? You were the one who called the police?'

Russell nodded.

'Calvin and me have had a long chat,' Barratt said. 'I've got it all written down.'

The DC's tone was placatory, as though reassuring a small child and Russell shot Barratt a grateful look. Kate understood. Russell probably had mild learning difficulties which explained Barratt's gentle tone. Barratt was good with people, seeming to have an instinctive understanding of what would work with each individual and Kate valued his adaptability and insight.

'That's fine,' Kate said. 'I just want to clarify a few things if that's okay?'

Russell nodded again, chewing his thumbnail as he studied her face.

'Have you got a record of who rented the storage unit where you found the remains?'

'On the computer.' Russell's face became more animated as

he explained. 'Mr Hibberts showed me how to put the details in. I'm good with computers.'

'Can you show us?'

Russell got up and led the way back through to the reception desk. He sat down in front of an ancient PC and his fingers danced across the keyboard. 'Here,' he said, jabbing his finger at the screen.

Kate leaned over his shoulder.

'In this column is the unit number – thirty-six. The rental period agreed was one hundred and eighty days from October the first. Amount paid – six times the monthly fee – three hundred pounds. Name Martin Short. Address 62 Kimberley Avenue, Thorpe.'

'How did he pay?' Kate asked as Barratt texted the name and address to their colleague at Doncaster Central. She knew that if he'd paid by card or bank transfer the man would have found it more difficult to hide his identity and he might have left an electronic trail that one of her team could follow. She wasn't convinced that the name or address would be real – not considering the contents of the storage locker.

'See the green asterisk?' Russell jabbed at the screen again. 'That means he paid cash.'

'Is that common? Do a lot of people pay cash?'

'Sometimes,' Russell mumbled. He kept his eyes on the screen and Kate sensed his discomfort.

'What sort of people?'

'Friends of Mr Hibberts – my boss. He sometimes lets them pay in cash.'

'So, this man, Martin Short, was a friend of your boss?'

'No. He wasn't a friend of mine.'

Kate turned to see a short, muscular man in an expensively-tailored dark suit leaning round from the reception desk. His dark blond hair was slicked down above a narrow face and his large front teeth gave him a rodent-like appearance. She hadn't heard him come in and, judging by the startled look on Barratt's face, nor had her DC.

'I'll take over for now, Calvin,' Hibberts said to his employee. 'You wait in the back room.'

Russell got up from his chair and did exactly as he was told. Hibberts took Calvin's seat and turned it to face Kate. 'I have no idea who this man is,' he began. 'Calvin must have made a mistake. And what he told you is only half true. I have, on occasion, allowed friends to use this facility as emergency storage. And they have sometimes paid cash. It's not the way I normally run my business and I can only assume that Calvin got the wrong end of the stick when this...' he glanced at the screen, '... Martin Short, made his booking.'

Kate wasn't at all convinced by the 'favours' that Hibberts sometimes did for his 'friends'. It wasn't uncommon for people to use storage facilities like this one to house stolen goods until they could be sold on. She wondered just how many green asterisks there were in the records.

'You think Calvin just assumed that this man was a friend of yours because he was offering cash?'

Hibberts shrugged. 'I don't claim to know what goes on in Calvin's head. You probably noticed he's a bit simple. Nice enough, but not the sharpest tool in the box.'

And probably easy to confuse and manipulate, Kate thought, trying not to react to the word 'simple'.

'I'm going to need access to your records,' she told Hibberts. 'And any CCTV footage you have from around the time unit thirty-six was rented.' She'd noticed a camera placed high up above the main entrance. It was trained on the desk and would, presumably, record customers coming and going.

'Doesn't work,' Hibberts said, pointing to the camera. 'It's just for show.'

Kate wondered how long the camera had been inactive. And if that was in any way linked to Hibberts's cash-paying clients not wanting a record of their transaction.

'Calvin's got a good memory, though,' Hibberts continued. 'He's great with numbers and stuff. He might be able to give you a good description.'

'My colleague has already spoken to him,' Kate said, as Hibberts stood up and reached out to open the door behind the desk. 'Mr Russell has told him everything that he can remember.'

She was about to ask Hibberts a few probing questions about his business dealings when Barratt stuck his head round the door of the back room.

'Sorry to interrupt but I think you need to get back up to the body. Dan's just texted down. Looks like they've found something that might help us to identify the victim.'

5

Hollis held up a plastic evidence bag as soon as Kate crossed the threshold of the storage area. He looked oddly as though he were trying to ward her off with the contents of the bag instead of allowing her to see inside.

'What is it?' Kate asked, taking the package from the DC and holding it up so that the light from the corridor would illuminate whatever was inside.

'It's a locket,' Hollis said. 'It was found in the box with the torso. There's nothing inside it. The SOCOs have taken photos of it *in situ* so you can have a look later. It didn't look unusually placed to me, though. The chain was all tangled up with the locket underneath.'

Intrigued, Kate turned the bag over so that she could get a better view of the gold object. It was heart-shaped and roughly the size and weight of a pound coin, with a fine chain attached. One side was engraved with an intricate rose design, the other was hallmarked and appeared to have been scratched or engraved.

'I think it's got an inscription on one side,' Hollis said. 'Hang on.' He pulled his phone out of his pocket and flicked the screen, scrolling through a series of photographs.

'Look at this one.'

The letters were unclear in the picture but there was definitely something on the back of the locket. Kate tilted the item slightly, but she couldn't make out whether she was seeing letters or numbers or just a design.

'Dan. Torch.'

Hollis tapped the screen and passed her his mobile with the torch activated. At first Kate couldn't get the light to stop reflecting off the plastic surface of the bag then, briefly, she got the angle just right and the scratches formed shapes that made sense.

'MS + DW 12/4/76. Write it down, Dan, before I lose it.'

She checked the front of the locket again in case she'd missed something, but the light only added more detail to the rose design.

'It's really beautiful,' she said, passing the phone back to Hollis. 'Must've been expensive.' She watched as he knelt and placed it carefully with the other evidence bags.

'So, we've got a date and some initials,' he said, straightening up and bending backwards slightly as though his back was stiff. In the close confines of the storage room, Kate was struck by Hollis's height and his slim frame. They'd been working together for a couple of years now, but she was still sometimes shocked by the size of him.

'I'll get Sam onto it,' Kate said, digging in her jacket pocket for her phone. Sam Cooper was another DC on her team and her data mining abilities were fast becoming the stuff of legend. 'If she can have a look through the register of births, deaths and marriages she might be able to put names to the initials, especially with a specific date.'

'Get her onto Martin Short as well,' Hollis suggested.

'Already done. I'm going to head back to base to see what she's dug up so far. You stay here and see if anything else turns up. Have a chat with Matt as well. He might decide that we need to bring Calvin in for formal questioning.'

Hollis gave her a grin and a mock salute as she left.

Cooper was staring at her monitor when Kate arrived in the team office. The woman seemed frustrated as her fingers pecked frantically at her keyboard, looking more like a sixth-former trying to complete an overdue assignment than a police detective doing research.

'Found anything?' Kate asked, placing a latte carefully next to Cooper's mouse hand. She knew that the DC wouldn't have taken a break since Kate and Barratt had texted her the information, so the coffee was more a necessity than generosity.

Cooper looked at the cup and then up at her boss, blue eyes not quite focused on Kate's face as if she was still lost in whatever section of cyberspace she'd last inhabited.

'Not a thing,' Cooper said, running a hand through her short blonde hair and adding to the spikes and angles that suggested that she'd done this a few times already. 'I've got a list of Martin Shorts as long as the Doncaster phone book – it's not exactly an unusual name. He might as well be called John Smith. I'm working outwards using the storage place as a locus, but even that's given me twelve within a ten-mile radius. And none of them live at the address that the suspect gave. In fact, none of them live in Thorpe.'

Kate thought about the implications of Cooper's comment about John Smith. 'Alias?'

'I'd put money on it. You don't go to the trouble of paying

cash in advance for something like this and then give your real name.'

Sam took a big drink of her latte and glared at her monitor as though she held it responsible for her lack of progress.

'Why choose that name?' Kate asked, thinking aloud. 'It must mean something to him. He'll have known that the body would be discovered sooner or later and that we'd search the records.'

Cooper shrugged and took another gulp of her drink. 'Could be anything. His favourite uncle, a teacher, somebody he doesn't like and wants to implicate.'

'Or somebody that he admires? Somebody well known?'

'There's an actor called Martin Short. I think he might be a bit obscure though.'

Kate didn't recognise the name. 'What's he been in?'

Cooper clicked on the toolbar at the bottom of her screen and a window popped up displaying a vaguely familiar face. 'He's Canadian. Comedy actor. *Father of the Bride, The Santa Clause 3, The Three Amigos, Three Fugitives...*' Kate tuned as Cooper continued to read the 'filmography'. If the name had been chosen for a reason, it was obscure and perhaps only apparent to their suspect. Perhaps he was a comedy fan, or he liked Canada. If they couldn't identify the man who'd rented the storage unit, they might have more luck with the locket.

'What about the initials that I sent you?' Kate asked. Cooper opened another window to reveal columns of names on what looked like photocopied pages that had been badly scanned. She pointed to a name on one line.

'Here. There's a Dennis Wilson, married a Moira Shackleton. But the date's wrong. It's November 1976 not April. I looked through April and there's nothing close. I'm only looking in the local area though. Checking BDM across the country will take a while as the records are scanned in versus being inputted on a keyboard. A few local authorities might be more up to date, but I doubt it. Who's going to pay somebody to type in lists of people who got married years ago?'

'So, I need to get a team together to read through the records and to check out every Martin Short in the area. Great. The DCI will love that.'

Cooper tried and failed to disguise a smile as she stared at her screen.

'Don't you dare,' Kate said, delivering a gentle backhanded slap to Cooper's shoulder.

She knew what was amusing the DC. Two months ago, Kate's old boss, DCI Raymond, had retired. Kate had locked horns with Raymond on a few occasions, but their relationship had been reasonably amicable and she'd been sorry to see him go. His replacement was very different in many ways. DCI Priya Das was a tiny woman in her early forties and was a whirlwind of energy. Fast-tracked through CID, she'd already made a name for herself as a DI in Nottinghamshire through her involvement in several high-profile cases. In her new role, she'd implemented a new regime of daily meetings with the DIs at Doncaster Central, regardless of caseload, and she insisted on each team of detectives holding a briefing every morning with minutes being forwarded to her before 10am.

There had been some grumbling among various ranks, but Kate hadn't joined in. She was already holding daily meetings with her team and Sam was happy to type up the main points as they were discussed and send them to the DCI. Her own meetings with Das tended to be supportive and productive – certainly nothing to complain about. Kate's compliance had gained her a whispered reputation as Das's favourite and it was this that was causing Sam to smirk.

'We'll need at least half a dozen people,' Kate said. 'I'll see if DCI Das will provide a few civilian investigating officers so that we don't need to get uniformed staff tangled up in this. We can use the uniforms to check out the Martin Shorts in the area before I contact other forces to check nationally.'

Sam nodded. 'What's my next job?'

'This woman's come from somewhere. I want you to check mispers for the past six months. I'll text you age and identifying features – not that we've got much. It looks like she might have been in her seventies or eighties and she's wearing a nightgown, wedding ring and the locket.'

'Nightgown might suggest hospital or some sort of residential care facility,' Cooper mused. 'I'll check if any of the local ones have had anybody go wandering off.'

'Nice one,' Kate said. 'I'm going to Thorpe to check out this address. There has to be a reason why "Martin Short" chose it. Somebody methodical enough to cut an old woman up into bits and put each one in a box won't be the sort of person to do things on a whim.'

6

The street lights came on just as Kate pulled into Crosslands Avenue – the wide street that ran the full length of the Crosslands Estate – bathing the damp pavements in orange light. She slowed down as parked cars narrowed the road and she was forced to pull in to let the single-decker bus that served the estate pass her on its way to the row of shops further along the street. It hadn't been like this when Kate was growing up. In the seventies and early eighties few people had owned cars and the houses had still been surrounded by privet hedges. Now, many of the hedges had been pulled up to make way for brick paving to accommodate some of the vehicles but, clearly, most families owned more than one car.

Kimberley Avenue was only two streets away from where Kate's father had lived until he'd moved her and her sister south at the height of the miners' strike. The houses were all red brick – only a handful of owners had covered the original façade with stone cladding or pebbledash – and their uniformity was somehow reassuring to Kate as she pulled in opposite the address that she'd been given.

She sat in the car for a few minutes, studying the house. A

largish semi – like most houses on the estate – it sat behind a well-cared for front garden which was mainly lawn with a small round flower bed in the middle. Kate could see where last year's roses had been cut down – the dark brown stems pushing up from the soil like the claws of a subterranean beast. Three steps led up to a uPVC front door and a concrete path led up to the side of the house to where the back door would be, inset into a small porch area. The house was exactly like the one that Kate had lived in, except for the addition of double glazing and a steaming vent which suggested central heating.

Kate's Mini gave a muted chirp as she locked it. She crossed the road to number 62. The pathway was starting to glaze with ice – a thickening strip of white perfectly mirroring the shape of the hedge that ran next to it – so she had to tread carefully as she negotiated the smooth concrete. She stopped at the steps, suddenly indecisive. When she'd lived on Crosslands Estate, hardly anybody had used their front door. In her dad's house it was locked and bolted and anybody knocking was told to come round the side. What was the correct approach now? She was torn between her feelings of being a local, somebody who belonged, and being a police officer, a formal caller.

Decision made, she stomped up the steps and, in the absence of a doorbell, tapped sharply on the front door.

The net curtain in the living room window was pushed back and a face appeared. Kate couldn't make out much detail, but it was joined by a hand pointing to her left.

'Go round to the back door,' the occupant said, over-enunciating every word as though speaking to somebody who might not be able to hear or understand.

Smiling to herself Kate followed the instruction.

The back door opened before she had a chance to knock and a short, elderly man frowned at her from a narrow gap between the door and the jamb.

'Can I help you?'

Kate showed him her ID and explained who she was before asking if she could talk to him inside. At first, the man looked like he might refuse. His frown deepened as he considered her request but, eventually, he pushed the door further open and invited her inside, leading the way into the kitchen at the back of the house. 'I suppose you want a cup of tea?'

'I'm fine, thanks,' Kate responded.

'Well, have a sit down then and tell me what this is about.' He sat down at the table and pointed to the chair opposite which was occupied by a large white cat. 'Just shift her off,' the man instructed.

Kate bent down and gave the cat a gentle shove. Its amber eyes opened and it blinked at her resentfully before pouring itself to the floor at what seemed like a deliberately leisurely pace.

'So, what's this all about?' the man asked. His manner wasn't quite belligerent, but he didn't seem overly inclined to co-operate. Kate put him in his late sixties or early seventies. His bald head was covered in freckles and his eyes, behind thick-framed glasses, were light grey and suspicious.

'Can I ask your name?' Kate said.

'Jim. Jim Taylor.'

'Does the name Martin Short mean anything to you?'

His eyes flicked off to the darkening window as he gave the question serious consideration. 'Wasn't he an actor? He was in one of those police series on telly. And before that he was in *The Professionals*.'

'That was Martin Shaw.'

The man shrugged as if to indicate that he really couldn't tell the difference.

'Your address and the name Martin Short were given by somebody who rented out a storage unit near Doncaster. The storage unit is now the focus of an investigation into a serious crime.'

'What sort of crime?'

'I can't discuss the details.'

The man smacked his thick lips together as he considered what he'd just been told. 'Murder then, I expect. Sorry I can't help.'

'Who else lives here, Mr Taylor?'

'Just me.' Taylor's expression darkened. 'It used to be me and my wife, but she divorced me fifteen years ago. Took up with a hairdresser from Bawtry.'

'Children?'

'Nope. It was just the two of us.'

'And how long have you lived here?'

Another glance at the window. 'Must be getting on for twenty-five years. I was made redundant from Mason's and I used most of the money to pay for the house. Bought it outright from a fella who'd bought it off the council. I reckon he must've made a fair profit even though I didn't pay that much compared to what it's worth nowadays.'

'I don't suppose you remember his name?' Kate asked.

'I never met him,' Taylor said. 'Did it all through solicitors. I think one of the neighbours said he was a teacher at one of the local schools and he'd moved to somewhere the other side of Donny. It'll be on the Land Registry documents though, I'd have thought. I'll have seen it written down, but it didn't stick.' He sat back in his chair and smiled at her; Kate could see that he was pleased to have come up with something that she might not have considered.

'Obviously we'll check the Land Registry,' Kate said. 'It would have been useful if you'd actually known him. But his name definitely wasn't Martin Short?'

'I'd have remembered,' Taylor said. 'Because of the actor.'

Back in her Mini, Kate texted Cooper with the results of her visit and an instruction to check the Land Registry. She thought about what Taylor had said about the previous owner of the house being a teacher – something had ignited a tiny spark of memory. Her sister, Karen, had been taught by somebody who lived on the estate. Kate had a vague recollection of bumping into him at the shops during the holidays and Karen being scarlet with embarrassment. She checked her watch. Half past four. Most of the time she would have had to do a quick calculation according to which time zone her sister was living in, but Karen had been back in the UK for the last two months, teaching refugees in Manchester. It was worth a try.

Karen answered the phone on the fourth ring. 'Hi, sis!'

Kate hated being called 'sis' and was convinced that was why Karen insisted on using the epithet.

'Hi, Karen. How's things?'

'Fine. But it's the middle of a work day so I doubt that you're ringing to see how I am. What's up?'

Kate smiled to herself. Karen had always been astute. She should have known that her sister would realise that she was ringing for a work-related reason.

'Got me,' Kate admitted. 'I'm in Thorpe and I'm trying to find out about a teacher who might have lived on our estate. Probably Kimberley Avenue.'

'Oh, God! Mr Whitaker! We bumped into him in the holidays once. I was mortified. I hadn't really thought about teachers having lives outside of school.'

'You remember him?'

'He was my teacher when I was in fourth year at Sheffield Road Juniors. I thought the sun shone out of his bum. He was hunky too.'

'Hunky?' Kate was surprised to hear that her sister had thought of a teacher in this way.

'Well, that's in retrospect. I suppose I had a crush on him. He played the guitar in lessons and sang Beatles songs. Funny, I haven't thought about him in years.'

'How old would he have been?' Kate started doing maths in her head. Karen would have been in fourth year around 1981 – Kate would have already started at Thorpe Comp.

'No idea. Everybody over twenty seems ancient when you're that age. I suppose he might have been in his thirties. I probably saw him around after I left but my fickle heart had moved on to the wonders of manhood on offer at the comp.'

Kate laughed, remembering those 'wonders' – lanky, spotty teenage boys who were obsessed with twanging the bra of any girl who came within range. 'I don't suppose you remember Mr Whitaker's first name?'

Silence at the other end of the line while Karen thought about the question. 'Not a clue, sorry. You know what it's like when you're at school. Teachers' first names are a big secret. The staff at Sheffield Road used to call each other Mr and Mrs So-and-so in front of the kids. I might never have known his name.'

'Might it have begun with a D?' Kate prompted, thinking about the locket found on the dismembered body.

More silence.

'No, sorry. If I ever knew it, it's been completely wiped from my memory. You could always ask at the school.'

'Okay. Does the name Martin Short mean anything to you? From school, or the estate?'

'Doesn't ring a bell. There's an actor called Martin Short. He was in something I watched on Netflix recently – a film with Steve Martin. Can't remember much about it though. There were a lot of sombreros.'

'*Three Amigos*?'

'That was it! Don't bother – it was a bit tedious. Look, I'm sorry but I need to get back to work. I've got a class in ten minutes.'

Kate thanked her sister and hung up. Martin Short was still a mystery but at least she had a possible identity for DW.

7

'David Whitaker,' Kate said, tapping on her laptop until a copy of a Land Registry document was displayed on the whiteboard at the front of the incident room. 'Previous owner of 62 Kimberley Avenue.'

The four members of Kate's team stared at the document as though memorising every word. It had taken Cooper only a few minutes to find the details of the house's previous owner and his identity corresponded with Karen's memory of her teacher.

'So, he's the DW on the locket?' Barratt asked.

'It's a strong possibility,' Kate confirmed.

Barratt nodded, the dipping of his head revealing the growing bald spot on his scalp. This combined with his hooked nose had inspired O'Connor to start calling him Monty after the Simpsons character Mr Burns. It wasn't a nickname that Barratt appreciated and Kate had already made a mental note to have a word with O'Connor. Hollis was drawing a circle around something that he'd written on his notepad, his pen going round and round as though he was trying to use it to carve a hole through the rest of the pages.

'Something to add, Dan?'

Hollis looked up, his blue eyes brilliant in the morning sun cutting a blade of light across the room through the one small window. 'If he's DW then who's MS?'

'Margaret Simpkins,' Cooper leapt in, eager as always to share the product of her data mining. 'They married in 1966. The locket must be an anniversary present.'

Cooper had shared this information with Kate before the briefing and Kate had been impressed with the DC's ability to think laterally. She'd had no luck with the date on the locket, so she'd searched backwards in five-year blocks in case it was a gift marking a significant milestone in a relationship.

'And are we assuming that the body is that of Margaret Simpkins?' Barratt wanted to know.

'We're not assuming anything but that's certainly a line of enquiry that I want you to follow up. So far Sam can't find David Whitaker or his wife in any of the online registries. They disappear after 1985. Matt, I want you to go to their last known address and find out anything you can. They only lived there for a couple of years, but you never know – somebody might remember them. I'll text you the details.

'Sam, I want you to get on to the Department for Education and see if you can dig up anything about Whitaker's employment history. Also try to find out about Margaret. It's possible that she might have family somewhere local. She'd be in her seventies by now but that doesn't mean that there's not a brother or sister out there somewhere. If nothing else, we might be able to get a DNA comparison for the body. Steve?'

O'Connor looked up at her expectantly.

'Back to the storage place. There's something dodgy going on there and dodgy's your middle name.'

The other three grinned. DS O'Connor was well known for his links with Doncaster's seedier side. If a case involved drugs, prostitution or anything else unsavoury, O'Connor always had a contact or two who could steer him in the right direction.

'Already put some feelers out,' O'Connor said, stroking his dark red moustache in a way that reminded Kate of a cartoon villain.

'Dan, I'm going to have a quick chat with the boss then we're going to Sheffield Road Junior School. My sister remembers Whitaker as being 'hunky' and charismatic. He obviously made an impression. There might still be somebody at the school who remembers him.'

Hollis nodded and stood up, shooting the cuffs of his suit jacket and checking the creases in his trousers. Kate smiled. Hollis might have been through a rough time, but he seemed more like his old self every day.

The school was very much how Kate remembered it from her childhood except that the rickety prefabricated classrooms that had been perched on the upper playground to accommodate an excess of pupils had been replaced by a single-storey brick building. The other change was the name. Now part of a chain, the school was called The Thorpe Danum Academy and emblazoned with a logo depicting a Roman centurion.

Kate and Hollis followed signage around the outside of the school to the main reception. The playgrounds and other entrances that, Kate remembered, led to the separate toilets and changing rooms for boys and girls were inaccessible to visitors, enclosed behind green mesh fencing.

'Funny how times change,' Kate mused aloud. 'When I was at school here anybody could come and go. Both gates were propped open and there wasn't an official reception – just a desk outside the head's office.'

'Stabbings, shootings and abductions,' Hollis responded. 'Too many nutters on the loose nowadays – schools have to protect their kids otherwise they fail the Ofsted.'

'Cynical.'

'True though.'

Kate didn't want Dan to be right, but she'd heard too much about schools whose staff hadn't been able to respond quickly enough to attacks and invasions and then been blamed for students being harmed. Too often the culpability culture seemed to lead to the right measures for the wrong reasons.

The security continued beyond the double doors which led into the school reception – a space which Kate vaguely remembered as being the stockroom and which she'd always loved whenever her teacher sent her to get a set of exercise books or a new tin of powder paint. Nick still sometimes commented on her stationery fetish and she had no doubt that it had begun here. Now though, walls had been demolished to create an airy space which had a welcoming feel until the visitor noticed the door next to the enclosed counter – a door that could only be opened by a swipe card. Nobody was getting through if they didn't belong.

The woman behind the desk greeted them with a wide smile, but her eyes were slightly suspicious and Kate pictured what a strange couple she and Dan must make. Him in his thirties, tall, blond, good looking and well-dressed; her a head shorter than Dan, fifty, greying roots because she'd missed her last hairdresser's appointment due to work commitments, a navy trouser suit that she'd had for at least three years and sparse make-up that she had applied before she left her flat and hadn't bothered to check since her morning meeting with Das.

'Can I help you?' the woman asked, and Kate immediately saw why she'd been given the job as gatekeeper. She was probably only a few years younger than Kate, her dyed dark hair and understated lipstick gave her a no-nonsense appearance and her white blouse and dark trousers almost amounted to a uniform. Everything about the woman said that she was prepared to be professional, but she wouldn't be messed with.

'DI Kate Fletcher and DC Dan Hollis,' Kate introduced them, showing her ID and waiting while Dan did the same. 'We're investigating a complex case and we were wondering if there's anybody here who might remember a member of staff from the nineteen eighties. I know it's a long time ago, but it is very important.'

The receptionist narrowed her eyes slightly as she stared at Kate and then glanced at Hollis. 'That's more than thirty years ago.'

Kate nodded.

'You'll have to talk to the head.'

'Might he have a list of former staff?'

The woman smiled. 'Better than that. He's been here since the late eighties. He might be able to help you. Have a seat and I'll see whether he's available.'

The woman watched until they'd both sat down on uncomfortable plastic chairs then she picked up the phone. She turned her back so that her conversation with the head teacher couldn't be easily overheard then turned back and put the phone receiver down. 'He'll be a couple of minutes. He's got a half-hour gap in his schedule. I'll need you to sign in.'

She pointed to a monitor and keyboard next to the reception desk. 'Just type your name and your employer and I can print you out a visitors' badge.'

Kate allowed Dan to go first and by the time she'd signed in and been given a badge on a bright red lanyard, the mysterious door opened and a tall man stepped through. If Kate had spotted him on the street she'd have immediately decided that he was a head teacher. Tall and slim, he was dressed in a dark grey suit, the fabric cut through by a shimmering pinstripe. His lilac shirt was complemented with a dark purple tie, all of which highlighted his ruddy complexion and amused-looking green eyes. His greying hair was thick for a man in his fifties and whatever style he'd been hoping for had obviously rebelled into an unruly mop. Kate could imagine that he was popular with his staff and the beaming smile of the receptionist confirmed this opinion.

'Detective Inspector Fletcher?' he asked, looking from her to Dan and back again.

Kate took two steps towards him and held out her hand which he shook firmly as he introduced himself as Wayne Campbell. She introduced Dan and then followed Campbell through into the main part of the school.

The familiarity caught Kate's breath as they stepped into the main hall. Suddenly she was nine years old again and trying not to cry as her teacher told her how sorry she was to hear about the death of Kate's mum. Except she'd not been Kate then, she'd been Cathy Siddons and she'd been swamped by her grief and confusion.

'Weird being back, eh?' Hollis said with a grin, but Kate couldn't answer. Everything was the same and everything was different. Classrooms led off the hall, each one guarded by a red door with a window in the top half and, beyond the doors, Kate could picture the teacher in each room. Ms Shaw in the room opposite, Mr Dawson's room in the corner, Mrs Dalston to her left and to her right the tiny staffroom that Kate had been allowed to enter when she'd been selected for extra maths tuition. She still pictured the dusty chairs and smelt the fog of cigarette smoke whenever she tried to work out a percentage.

The hall was lit from above by a huge skylight made up of at least twenty panes of safety glass, most covered in bird droppings – Kate remembered them being replaced when she was in second year after one cracked after a storm. When she was seven, Kate had been puzzled to learn that the huge glass construction was called a skylark – it was three years before she learnt the real word.

'... So, as you can see...' Campbell was obviously saying something about the school but Kate hadn't heard a word of it.

She apologised with a smile. 'I'm sorry. I haven't been listening. I haven't set foot in here for over thirty years – it's a bit overwhelming.'

She saw that Hollis was looking at her oddly and knew that she'd be in for some serious teasing later.

'You were a pupil here?' Campbell turned to face her, his face a mix of puzzlement and interest.

'Yep. When it was Sheffield Road Juniors. I left in 1979.'

'And it hasn't changed much?'

Kate looked around again. The layout was exactly the same; even the wood panelling on the hall floor was the same faded beige. 'Not really. Although I bet I'd see a lot of differences if I went into any of the classrooms.'

Campbell seemed reassured by this, as though he thought he could claim responsibility for progress, and he gave her another broad smile as he led the way to his office. 'And did you spend much time in here?' he asked, opening the door and ushering the two detectives inside.

'Thankfully not,' Kate responded. She had been summoned to Mr Turner's office twice during her time at the school – once for getting into a fight with a boy in the year above and once for the head teacher to offer his condolences after her mum died.

'Glad to hear it,' Campbell said, taking a seat behind the light wood desk that dominated the room and gesturing to two hard-backed chairs opposite.

'Cheryl says you want information about somebody who used to work here? A former teacher?'

'That's right,' Kate said, and noticed that Hollis had taken out his notebook. 'David Whitaker. He taught here sometime in the seventies or eighties – maybe up to 1993 or so?'

'Dave Whitaker,' Campbell said softly. 'Haven't thought about him for a long while.'

'You knew him?' Kate prompted.

'He worked here when I first started in 1987. He taught the fourth years. I think he left in the early nineties.' The head teacher's manner had changed subtly. The openness and welcoming smile had given way to wariness as suddenly as a door being closed, blocking out the sunlight.

'What was he like?' Hollis asked. 'Was he a good teacher?'

'I suppose so. I was young and idealistic at the time and had my own ideas about education. Whitaker had probably been teaching for a decade or so by then – practically a dinosaur.' A shadow of his former smile appeared.

'Did he get on well with the other staff and students?'

Silence.

'Mr Campbell? Was David Whitaker not well liked?'

Campbell's expression had completely closed down. 'You know, don't you? Is that what this is about?'

'Know what?' Kate suddenly felt sick. She could only think of one reason why her question had made Campbell uncomfortable.

'Has he been arrested?' Campbell's voice was little more than a whisper. 'Have you finally got some evidence?'

He looked down and Kate followed his gaze to his hands which were trembling. He wrapped them together and took a deep breath. 'A number of us thought that David Whitaker's interest in his students was inappropriate. He was in charge of the end-of-year residential and there were rumours about his behaviour. I suppose I first heard them a couple of years after I started. Nothing specific and nothing was ever proven. Most of the staff were glad when he left – I think the head at the time had been trying to get rid of him for years.'

'He was a paedophile?' Hollis asked.

'Honestly? I don't know. As I said, there were rumours, but I don't think there were ever any formal complaints or accusations. He was taken off the residential a couple of years before he left. I don't know what excuse the head used but I remember Whitaker wasn't happy about it.'

'Did you know his wife?' Kate asked.

Campbell shook his head. 'To be honest, I didn't have much to do with him after the whispers started. I was young and new to teaching – I couldn't afford to risk any of that rubbing off on me. Can I ask what this is about?'

Hollis gave him the usual line about not being able to comment on an ongoing investigation, but Kate felt that she owed the man something after making him remember something so uncomfortable. 'We're involved in a possible murder inquiry,' she admitted. 'Some of the evidence may have a link with Whitaker or his wife. A person of interest gave Whitaker's former address as their own and also a false name. It's just one possible line of enquiry, though.'

'Not a child?' Campbell asked, his face ashen.

'Not a child,' Kate confirmed. 'But I really can't say anything else. Unless the name Martin Short means something to you?'

Campbell gnawed on his thumbnail as he gave her question serious thought. 'I don't think so. Not a member of staff. Could be a student though – I can't remember them all.'

'Funny. Nobody seems to have heard of him,' Hollis mused. 'Apart from as one of Steve Martin's sidekicks in *The Three Amigos*. Canadian actor apparently.'

'*Three Amigos*?' Campbell was suddenly animated again. 'The film?'

He stood up and turned to the window behind his desk. 'I remember The Three Amigos.'

'Pile of rubbish according to Netflix,' Hollis said.

Campbell turned back to them, his expression earnest. 'Not the film. In my first year here, we had a trio of kids that called themselves The Three Amigos. They were inseparable. Did everything together. God, I haven't thought about them in years. Two lads and a girl. Everybody wanted to join their little gang, but they kept themselves to themselves. Dusty, Lucky and Ned – they named themselves after the characters in the film. Except,' he paused. 'Except they fell out. I remember a big fight between the two boys. Just before the end of term, before they left. I expect they were scrapping over the girl. It was the first time I'd had to step in and break up a proper fight. I remember being really nervous.'

Kate was only half listening. There was a link between the false name and David Whitaker. The Three Amigos. Three children who would have been on one of Whitaker's residential trips at the end of their time at the school. Three children who may have had a reason to want to hurt their former teacher.

'I'm going to need names,' Kate said.

Dusty had to admit it had been a really good few days, even though she'd spent part of the time wishing she could have shared a tent with Lucky and Ned instead of dopey Angela Fox. She understood why it wasn't allowed. They'd had the 'sex talk' last month; boys and girls in separate rooms with a teacher of the appropriate gender. When she'd met up with the boys at playtime they'd been giggling about something that their teacher had said, but she'd stayed silent. The female teacher had impressed upon the girls that the information she'd shared wasn't to be discussed with the boys, but it wasn't obedience that kept Dusty quiet. For once, she agreed with the teacher – she didn't need to emphasise the ever-increasing difference between herself and her closest friends.

She'd still spent all her time with them though. They'd been on hikes, kayaked on a reservoir and even tried abseiling from a disused railway bridge earlier that day. There had been some drama when Mrs Dalston had misjudged the rope and had fallen the last few feet, landing awkwardly on one ankle. An ambulance had been called and the teacher had been rushed off to hospital with one of the staff from the outdoor centre – the rumour mill was circulating the possibility that she wouldn't be back until the following morning; if at all.

Dusty gave the raft a quick inspection. It was the last challenge of the trip, one final task to perform in teams and Dusty thought she, Ned, Lucky and Angela had a decent chance of winning. The craft looked solid enough despite their lack of understanding of knots and the slightly dodgy-looking tilt to one side. They'd been given huge plastic containers which looked like a giant's milk bottles and a range of wooden planks and sticks as well as various lengths of coloured nylon climbing rope and some thick, silver tape. They'd lashed planks across two of the barrels and done the same with another pair then joined the whole thing together with two further planks so that the plastic containers looked almost like wheels supporting a rickety platform. Two plank oars were to be their means of propulsion as they negotiated their way downstream. The site staff had hammered a wooden stake into the riverbank about five hundred yards from the clearing where the last-minute finishing touches were being added to the mongrel craft. The race was first past the post. The first team to get from the clearing to the marker post without capsizing were the winners. Dusty was determined that her team would take the crown and the promised extra helpings of pudding at teatime.

The boys were having a great time: whipping each other with the rope, threatening to push each other into the river and making as much noise as possible but Dusty tried to keep focused on the task. They'd been forced to be a foursome – Angela had been made a member of their team for the past few days because she was sharing a tent with Dusty – but the other girl seemed hesitant about joining in. Dusty understood why. The three of them had been such a tight little clique for so long that it was impossible for anybody else to become part of the group. And that was the way that they liked it. She did feel a bit sorry for Angela though and had tried to get her involved in tying the barrels together, but Ned and Lucky had just made fun of her so Angela had mostly been watching their progress from an upturned barrel on the riverbank.

'We'll need you to row,' Dusty said, plonking herself on the dusty ground next to where Angela was sitting and slapping her hands together to remove some of the grime. 'There have to be four of us on the raft or we can't win.'

Angela looked at her, strands of dark hair sticking to the sheen of sweat on her forehead.

'So, I will be of *some* use then?' Her eyes were glassy with tears and Dusty realised that the girl was far more upset about being left out than she'd seemed.

'Look,' Dusty said. 'The lads are just being lads. You know what they're like.'

Angela shook her head. 'It's not just them. You've practically ignored me since we got here. It's not my fault that you can't share a tent with your mates, you don't have to be so horrible to me.'

Dusty knew that Angela was right. She had been focused on Ned and Lucky and she had ignored her tent-mate. It wasn't that she didn't like Angela: it was just that nobody else was as important as her two friends, but Dusty knew all that was going to change in a few months and she would have to get used to being on her own – or make some new friends.

'You're right,' she admitted to Angela. 'Look, we'll do the boat race and then me and you could go for a walk – leave the lads to it for a bit.'

Angela just shrugged.

'Okay, how about you sneak out with us tonight? We're going for a night walk. It's the last night so even if we get caught there's not much that the teachers can do.'

'Why?' Angela asked. 'What's the point? It's the same place only at night. What's different?'

'We just thought it'd be fun. Sneaking around while everybody's asleep.' Dusty could hear how stupid their plan sounded as she tried to explain it to Angela. Really, what *was* the point? But they'd agreed and they couldn't back out, especially now Angela was in on the secret.

'It's daft,' Angela said. 'If you get caught you'll get into real trouble with the teachers. I think I'll just get some sleep.'

Dusty wanted to agree with her, to keep her on side, but a shout from the riverbank indicated that the race was about to start. Angela hopped off her upturned barrel and, with a grin, held out her hands to haul Dusty to her feet. Dusty accepted the gesture as an offer of truce and the two girls headed towards the river.

'All hands on deck!' Ned yelled as Dusty and Angela approached. The two girls clambered onto the rickety craft and tried to find places to kneel whilst maintaining the balance of the raft.

'Ready?' one of the camp staff yelled.

Shouts from every raft indicated that all the teams were in place. Dusty glanced across to the opposite bank where Wheezy and his team had constructed something that looked like a cross between an oversized dustbin and the Starship Enterprise. Suddenly, she had no desire to win. She didn't care. It was just a stupid race and all the pudding in the world wouldn't change the future; the future without her two best friends.

'On your marks…'

The countdown continued.

'Get set. Go!'

At first, Dusty could see nothing but water. It was everywhere, splashing up at her face and pouring down her arms as she paddled. Gradually, shapes started to form – the other rafts were jostling ahead of them.

'Faster!' Ned yelled. 'Give it some welly!'

Dusty grabbed the plank oar as hard as she could and thrust it into the river. Glancing across at Angela she saw that the other girl was doing the same, paddling as hard as she could.

And then disaster struck. Angela's oar caught on something and acted like an anchor, spinning them around and slowing their progress.

'Pull it out!' Lucky yelled pointing frantically at the plank of wood. Ned leaned across and yanked, trying to free up the raft but the motion caused the whole craft to buckle and Dusty saw one of the ropes starting to slip from where it held one of the barrels in place.

'Abandon ship!' she yelled, shoving Angela towards the river-bank. She watched as her tent-mate jumped to safety, followed by Lucky. Ned was still struggling with Angela's oar.

'Come on!' Dusty yelled. 'It's going to sink! It's a pile of crap!'

Ned scowled at her and clung on defiantly while she grasped at a tree root and hauled herself onto the damp, muddy grass. She turned and watched as the raft finally pulled free and then spun slowly in the river before the two barrels pulled apart leaving Ned with nothing to balance on.

'You prat!' she yelled at him as he gave her a two-fingered salute and leapt into the water.

It wasn't deep – probably only up to Ned's thighs – but he stumbled and sank briefly beneath the surface before reap-pearing with a broad grin.

'A captain always goes down with his ship,' he said before stumbling slowly to where his friends were waiting.

'Who made you captain?' Lucky asked, reaching down and splashing him with river water.

'Well, I didn't see any of you lot trying to save us.' He hauled himself up onto the muddy bank and looked down at his clothes.

'Shit. I'm soaked through. I'd better get–'

'Oy! You boy!'

All four of them turned instinctively in the direction of the voice. It was one of the camp staff – the one that Lucky had nick-named Sergeant Major Furry because of his thick beard and moustache.

'Get here – now!'

Ned stood up and sighed loudly. 'Looks like I'm not getting extra pudding tonight.'

He'd only taken three paces towards the man when a figure appeared from the trees.

'Leave him. I'll sort him out.' Mr Whitaker looked round at the group of children and gave them a theatrical wink. 'No need to get the sergeant major involved, eh? Come on, lad. Let's get you out of those wet things.'

Dusty watched as Ned allowed the teacher to lead him away towards the circle of tents. Her friend looked both scared and relieved at being rescued from what could have been a serious telling off. She noticed that Ned didn't even flinch when Mr Whitaker put an arm around his skinny shoulders.

8

'I can't work out if that was a waste of time or our best lead yet,' Hollis said with a wry smile as he opened the driver's side door of the pool car. 'Are we really looking for a group of kids who were fans of an obscure eighties film?'

'Honestly? I have no idea,' Kate admitted. 'But the pieces seem to fit together.'

It did seem unlikely, but the link was there. The problem was that Wayne Campbell couldn't remember the names of the three children and he thought that the school records from the eighties had been stored by the local authority in Doncaster somewhere. He didn't remember the girl's name and his memory of the two boys was very murky. He thought that one might have been called Lee or Liam and the other might have been a Nick or a Neil but he couldn't be certain. It was a start though, something to work with. If they could get a name they might be able to get hold of the old registers and do some cross referencing.

Kate pulled her phone out of her jacket pocket as Hollis put the car in gear. A text from Barratt – nothing useful from his visit to the Whitakers' last known address, he couldn't find anybody who remembered the couple. She hit 'contacts', intending to get Cooper to look into school records or Facebook or any other sources she might have access to in her cyber world, but before she could scroll to Cooper's number, the phone rang in her hand.

'Cooper? I was just about to ring you.'

'Whatever it was I think you'll want it to wait,' Cooper said cryptically. 'I've found David Whitaker. He's in the system but he's changed his name.'

Kate's mind was already trying to get a fix on Cooper's statement. 'In the system' was their shorthand for somebody who had a criminal record. Whitaker had been arrested and charged with something.

'Details, Sam.'

Cooper reeled off Whitaker's criminal record. It wasn't much but it was serious. He'd been charged with grooming a child for sexual purposes and he was currently in HMP Wakefield serving six months – due for release in three weeks' time.

'Sorry it took so long,' Cooper said. 'It took a while to find out that he'd changed his name. He's David Wallace now. Changed at around the time he moved from Thorpe. My guess is that the rumours got too much for him and he wanted a fresh start, but he couldn't change what he was.'

Kate noted the bitterness in Cooper's tone. Nobody on her team, and probably nobody on any force in the country, liked dealing with paedophiles, and this case now had that taint, that bad taste in the mouth.

Cooper was still speaking. 'So that's how I missed him. I couldn't find David and Margaret Whitaker, so I went back to the electoral register looking for any combinations of Margaret and David in the local area. I just tried W surnames on a hunch. I set a programme up to do the heavy lifting and there he was. I've found the deed poll documents so it's definitely him.'

'Nice work,' Kate said. 'Did you get a last known address? We need to check to see if his wife still lives there.'

'Done. She went into a nursing home two years ago. I rang them and they were a bit cagey at first, but it seems she was discharged in September. They won't give out any more information over the phone. I'll text the details. It's in Rawmarsh. Wallace's address is listed as a flat in Bentley.'

Kate thanked Cooper and hung up, trying to work out their next move. Somebody needed to go to the nursing home and she needed to get somebody out to Wakefield Prison at some point to see what Whitaker, or Wallace, might know. But he wasn't going anywhere – he could wait for a while. The nursing home should be their priority if they were going to make a positive ID on the woman's body and it was looking more and more likely that it was Margaret Wallace. A text pinged in and she gave Hollis directions to a street in Rawmarsh, a small town near Rotherham.

'I'll give them a ring and let them know we're coming,' she said. 'They might be a bit more co-operative face to face.'

Hollis nodded his agreement before turning down a side street and executing a U-turn.

The Nook nursing home was at the end of a quiet cul-de-sac off the main road through Rawmarsh. It looked like it might once have been the home of a Victorian industrialist or a minor member of the aristocracy and was entirely at odds with the empty shops and graffiti-covered bus shelters of the main street. Set back behind a low wall it dominated the short road and its red-brick gate posts seemed somehow threatening rather than welcoming. Hollis navigated the car into a small car park and sat for a moment staring up at the building.

'Do you think they handcuff the old people to their beds in there?' he said, gazing at the huge bay windows that flanked the door. 'It looks a bit forbidding.'

'It's just an old building,' Kate said. 'It's probably been gutted inside. It's rare to find one still run by the NHS these days so I'm expecting functional rather than opulent. Surprised the building hasn't been sold off.'

Her prediction turned out to be true. As soon as she approached the main door she saw that any sense of the building's former charm had been undermined by the modern barrier of hardwood and wire-crossed safety glass. Next to the door was a buzzer and an intercom box.

'Security looks tight,' Hollis mused, echoing Kate's own thoughts as she pressed the button. If the body of the woman in the storage unit was that of Margaret Wallace, how did somebody manage to get her out of The Nook? Unless she left of her own accord.

'Help you?' the intercom crackled into life.

Kate explained who they were and was told to wait. Less than half a minute later the door clicked open and a young man in dark blue trousers and a matching polo shirt with the NHS logo on the breast peered out at them.

'Police?' he asked, his tone more interested than concerned. Kate showed him her ID and he pushed the door open so that they could pass through into a bright foyer area. 'Sorry to keep you waiting,' the man said. 'Can't be too careful.'

'Is that standard?' Hollis asked. 'People have to ring the buzzer and then wait to be let in?'

The man looked at Hollis as though he couldn't quite believe he'd heard such a ridiculous question. His face flushed, making his blue eyes stand out against the pink flesh. 'Of course. We can't have people wandering in off the street.'

'Or wandering out, I suppose?'

Kate turned and noticed that the door had locked firmly behind them. There didn't appear to be an obvious way to open it from inside but there was some sort of sensor on the wall next to the handle.

'How do people get out?' she asked.

'They ask at the front desk. A member of staff has to come down and scan their fob.' He indicated a small, barrel-shaped object attached to his ID lanyard where, Kate noticed, his name and a photograph were displayed. Mark Harrison. She made a mental note of his details – just in case.

'Mr Booth's office is just through here,' Harrison said, leading them down a short corridor which was noticeably less well-lit than the foyer, as though the occupants of the offices didn't want to be noticed. Or bothered. 'I assume he's expecting you.'

Harrison tapped on the door and then pushed it open without waiting for an invitation, showing them into a small office which looked like it might have been an understairs scullery in the house's previous life. A fluorescent strip light buzzing faintly on the ceiling and a tiny window on the wall behind the occupant's desk were the only sources of light and, as Hollis squeezed in behind Harrison, Kate had a sudden flutter of claustrophobia. She didn't want to be squashed in there with the three other men, but she had little choice. To her relief, as she crossed the threshold, Harrison pushed past her back into the corridor.

'I'll leave you to it,' he said with a faint smile.

Kate turned her focus to the man behind the desk. In his fifties, bearded and ruddy complexioned, Booth frowned up at them. He hadn't bothered to stand up – perhaps aware of the tightness of the space – and he didn't invite her and Hollis to sit down.

'Mr Booth?' Kate asked, despite the nameplate on the office door.

The man nodded. 'You're the policewoman who rang earlier?'

Kate saw Hollis's lips curl slightly at hearing his boss described as a policewoman, but he managed to keep a straight face as he introduced them both, emphasising the *inspector* in Kate's title.

'Is this going to take a while? Should I get another chair?' Booth looked around as though expecting one to magically appear from somewhere.

'We're fine,' Kate reassured him, edging Hollis out of the way so that she could sit down. He stepped round her and stood by the door, arms folded, like the world's gangliest bouncer.

'Mr Booth, as I told you on the phone, we're here about a former resident, Mrs Margaret Wallace?'

Booth nodded enthusiastically, causing a lock of his greying hair to fall across one eye. 'I've got her details here.' He opened the folder that sat on his desk and scanned the first page. 'What exactly did you want to know?' Booth's manner suggested that there was nothing unusual in the folder, nothing that was causing him any alarm.

'How long was she here?' Kate asked. Booth checked his notes.

'Just over two years.'

'And the reason?'

Booth glanced up at her. 'I'm afraid I can't divulge medical information about residents, or former residents.'

Kate nodded. She'd expected this. 'I understand. Can you tell me when she left?'

Another glance at the notes. 'Just under three months ago. 4th September.'

'And where did she go? Was she hospitalised or transferred to another residential facility?'

'Oh, no,' Booth said with a smile. 'Her niece collected her. She'd been living abroad and had just come home. She wanted Margaret to live with her.'

'Her niece?'

'I know. Some people are so selfless. She seemed very concerned about her aunt and wanted to look after her herself.'

'You met this woman?' Kate asked.

'Of course.' Booth smiled at her. 'I did the discharge myself.'

Kate heard Hollis turn over a page in his notebook. This could be crucial. If they could get a description or any other information, it might help them to piece together the connection between the supposed niece and whoever had rented the storage unit.

'Could you give us a description?'

Booth shrugged. 'It's a little while ago but I remember she had shoulder-length blonde hair, late thirties or early forties. Medium height, medium build. She was very pleasant to deal with.'

It wasn't much. 'What about her voice? Did she have a local accent?'

'Northern, definitely. Possibly local with the edges worn off by all the travelling she'd done. She'd been in the Americas for a few years.'

'How did you verify her identity?' Kate asked.

Booth looked over Kate's shoulder, his eyes focused on the middle distance, clearly trying to remember. 'Driving licence, I believe. She didn't have her passport because she'd sent it off for renewal as soon as she'd arrived home. She also showed me a credit card and a utility bill to prove where she was living.'

'So, you have an address for this woman?'

Booth pulled his keyboard towards him and typed something. He glanced at his monitor and typed again.

'Are all your records computerised?' Hollis asked.

Booth nodded, distracted by what he was doing.

'Everything?' Hollis persisted. 'Admittance, deaths, all that?'

'Yes,' Booth said. 'Our system is kept up to date with all the details of our residents.'

'So, you'd have had a record of the niece before she turned up. You wouldn't have just taken the word of a stranger, if the resident didn't have all their faculties say?'

Booth frowned. 'I don't know what sort of place you think I'm running here,' he said. 'Under no circumstances would we release a vulnerable resident unless we followed proper procedures. It's not as if somebody could just walk in off the street and call themselves a relative.'

'So, how did you know this woman was Mrs Wallace's niece?'

Booth turned the screen so that Hollis could see it, a smile of triumph in his eyes. 'Here. She was listed as a family member when Mrs Wallace was admitted two years ago.' He pointed to the relevant piece of information.

Kate leaned round so that she could see where Booth was pointing. A passport-style photograph of an elderly lady stared out at her from the top left-hand side of the screen – her eyes looked vacant. Next of kin was recorded as David Wallace with an address in Bentley and, under 'other', was the name Stephanie Martin with an address which looked Spanish and another in Thorpe.

'That makes no sense,' Kate said. 'Wouldn't the husband have had to be involved?'

'It's perfectly straightforward,' Booth said, sounding slightly defensive. 'Our residents are elderly so, usually, their spouses are also elderly – if they're still alive. We always ask for the name of another relative who can act as next of kin if the spouse dies.'

'And if the spouse is still alive? Surely you would check with them first?'

'Of course,' Booth looked affronted, as though Kate was suggesting that he hadn't done his job properly. 'But, as you can see, the husband is dead. He died almost a year after Mrs Wallace came to stay with us.'

Next to the name David Wallace was the word DECEASED in red upper-case letters and a date in 2018.

9

'Who has access to these records?' Kate asked.

The care home manager, Booth, rubbed his chin. 'Myself and the admin staff. Medical staff can see the records, but any alterations have to be authorised by admin. Family members are verified at the time of admittance – we usually ask for a passport, birth certificate, marriage certificate. We have to be as thorough as possible – we can't have somebody being admitted in error and we need to know exactly who to contact in case of an emergency.'

'But this Stephanie Martin claimed to have been living abroad. How would you have been able to verify her identity if it was Wallace who brought his wife into your care?'

Booth sighed and tapped at his keyboard again. 'Our records show that Mr Wallace brought a copy of his niece's birth certificate along with documentation proving that she was Mrs Wallace's niece through her sister, Deirdre. The information was entered by our registrar two days prior to Mrs Wallace coming to live here. You can see that the appropriate boxes have been ticked.'

Kate glanced at the screen, more interested in the process

Booth was describing than the result. 'No scans of the documents?'

Booth tapped a couple of keys. 'No. That is slightly irregular. Possibly an oversight or it's possible that the client didn't want the documents scanned – that is their prerogative.'

'I'd like copies of this, if possible,' she said. 'Could somebody else have entered this information, at a later date? Or could somebody have changed it?'

'I don't see how. The system logs the ID of the person entering the data – as you can see. If I changed this, it would then show that I'd made a change and the date.'

Kate was struggling to make sense of the information. Surely Wallace must have known the niece if he showed the admin staff the documents. And the name, Stephanie Martin. Steve Martin was one of the actors in *The Three Amigos*. Somebody was taking the piss.

'Do you have somebody who maintains your IT system, or do you use an outside company?'

'We use Don Valley Data – they're based in Doncaster. It's part of an NHS contract.'

'And do you have a lot of IT issues?'

'We're a small organisation, DI Fletcher. Our in-house network consists of less than twenty PCs and maybe two dozen staff laptops. We don't have many IT problems.'

'Can staff access your system remotely? When they're at home, or off-site?' Hollis asked. It was a good question. If remote access was enabled, then it opened the system up to being hacked much more easily.

'No. There's no need. Patient medical records can be accessed via the NHS system in case of a medical emergency. It's all very secure – we just get regular usage updates, that sort of thing. What exactly are you looking for?'

'We're investigating a murder, Mr Booth. There may be a

connection to The Nook but we're yet to establish what that connection might be. I'd appreciate it if you could get the information I've requested, plus details of your IT provider. I'd also like any CCTV footage you have from the days that Mrs Wallace was admitted and discharged. If there's anything else, I'll be in touch.'

Kate stood up, denying Booth the chance to respond to her request and Hollis opened the door. 'We'll wait in the foyer, if that's okay.'

'Did you get a good look at the niece's address?' Hollis asked as soon as they were out of earshot of Booth's office.

'Kimberley Road in Thorpe. Same as the one given at the storage place. We know that's a dead end.'

'Not that one. There were two. When she was supposedly abroad the niece was living in Mexico – where that bloody film's set. It all comes back to those three kids. Somebody must have accessed those records and altered them.'

'There is one thing you're missing,' Kate said.

Hollis frowned at her.

'We're looking for a niece. A woman. Calvin Russell told us that a man made the booking for the storage unit where the body was found.'

'An accomplice?'

'Or Russell's not what he appears to be. He did say that he got the job because he was good with computers.'

Hollis was silent for a minute and then shook his head. 'Can't see it. He looked genuinely shaken up. And the way his boss treated him – like a little kid.'

Kate wasn't as convinced. There was a pattern to this, and she didn't like it. It felt like every step forward they took presented them with a new piece of the puzzle but she couldn't see the whole thing. The niece obviously wasn't who she claimed to be but then who was she? What was her role in this? Was she working with Russell and if so, what was the motive?

'I'm going to get Barratt to bring Russell in,' she said to Hollis. 'My gut isn't telling me anything, so we need to act rather than theorise.'

She dialled Barratt's number on her phone and turned away from Hollis as she waited for the other DC to pick up. Scanning the bright wallpaper and vases of fresh flowers she wondered what could have drawn a murderer here – to a place of the elderly and the dying.

'Kate?' Barratt finally answered.

'Bring Calvin Russell in. I want him formally questioned.'

Silence.

'Did you get that?'

'Of course,' Barratt sounded flustered, as though he didn't want to talk to her.

'Something wrong, Matt?'

'Nope,' he responded, a little too quickly. 'I'll get on to that.'

Kate hung up and dialled Cooper's number.

'Sam? Clear the decks. I've requested CCTV from The Nook from the days that Margaret Wallace was admitted and discharged. And I want you to find out anything you can about Don Valley Data. See if you've got any contacts who might be connected with them.'

Cooper didn't respond.

'Sam? What the fuck's going on? First Barratt sounds like he's away with the fairies and now you.'

'Sorry,' Cooper mumbled down the phone. 'CCTV and Don Valley Data. Got it.'

'Good and–'

'Kate, I think you might be in bother,' Cooper blurted out.

'DCI Das's been in here looking for you and she's not happy. She was at the PM of the body from the storage locker this morning and got back ten minutes ago with a face like thunder. Has she rung you?'

'I don't think so.' Kate hadn't felt her phone vibrate during the interview with Booth. 'Shit! We were in a cupboard under the stairs. I bet there was no signal.'

She ended the call and scanned the screen of her phone expecting to see a red exclamation mark next to the handset icon. Nothing. No missed calls and no texts. Maybe Cooper was imagining things. But Barratt had been a bit off as well.

'DI Fletcher,' Booth was walking towards her with a slim folder of papers. 'Here's the information you requested. I've included the phone number of the IT company. I'm afraid the CCTV footage might take a couple of hours, but I'll get it to you by tomorrow.'

'I'll send somebody over by the end of the working day with a memory stick,' Kate said, unwilling to allow Booth to dictate a timetable. 'Please have it ready. And thanks for this.' She waved the folder at him and started walking to the door. Mark Harrison appeared from behind the reception desk and flashed his key fob at the sensor, allowing them out into the chilly November air.

'Well, that was–' Kate's phone buzzed in her pocket. She checked the screen. Priya Das. It looked like Sam had been right.

'Fletcher?' Das barked at her. Kate knew she was in trouble – the DCI never used her surname. 'We have a huge problem. You need to get back to Doncaster Central now. I'll see you in my office in half an hour and you'd better be prepared to turn everything on this case over to DS O'Connor until we get this mess sorted out.'

'What–' Kate started to ask but Das had already hung up.

JULY 1988

'Where's Ned?' Dusty whispered peering over Lucky's shoulder, trying to see if their friend was lurking in the gloom between the tents.

'Not coming,' Lucky said with a shrug. 'Says he doesn't feel like it.'

'What's up with him?'

'Dunno. He's wrapped up in his sleeping bag. Told me to fuck off when I tried to get him out.'

Dusty was puzzled. This night walk had been Ned's idea. There was no way he'd back out without a good reason. He'd been weird at teatime as well. He hadn't eaten much and had hardly spoken to anyone as far as she could tell. She hadn't been sitting with him and Lucky because they'd been made to pair up with the person they shared a tent with so she'd had to put up with dopey Angela for an hour instead of sharing the meal with her friends.

'Is he not well?' she asked Lucky.

'I said I don't know!' Lucky snapped back a little too loudly, causing them both to look around in case they'd woken up one of the teachers. 'He didn't seem to want to talk to me, so I took his advice and fucked off.' Lucky's voice had lowered to a hiss and Dusty could tell that he didn't want to talk about Ned's emotional or physical state. It was another of the growing differences between them and an increasing source of friction. How many times had one of the boys laughed when she tried to explore their feelings? She had laughed herself, but she knew that none of them meant it – that beneath the surface there were things that were becoming more difficult to talk about as they grew up. And feelings were very much off limits.

But she couldn't let it go. She didn't know why. Maybe it was Lucky's blasé attitude to his friend's distress or it might have been her own bloody-mindedness – Ned had planned this so the least he could do was to turn up. She tiptoed over to the boys' tent and unzipped the front flaps as quietly as she could manage.

'Ned?'

She couldn't see much inside except for a large dark lump which she assumed was Ned.

'Ned!' she hissed again, sticking her head and shoulders through the gap between the hanging folds of fabric. 'Since when are you a chicken? This was your bloody idea so get yourself up and come with us.'

The lump moved slightly and Dusty heard a muffled sniff. 'Ned? What's up?'

A sigh from the lump. 'Nothing's up. I've just changed my mind. Leave me alone. You and Lucky go.'

There was nothing else to be said. If Ned didn't want to talk and didn't want to go with them there wasn't much that Dusty could do about it. She couldn't spend all night arguing with him about it either – the first hint of raised voices would be sure to send an adult in their direction.

'And zip the doors up,' Ned said as Dusty withdrew her head.

'Well?' Lucky asked as Dusty crept back to where he'd been waiting in the deep shadows under a huge tree.

'He's not coming,' she said. 'It's just us.'

'Okay, so what do we do? This was Ned's plan. Where shall we go?'

Dusty looked around. Her eyes had adjusted to the light and she was surprised that there were still faint streaks of pink and orange in the blue-black sky. The tents were a huddle of pale shapes on the silvery parched grass, turned metallic by the light from a three-quarter moon. It was tempting to just run around them yelling, to give everybody a fright and then go back to bed, but she didn't think that was what Ned had in mind and she felt a strong spark of loyalty to him despite his resistance to her questions.

'Let's see what the teachers are up to,' she whispered, nodding towards the solid black block of the wooden building which housed the staff accommodation. 'I bet they're all still up drinking and playing cards without Mrs Dalston to keep an eye on them.'

There had been a sense of shock in the camp earlier when the instructor who'd taken their teacher to the hospital had returned without her. He'd spent some time reassuring the students that Mrs Dalston would be fine – it was a clean break and she'd be in plaster for a few weeks but no permanent damage. It had still felt a bit strange having tea without her, though.

There was just enough light for her to read Lucky's doubtful expression. 'What if they catch us?'

'Then they'll just send us back to our tents. It's not like we're doing anything – just having a wander round.'

Lucky shook his head. 'I dunno...'

Shocked, Dusty saw that his eyes were wide, the whites clearly visible all round his pupils. Lucky was frightened. Whether it was the darkness or the fear of being caught by the adults, Dusty couldn't be sure but, now she thought about it, his voice had been trembling since they'd met up.

'Or we could just go back,' she said. 'We've been out and had a look around. There's not really much to do anyway. Maybe Ned had something in mind but it's not the same without him.'

The relief was obvious in Lucky's face as he nodded his agreement. 'Okay,' he said. 'If that's what you want.'

And suddenly Dusty was furious. *If that's what you want.* Putting the blame on her when he was obviously scared stiff. Well, she wasn't going to let him get away with that. 'No, it's not what *I* want. *I* want to go and spy on the teachers. I only said it because you're shitting yourself. Come on.'

She walked towards the shadow of the building imagining

that it was a huge mouth waiting to swallow her up in its darkness. She didn't bother to see if Lucky was following her, she didn't care. He could do what he wanted but she wouldn't let him get away with making out that she was the one who was scared.

'Dusty?'

She turned round and Lucky walked into her. 'What?'

'Slow down. They'll hear us if you keep stomping about like that.'

'A bit late for that,' said a deep voice from the darkness.

Dusty took a step away from the sound and trod on something behind her.

'Shit! That was my foot,' Lucky yelped.

'You don't know what pain is, you little cunt,' said another voice, this time from behind Lucky. 'But you're about to find out. Think you can get away with breaking the rules?'

Dusty turned to see Mr Whitaker emerge from the deepest of the shadows. 'You c-c-can't talk to us like that,' she stammered. 'I'll tell my mam.'

'And *I'll* tell her that you were trying to steal cigarettes from the staff. That *is* why you're out here at this time of night, isn't it?'

'No!' Lucky squawked. 'We just wanted to see what it was like in the dark.'

'You need to keep them quiet,' the mysterious voice behind Lucky said. 'We don't want the other kids waking up.'

Dusty saw Whitaker nod and then, without seeming to move he'd caught the top of her arm in an iron grip.

'Right, you two. Let's show you what happens to naughty little children who can't do as they're told.'

She tried to resist as he pulled her towards the building, but he was a grown man and much too strong for her. A door opened in front of her, spilling dull orange light out onto the grass. A huge figure was silhouetted in the rectangle of brightness – the sergeant major. He crossed his arms and leaned against the door jamb as though he had been expecting them and, as they got closer, Dusty could see that he was grinning to himself. She looked back over her shoulder and saw Lucky's pale face contort with pain as he struggled with a member of the centre staff. The one who'd taken Mrs Dalston to the hospital.

For a second she considered shouting for help. But who would come? There were no other adults within earshot and none of her classmates would be able to do anything – they were just a bunch of kids.

There was nobody here to help them. Nobody at all.

10

P riya Das was the polar opposite of Kate's previous DCI, Bill Raymond. Raymond had been an imposing figure and his physical stature and forceful personality had gained him a reputation as someone not to be crossed. Where Raymond had been tall and broad, Das was tiny. Where Raymond had been loud and sometimes belligerent, Das was softly spoken and showed others due consideration in discussion. And where Raymond had been 'old school', Das was keen to embrace new technology and cutting-edge methods of investigation. That was one reason why she'd wanted to attend the post-mortem of the body from the storage facility – it was a puzzle and, Kate knew, Das loved a puzzle.

Now facing the DCI across Raymond's old desk, Kate felt like she was being assessed to see exactly where she fitted into some bigger picture. Das's dark brown eyes stared into her own as though trying to read Kate's thoughts, allowing Kate time to study her boss and to try to work out what was going on.

Despite her small build, Das appeared to have the knack of dressing for maximum impact. Almost as soon as they'd met, Kate could see that she was a woman who knew exactly which clothes and make-up suited her and how to use that knowledge to her own advantage. Today she was wearing a dark grey suit, appropriately sombre considering she'd attended a post-mortem but, underneath, she wore a deep red blouse which complemented her dark skin and minimal make-up. It was a slash of colour that flashed a warning to anybody who thought they might be able to intimidate or manipulate her.

Das's short black hair was styled into what some might describe as a pixie cut but nobody who knew the woman would dare associate her with a playful sprite. Priya Das was a woman to be reckoned with and Kate was now facing a reckoning of her own.

'Ma'am, if I could just ask what exactly–'

'Sit,' Das barked, pointing at a chair while she remained standing by the window. Backlit by the fading sunlight she was a blur of red and black.

Kate did as instructed and waited for the onslaught of Das's wrath. She wasn't sure what she'd done but she had no doubt that, whatever it was, the DCI felt justified in treating her like this. Sam hadn't been wrong when she'd hinted at Kate being Das's favourite, but it looked like that was firmly in the past.

'Chris Gilruth,' Das began. 'You knew him?'

'I worked with him in Cumbria,' Kate said, trying to keep the details of her relationship with Chris as simple as possible.

'You also found his body a few days ago.'

So, it *had* been him. Even though she'd been expecting it, the grief was a blow. Images of Chris played in her mind on fast forward until that final one – the body on the wet hillside at dusk.

'I didn't find the body. An elderly couple spotted it when they were heading back to their car. I wasn't even sure that it was Chris.' Suddenly this fact seemed important. Kate had just kept a vigil. She hadn't been the one to find Chris.

'It was. Cumbria Constabulary confirmed it this morning. A DCI Bland asked me to pass the information on to you.'

Kate nodded. This still didn't explain why Das was so angry.

'Bland also hinted that you and Gilruth had been a little closer than colleagues.'

Was that what this was all about – rumours of a workplace romance had got the DCI's back up? If so, her reaction was disproportionate to the supposed offence. Kate wouldn't have categorised her relationship with Chris as a romance.

'It was nothing, ma'am,' Kate replied truthfully. 'We were both having a rough time with our respective partners and things went a bit further than they should have. A few kisses and that was it. Chris wanted to make things work with his wife and I... well, I moved down here. I really don't see how a misjudged friendship a few years ago would make you want me off this current case. I'm sad about Chris but I hadn't spoken to him for three years.'

Das shook her head. 'It's not that. Not *just* that. We got DNA back on the body from the storage place. Kailisa talked me through it as the results came back while I was at the PM. All the body parts are from the same victim – which is good news. She wasn't on the database but Kailisa had asked for a familial match as well in case we could track down a relative.'

'And one turned up?'

'Indeed,' Das said. She stepped away from the window and sat down opposite Kate.

'The dismembered woman's DNA flagged a match with a police officer who was living in Cumbria. She was Chris Gilruth's mother.'

Kate closed her eyes as the room started spinning. Nothing was making any sense. How could the two be linked? An accident in the Lake District and a murder in Doncaster? How could the dismembered body be Chris's mother?

Then she saw what Das had seen. The connection was her, Kate. She'd known Chris and she was involved in the investigation into the murder.

'I'm afraid there's more,' Das was saying. 'Gilruth's body underwent a PM because of the circumstances of the discovery. Kate, I'm really sorry but Chris Gilruth was murdered. The local team think he was approached by somebody who stabbed him in the chest – possibly under the guise of asking for directions. The details are sketchy. They think he might have been pushed from a height in order to prevent his body from being discovered. His wife had reported him missing three days before he was found and Mountain Rescue had been out looking – it's likely that the heavy rain washed the body down the hillside.'

'He was killed?'

Das nodded.

'And his mother? But that makes no sense. Chris's mother lived near Kendal. I met her. How did she turn up dead in Doncaster?'

'I don't have any other details.' Das was almost apologetic. 'But I need to take you off this case until things are a little clearer.'

'No.'

Das raised her eyebrows. 'No?'

'The dismembered body is Margaret Wallace also known as Margaret Whitaker. I'm almost certain of that – Sam's spent a lot of time digging and she's rarely wrong. How can she be Chris's mother? I met Chris's mother.' Kate knew that she was repeating herself, but she could only go round in circles with the information that she had. 'Hang on. Surely Cumbria Constabulary have been in touch with Chris's family. They'd know if his mother was missing as well. His wife would have known. You need to find out. Her name was Maureen Gilruth and she lived in Staveley. You need to find out.'

Das made a note on the jotter on her desk. 'I'll contact Bland and see what he says. I understand how upsetting this is for you but, until we've conclusively established the identity of the dismembered body, I feel I need to keep you away from this case. If the press get hold of the link, they'll have a field day.'

So that was the problem – bad publicity. She'd come to expect this from Raymond but she'd hoped that Das could think a little more creatively.

'Listen,' she tried again to make her case. 'Dan and I have been to a nursing home where Margaret Wallace was staying. She was discharged from there by a woman claiming to be her niece. Dan's got the records, including a fairly recent photograph. Her husband's serving six months in Wakefield for a grooming offence. He could identify the body if the photograph is inconclusive. If this woman is Chris Gilruth's mother, then I'm almost certain that she isn't the woman I met in Cumbria. And if she is his mother, what are the chances that David Whitaker or Wallace, whichever you prefer, is his father?'

Das tapped her pen on the desk, her eyes focused on a point somewhere above Kate's head. 'Okay,' she said eventually. 'I don't want to kick you off the case, Kate. I was just so bloody angry when I thought you hadn't told me about the connection between Gilruth and our body.'

'But I–'

'I know, you had no idea,' Das said, holding up a hand. 'But it's still a hell of a coincidence. I need to check through the notes that Hollis got from the residential home – I can send the photo to Doctor Kailisa to see if he can confirm identification. With a provisional ID we might be able to access her dental records if the husband will give consent. I'll get Kailisa to see if there's a DNA match between Gilruth and Whitaker as well – that might take a bit of time. I'll ring Bland and see what he can tell me about Maureen Gilruth. But, until I can get this clear in my head, I want you to take a break from it. In fact, go home now and take tomorrow off. It's not official and I don't want to have to make it official, so stay away until I ask you to come back. I'll ask O'Connor to take up the slack.'

Kate wasn't mollified. It felt like she was being suspended even though she knew that Das was actually trying to spare her some trauma. 'What about the leads from the nursing home? We need to get CCTV and to follow up on the addresses for the niece.'

Das sighed. 'Kate, you run a tight team. I know they all have their own skills and talents and I know that a lot of what they're capable of is down to your mentoring. Trust me and trust them.'

Das was right. Every member of the team could follow up on the information they already had without even being asked. Cooper would check the CCTV. Barratt would organise the interview with Calvin Russell. Dan would follow up the DNA and organise for Whitaker to ID the body if necessary. And O'Connor? Well, maybe he'd enjoy being in charge for a few days – although Kate found that a little unlikely.

She'd run out of arguments.

'Kate,' Das said softly. 'Go home.'

11

When Kate pushed open the door to her flat she could hear the radio, and steam was drifting into the hallway from the kitchen. Nearly a year on and she still hadn't got used to finding Nick making dinner when she got home. Not that he was there every night. She loved him but she also loved having time and space to herself and she was glad that she'd found somebody who could respect that. Even on the rare nights that she stayed at his house he'd never smothered her or tried to persuade her to move in with him.

Her flat was the better option for both of them – close to Doncaster Central and five minutes from the hospital where Nick worked as an oncology specialist – but they both agreed it was far too small. Kate thought that they might, eventually, live together, but that was still quite a way into the future.

'What's for tea?' she asked, pushing the kitchen door wider open. Another blast of herby steam welcomed her.

Nick turned, his dark hair plastered to his forehead by the damp heat of the kitchen and Kate felt her pulse quicken. Nearly a year and he could still take her breath away. 'Moussaka? I'm just making the sauce.'

She laughed and stepped forward to wrap her arms around his waist. 'Moussaka, isn't that a bit of a cliché?'

'What, I'm not allowed to cook Greek food because I'm Greek? Then you can't make shepherd's pie, or Yorkshire pudding, or fish and chips.'

Kate grinned at him. 'Deal. No cooking for me.'

He smiled back at her. 'You're early. This was supposed to be in the oven by the time you got home. Everything okay?'

She paused before answering. How could she explain how shit everything was without giving out details of the case? Eventually she opted for, 'Not really, but I can't talk about it.'

Nick nodded and turned back to the cooker to stir his sauce. 'Tough case?'

'Something like that. I heard that the body in Langdale was Chris Gilruth. I'd been expecting it, but it still came as a bit of a shock.'

'I'm sorry,' Nick said without turning round. They'd spoken about Chris the evening of the discovery of the body, but Kate hadn't told Nick everything. He thought that she and Chris had just been colleagues.

'Das sent me home.'

Nick turned to face her again, frowning this time. 'How come?'

'Can you turn that off and come and sit down with me. I think we need to talk. There's some stuff that I want to tell you before you hear it anywhere else.'

'What sort of stuff?'

Kate shook her head. 'Not here. Turn it off and come into the sitting room.'

She walked down the hallway, hoping that he'd follow, and threw herself on the sofa in the lounge. This wasn't a conversation for a casual chat over the stove. This could be serious – if her relationship with Chris became common knowledge it could undermine her authority with her team, especially given the connection with the current case.

'What's up?' Nick joined her on the sofa and turned to face her.

'I haven't told you everything about me and Chris.'

'Me and Chris?' Nick pulled a face that was half smile, half scowl. 'I wasn't aware that there had been a "me and Chris".'

'There wasn't, not really. It was something and nothing.' She reached out and put a hand on his thigh, more to reassure herself than him. 'Before I moved back down here, me and Chris were close. We worked a couple of cases together, did some late nights and one thing led to another. I was still reeling from Garry's latest betrayal and Chris thought his marriage was over.'

Nick's eyes narrowed. 'One thing led to another? Did you sleep with him?'

Kate withdrew her hand and edged away from him. 'Oh, please don't tell me you're jealous. This was a couple of years before I knew you.'

'Did you sleep with him?' Nick repeated.

'It's none of your business – what I did before I met you and who I did it with. What the hell's wrong with you?'

Nick stood up and strode over to the window. 'It's not that,' he said, his back to her. 'I'm not jealous.'

'So, what's up?'

He turned to face her, his dark eyes serious. 'It's the hypocrisy. You told me all about Garry and how he went off with other women – but what about you?'

'Garry had left me,' Kate said, baffled. This wasn't like Nick at all.

'But Chris was married. You told me that he lived with his wife and kids in Kendal. You were upset for them when you thought the body was him.'

'And he went back to her. He made a go of it. Nothing we did hurt his wife because he went back.'

'Did she know? His wife?'

Kate shrugged. 'I have no idea. Two months after Chris said he wanted to make his marriage work I moved down here.' She thought she should tell Nick that she hadn't slept with Chris. That she'd wanted to, but they'd decided that it was a bad idea. They'd done the right thing. But she didn't need or want Nick's forgiveness just as she didn't deserve his judgement.

'I just don't think it's right, that's all,' Nick continued. 'You knew how it felt to be the other woman and yet you did that to somebody else's wife.'

'Jesus!' Kate spat. 'What's this? Your bloody orthodox upbringing suddenly kicking in? You have no right to judge me. You weren't there. You have no idea what happened or how I felt.'

'So, tell me,' Nick said, slumping in the armchair opposite the sofa. 'Explain.'

For a second, Kate was tempted. It was just a couple of kisses and *what ifs* but neither she nor Chris were really interested in a relationship and she'd been relieved when he'd told her that he didn't want to take it further, that he wanted his marriage to work. But the stubborn part of her brain and the part that was still stinging from the way Das had treated her conspired to make her shitty day just a little bit shittier.

'No,' she said. 'Why should I? I'm sick of having to defend myself and justify my actions – I get enough of that at work. What happened between me and Chris is *my* business, it's on *my* conscience and it's in the past. I've had a crap day and it's just getting crappier. I want you to leave.'

Nick flinched back, his expression one of surprise and hurt. 'But I...'

'Just go, Nick!' she yelled, marching out of the sitting room and shutting herself in her bedroom. 'And take your fucking moussaka with you!'

12

DC Matt Barratt felt almost sorry for the young man sitting opposite him in the interview room. Calvin Russell looked like a child who'd been caught shoplifting and been turned in by his parents to teach him a lesson. He sat with his chair pulled in close to the desk, sitting up straight as though trying to show that he was attentive and willing to co-operate. He'd removed his dark blue baseball cap and tried to smooth down his dark hair probably more out of habit than necessity given the shortness of the cut. His eyes flicked from Barratt to O'Connor who was sitting next to him and then to the two corners of the room that Russell could see from his position. He didn't look at the duty solicitor: didn't even acknowledge her presence until she spoke which seemed to make him jump slightly in his seat.

'I want it on the record that my client came in for interview willingly and that he is keen to co-operate with this enquiry,' she said as soon as Barratt had started the recording and got the formalities out of the way.

Barratt nodded. 'And, as you're aware, we're *not* conducting this interview under caution, but it is being recorded with Mr Russell's permission. Mr Russell claims to understand what that means and has stated his intention to co-operate.'

Barratt hadn't encountered Sherry Pines before but some of his colleagues had warned him that she was an absolute stickler for procedure and that she would call an end to the interview at the slightest hint of irregularity.

Pines nodded for Barratt to continue.

'Thanks for coming in so early, Calvin. It's important that we get on with this as quickly as possible.'

Russell nodded. 'Early is best. At least I won't miss too much work. Mr Hibberts says he'll pay me while I'm here, but I don't want him to think I'm skiving.'

Barratt gave him what he hoped was a reassuring smile. 'So, Calvin, on the day you discovered the body, you told me that you were good with computers. Do you remember that?'

Russell nodded. 'Yes.'

'Do you have any formal qualifications in information technology?'

'No.'

'You didn't do IT at school?'

'No. I didn't do very well at school. I always liked computers, though.'

'So, your knowledge of computers is self-taught?' Barratt felt O'Connor's foot tap his own. They'd agreed before the interview that Barratt would lead and also that he would let Russell answer fully, without prompting.

'I got a laptop when I was eleven – my sister bought it for me – and I learnt how to use it. It's not difficult really.'

'So, what programmes can you use?'

Russell grinned at him as though, finally, he felt on safe ground. 'I'm pretty good with all the Microsoft stuff. Word, Excel and e-mail. I like keeping things in order, so I use spreadsheets.

That's why Mr Hibberts took me on – he likes everything in order as well.'

Barratt made a note. This wasn't the information he required. 'What about the internet? Do you use it a lot?'

'Not at work.'

'Why's that?'

Russell glanced at his solicitor and blushed. 'Mr Hibberts caught me doing something I shouldn't have been, so he told me not to use the internet at work.'

Barratt struggled to keep his face straight. 'What were you doing, Calvin?'

Russell hung his head and mumbled something.

'I'm sorry, Calvin, I didn't hear you.'

'I was playing online games and I missed two important phone calls.'

'What were you playing?'

'Minecraft.'

Pines sat more upright in her seat and gave a theatrical sigh. 'Is this really relevant?'

Barratt tilted his head to one side and gave her his best patronising smile. 'I wouldn't be asking if it wasn't. So, Calvin, do you play games on your laptop at home?'

Russell nodded but Barratt saw little point in pursuing this line. Pines was right – this wasn't relevant – and he was unconvinced that Russell had the skills or experience to hack into a computer system and alter confidential records.

'What else can you do on a computer? Do you chat with other people, Facebook, Twitter?'

'I don't do that stuff,' Russell said. 'My sister, Clare, told me that there are some bad people out there who pretend to be friendly but they aren't. She said they might take advantage of me because I'm not very good with people. I just play games.'

This was getting them nowhere and Barratt could feel

O'Connor's seat vibrating as he twitched his leg up and down in frustration. In his previous interviews with O'Connor, the DS had taken the lead, but he felt like he'd formed a bit of a bond with Russell during their previous encounter and O'Connor had been happy to take a back seat. Barratt thought the DS had enough on his plate with Fletcher being AWOL – he knew that O'Connor preferred to do his own thing and he wasn't overly comfortable being in charge of the team. Fortunately for all of them, Fletcher had allocated jobs before she'd left the previous day, so her absence hadn't been felt too much so far. O'Connor had spent part of the day chasing information on the owner of the storage facility but didn't seem to have found anything helpful and this interview was looking like a dead end.

'Calvin, do you know what a hacker is?' O'Connor asked abruptly. So much for not asking leading questions.

Russell nodded. 'It's somebody who gets into other people's computers without permission.'

'And how would somebody do that?'

Russell looked blank.

'Come on, Calvin. How would somebody hack into a computer?'

Russell gave his solicitor a panicked look. 'I don't know.'

'Really. Somebody who's as good with computers as you claim to be, and you don't know how to get into somebody else's data?'

'No. And even if I did, I wouldn't. It's not right.'

Barratt was convinced – Russell's distress was completely sincere.

O'Connor nodded. 'I believe you, Calvin. But I just needed to check. Is there anything else you'd like to tell us about your job? Anything that might help us to find out who killed that old woman?'

Another glance at Pines. 'I don't want to say in case I get it wrong?'

Barratt leaned forward. This was interesting. Russell hadn't given any indication that he had any further information up until now. 'You can tell us anything,' he prompted. 'It won't get back to Mr Hibberts.'

'It's not about him,' Russell said. 'It's about the man who rented the storage locker. The one where the body was found.'

'Go on.'

'He didn't look quite right. His face and that. And his hands. That's what I noticed most.'

'In what way?'

Russell shook his head and sat back. 'I don't want to say.'

'Come on, Calvin,' Barratt lowered his voice. 'This could help us to catch whoever killed that woman before he kills somebody else. You could be a hero.'

Russell seemed to consider this for a few seconds then gave a hint of a smile. 'He wasn't really a man. Not properly. Or he might have been. I'm not sure. I know there's a word that you're supposed to use to be polite.'

'What word, Calvin?'

'I think he might not always have been a man. He might have been a transgender.'

'What makes you say that?'

'His hands were small,' Russell said, more sure of himself now. 'And his voice was quite high-pitched. He had a beard, but it was a bit scraggly.'

'Could he have been a woman dressed as a man? Are you sure he was transgender?'

'I suppose he could have been a woman dressed up. I just thought that's what we are supposed to say nowadays though – transgender.'

Barratt's mind was racing. This changed everything they

thought they knew about their suspect. If it had been a woman all along, it tied in with what Hollis had told them about the woman who took Margaret from the nursing home. They could be looking for a single female suspect. O'Connor had obviously had a similar thought because the leg was jiggling frantically. It was time to wrap up the interview.

'Calvin, would you be happy to work with a police artist? You could describe this person and the artist would try to draw them.'

'With a pencil?'

Barratt shook his head and grinned at the other man. 'No, on a computer. It's fascinating to watch.'

Russell returned his smile. 'Yes. When can I do that?'

Barratt explained that it would take a few days to organise, but it would be really helpful. He promised to be in touch and then summoned a uniformed officer to escort Russell and Pines back to the front desk.

'Well?' he turned to O'Connor who was frowning, deep in thought.

'I don't know if this is a breakthrough or a setback,' O'Connor admitted. 'We might know more when we get the image done. It does link with what Fletcher and Hollis found out yesterday though. I think I need to run this past Das. And I think we need to get Kate back as soon as possible – this is way too big for me to handle without her.'

13

K ate took a big gulp of coffee and logged on to her laptop. Her slightly fuzzy head and very furry tongue reminded her that she'd had too much wine the previous night but, without Nick to share the bottle, she'd felt justified in polishing it all off as it would only have gone to waste otherwise. And it wasn't like she had to get up for work the next day.

After Nick had left, Kate had slunk out of her bedroom to check the kitchen. Despite her instruction, he'd left the moussaka filling, the white sauce and the fried slices of aubergine on the stove top awaiting their final places, layered up in an oven dish. It would have been simple for Kate to have finished the process but instead she'd opened the bread bin, cut a chunk off a white loaf that she didn't remember buying and took it into the sitting room with the pan of meat and tomato sauce and a large glass of white wine.

She hadn't been able to shake the feeling that the key to the two murders lay in the past – in whatever Whitaker had done while he was working at Sheffield Road Juniors, possibly thirty years ago. She could see how somebody might want to kill his wife as some sort of twisted revenge but what about Chris Gilruth?

It was the time span that gave her the idea. She'd looked for anything that mentioned any sort of school reunion and her search had led her inevitably to Facebook. There appeared to be three groups connected with school reunions for Sheffield Road Juniors but, without a Facebook account, Kate had no access to any of them. She'd considered ringing Sam Cooper, but she'd had just enough wine to feel confident that she could manage this herself and ten minutes later she had a Facebook account in the name Cathy Siddons – the name she'd been known by all through her childhood in Thorpe. It hadn't been quite as simple as she'd imagined though. Each group was private and she had to send a request to join. After that it had been a waiting game.

Now, in the harsh morning light, with a mild hangover, Kate wondered if she'd been a bit rash. It was unlikely that any Facebook group would accept a new member who had just joined the site and had no friends and, even if she had been accepted, the chances of the group representing the correct school year accepting her were slim.

The message icon at the top of her Facebook homepage had a red tick next to it so she clicked on it to see who had contacted her. There were two messages, both from admin members of groups that she'd applied to join the previous evening. One simply informed her that she'd been accepted into the group and could now view status updates and the other was a message accepting her into another group but this time with a personal touch.

Hi Cathy. I don't remember you but there was a Karen Siddons in my year. Are you related?

'And that's why I don't do social media,' Kate muttered to herself as she clicked a link to the first reunion group and started scrolling down the page.

Some of the images on the page were breathtaking in their familiarity. Visiting the school had been a jolt but so much had changed that it had been possible for Kate to remember that she was no longer a child. Now, the constant scroll of photographs triggered memory after memory. Teachers, sports days, school trips – everything was a reminder of a childhood that had been almost ridiculously happy until her mother had died when Kate was nine.

She saw class photos – three irregular rows of children like a crumbling Aztec pyramid – the faces not quite familiar but the clothes and poses could have been from any class she'd been in for the four years that she'd been at the school. She did recognise some of the teachers, though, and was surprised to find that she could name most of the ones who had taught her, even though the photographs were from at least ten years after she'd left the school. Their hairstyles had changed, the faces were a little more lined, but they were still the same people who'd obviously left an impression on her.

And then she spotted Mrs Dalston.

Mrs Dalston had been Kate's teacher the year her mum had died and had been instrumental in helping her cope with the grief and sense of loss. She'd given Kate books to keep her occupied. Books that were for older children, books about loss and anger, and also books that were pure escapism.

Kate hovered the cursor on the photograph and was surprised when a name appeared – Liz Dalston. She'd been tagged in the photograph, which suggested that she had joined Facebook and was potentially still alive. Kate clicked on the image and it took her to the teacher's homepage – a few pictures which looked like they might have been from foreign holidays and two images of a scruffy-looking mongrel. Nothing from her days at Sheffield Road Juniors.

Kate was about to start trawling the second reunion page when her mobile rang. 'Sam, anything from the CCTV?'

She heard Cooper sigh at the other end. 'There's nothing from when Margaret was admitted or whatever they call it. The company doesn't keep the footage for that long. The day she left the cameras seem to have been on the blink. The recording is rooted in the IT system so, if somebody did hack in to change Margaret's records it seems likely that they went in again to destroy a section of the recording. It's too time-specific to be a coincidence. I think whoever we're looking for knows what they're doing.'

'What about Calvin Russell? Has Matt interviewed him yet?'

'Yep. He's not our hacker. But he did give us one interesting piece of information. He reckons that the person who rented the storage locker might have been trans.'

'Based on?'

'He claims that they looked more like a boy than a man and that the hands were quite feminine.'

'Could have been a woman in disguise,' Kate mused.

'The niece?'

'Possibly. But I'd bet a lot of money that I don't have that she's not Margaret's niece.'

'She's not,' Cooper confirmed. 'I've checked the family history as far as I can. There's no suggestion that Margaret had a niece, but she did have a nephew. You're not going to like this though.'

'Go on.'

'Well, for a start, Margaret doesn't have a sister called Deirdre – there's one called Maureen, though. And she has a son – Christopher Gilruth. He's registered as the child of Maureen and Duncan Gilruth. The father's dead but the mother lives near Kendal.'

Kate felt sick. Chris had told her that Maureen was his

mother, but the DNA was conclusive. Chris had been Margaret's son and Maureen's nephew. She wondered whether Chris had known the truth.

'Sam, see if you can find any record of Chris Gilruth having been adopted by his aunt. I'm not hopeful because things aren't always done officially in families, but you never know. And let me know when you've got a result on the father.'

Sam had gone quiet.

'I know I'm officially on leave,' Kate said. 'And I'm pretty sure you all know why, but I'd like to be kept in the loop until I get back. You've gone this far, contacting me this morning. Das seems to think that I'm connected to the two murders but it's all coincidence. I knew Chris in Cumbria, but I had no idea that the body we found was his mother. And I'm certain I've never met the woman.'

'I'll see what I can do,' Cooper offered. 'But I hope you're coming back soon. Das'll see sense, she really rates you, you know.'

They spent another few minutes chatting about how O'Connor had stepped up to lead the investigation and how he was doing a good job but it was obvious that he didn't want the responsibility. Kate had expected nothing less. O'Connor was a good DS in many ways and had proven his worth on Kate's last two murder cases, but he wasn't promotion material. He'd reached a level that he was comfortable with and seemed content to stay there.

Before she hung up, Kate gave the DC her new Facebook login details. If anybody could find anything in either of the groups, it would be Sam.

* * *

Do you know how difficult it is to cut up a body? I had no idea. The drugs were the simple part – I'd just crushed them up in her tea and she drank it all down without a murmur. I'd made sure to kill her upstairs as there was no way I could lug a body, even one as frail as her, up to the bathroom. Not that I'm not fit, but the stairs have an awkward turn just before the top and I'd have probably sent both of us tumbling to the bottom if I'd tried to negotiate it, and probably killed myself at the same time.

Funny, when I picked her up to put her in the bath, she hardly weighed anything. It was like lifting a shop dummy and only slightly less stiff. Everything I'd read suggested that rigor mortis didn't set in until a body had been dead for a few hours but manoeuvring the old lady into the bathroom was like trying to get last year's Christmas tree through a narrow doorway.

And then, when I got her in the bath, she went down with such a thump I found myself worrying that I'd hurt her. Stupid really.

I hadn't planned to kill her straight away. I'm not really sure that I planned to kill her at all, I just knew that taking her away from the home would torment him, her husband. Her bloody rambling convinced me that it was the right thing to do though. I didn't understand at first. She kept mumbling something about Christopher and how he never came to visit and how his father would have loved him so much. It took a while to realise that the father was him – Whitaker – and that Christopher was her son.

That changed everything. I thought I might keep her for a bit, to torment him when he got out of prison, but knowing that this woman had a child with that bastard was too much to take in. I did a bit of research on the family but there was no record of a child. So, she'd managed to get him away from his father before Whitaker could do anything? She saved her own child from the monster, but she stayed with him. She must have known what he was, but she did nothing to protect his other victims – only her son. A bit more digging led me to a sister who had a son called Christopher. So that was the arrangement, was it? The sister brought up the child in safety while Whitaker was free to do what he wanted; to destroy more lives.

That's when I knew it was right to kill the old lady.

I thought I'd be sick. Really, properly sick the minute I started cutting but, strangely, after the first cut, it didn't bother me. It was just a job that had to be done. I'd tried to read up on methods to cut up a body but most of the stuff I found online was a bit stupid – people blogging about disposing of bodies in basements after first dates that went wrong, that sort of thing – so I decided to approach it from a more practical point of view. It's just butchery after all, so I'd ordered the appropriate tools and read about how to reduce a cow to steak and ribs and other bits. A human body is no different really. The only problem was that I didn't want to have too many pieces to deal with. I stared at her, lying there in my bath, and imagined thick black lines where I wanted to cut. Ten pieces in ten boxes. Two each for the legs, two each for the arms, one for the head and one for the torso. Butchery.

I did the head first. Wouldn't you? It dehumanised the body – she was just meat once the head was gone. After that I took off both arms – the shoulders were a bit of a bugger though because I couldn't get *them to dislocate so I ended up cutting through the top of each humerus and then cutting through the lower arms just below the elbows. The knives I'd bought were excellent – really sharp – and the meat saw was a godsend.*

The legs were a bit easier. I'd learnt my lesson with the shoulders, so I didn't even try to dislocate the hips. Same with the lower legs; and then I was done. I wrapped the torso up in the nightdress – I'd left it on the bathroom chair so it didn't get too bloody – and then put everything in boxes. A quick swill round with the showerhead and everything was back to normal. I know I should have scrubbed the bath with bleach but there didn't seem much point. The police will work it out eventually.

The daft lad at the storage place didn't even blink when I asked to pay cash up front for six months. Everybody knows that Hibberts has run that place into the ground and it's only his dodgy customers that are keeping him afloat. Poor kid probably thought I was one of Hibberts's mates. He didn't seem to notice anything unusual about my appearance when he took my money, but I kept my back to the camera and my head down just to be sure.

And that was that. I stuck the boxes in the furthest corner of the space I'd been allocated, bunged some other random junk around them that I'd picked up from where somebody had done a bit of fly tipping near the old railway bridge, and went home. I know that the plastic bags and plastic boxes won't conceal the smell forever, but they'll probably give me a couple of months to get everything else sorted out.

The sense of relief was incredible. To finally have started to lift the burden that I've been carrying around for so long. Any doubts that I might have had vanished as soon as I got home. I had a purpose and a plan.

The son was much easier. How many times have you heard kids being

told to be careful on social media? And why don't adults think the advice applies to them? Well, male adults at least. Chris accepted my Facebook request almost instantly and had obviously been fooled by the photographs of mountains and walking gear that I'd uploaded. The photograph I'd chosen was of a hairy outdoorsy-looking man in his mid-twenties – easily copied from an advertising website – and Johnny Chase was born. It had been simple to find out Chris's routine and what he enjoyed on his days off and he'd been keen to describe his planned route across the Langdales.

I'm not much of a hill walker but we all have to make sacrifices sometimes, so I'd bought a pair of boots from one of the walking shops in Sheffield and spent a week or so breaking them in before I set up the fake profile. I also got myself a rucksack, a pair of walking poles and a map. The map was essential – not for navigation but because it was a key prop in my plan to get Chris close enough for me to ambush him. I'd thought long and hard about Christopher and it wasn't fair that he got to live his happy life while others had suffered so much. And what about his children? Were they safe from a man who had Whitaker's blood flowing through his veins? He was a policeman – the perfect cover, like being a teacher – God knows what sort of material he had access to, what sort of favours he called in. I thought, if I could talk to him, I'd know. I just needed to meet him. But I needed to be prepared to get rid of him if there was any doubt at all.

I'd been to the Lakes a few times when I was younger and I'd pored over the route until I felt like I could walk it with my eyes closed; then it was just a matter of booking a B&B for the same weekend that Chris said he was 'doing' the Langdales. I knew it was risky. There were so many things that could have gone wrong. He might have changed his mind, he might have a friend with him, there might be too many other people around...

All I could do was take the chance and hope for the best. If I failed, then I could set up another opportunity at a later date.

I'm not a great believer in signs and auspicious omens but the *morning I'd planned to 'bump into' Chris was cloudy with a high probability of rain. I'd checked in with him as Johnny the night before and he was still planning to attempt the route whatever the weather, claiming it would give him some much-needed 'head space'. Hoping that the rain would put a lot of people off I set out from the car park near Sticklebarn about an hour earlier than Chris's intended start time. It was a slog up to Stickle Tarn but, after a ten-minute rest I was ready for the next climb. I tried to picture Chris doing the route in the opposite direction, following the green diamonds of the Cumbria Way to Stake Pass before almost doubling back on himself to approach Pike of Stickle. I knew that he was planning a descent via Loft Crag and hoped to intercept him just before he started heading downhill where the crags fall steeply to the valley below.*

After the second steep climb of the day I settled down, huddled inside my waterproof jacket, with a flask of coffee and a slab of flap-jack. All I could do was wait and hope.

A few bedraggled walkers slogged past me with barely a glance, their eyes slitted against the drizzle. I pretended to be looking at my phone or my map as they passed, confident that all they'd see was an androgynous figure in wet waterproofs. After an hour and a half, I was about to give up. Two lone walkers had passed but neither of them bore any resemblance to Chris, and the weather was getting worse. I knew it would take me at least an hour to get back to my hire car and I didn't want to risk being on the path down from the tarn as darkness fell.

And then I saw him.

He was strolling along as though it was a lovely summer's day, clearly enjoying himself. I stood up and unfolded my map, fixing what I hoped was a puzzled frown on my face I turned towards him. As he got closer, I could see the resemblance to his father in the lines of his face and the cut of his jaw, but his colouring was all his mother. Could I really do this? Was it necessary?

'You okay there?' he asked. His face showed concern but his eyes...

his eyes were those of a monster. I'd seen those eyes before, and I knew what I had to do.

I shook my head, not trusting myself to speak in case he heard the tremble in my voice.

'Lost?'

I nodded and scanned the path behind him. Deserted.

'Where are you heading?' He took a few steps closer.

'Back down to New Dungeon Ghyll.'

'Okay.' Another step closer. 'If you head down here a bit and then swing left, you'll see a pitched path that'll take you all the way back down to the valley. It's a bit loose in places but it's not far.'

I pointed to the map, hoping to lure him closer.

'This one?'

As he studied where I was indicating I had a last check around. Nobody in sight.

'No,' he said. 'You need...'

His eyes widened as I slipped the knife up beneath his ribs and he looked puzzled as he slumped towards me. I used the momentum of his collapse to enable me to guide him towards the top of the crags and then I pulled out the knife and let him go. It took a few seconds for him to tumble and slide down to an outcrop of rock where his body seemed to lodge in the scree. His red jacket was visible from where I was standing – he would be easily found. I probed this piece of information, trying to work out whether or not it was to my advantage, but before I could decide, he slid further down and disappeared from my sight. Good enough.

I wiped the blade of the knife on the wet grass and then slid it back into the inside pocket of my jacket. Shouldering my rucksack, I headed back down to the valley where I hoped a drink and a good meal were waiting for me in one of the pubs.

14

K ate was on her third coffee of the day and her second hour of BBC news when her phone rang. She picked it up and glanced at the screen expecting Cooper or Hollis.

Priya Das.

'M-ma'am?' Kate spluttered in her hurry to answer the call.

'Fletcher,' Das began and Kate's heart slowed down. She'd been hoping that Das had been calling to invite her back to work, to pick up the reins of the case again, but the use of her surname was as chilling as a cold shower. 'I've spoken to Chris Gilruth's aunt in Cumbria. She's the one who brought him up – not his biological mother. I had to tell her about her sister. Not the details of course – she's got enough on her plate with the death of her son – but I told her that we think her sister's body has been found. She didn't seem overly upset but I think she might be able to help us make sense of this case and the one in the Lakes.'

Kate kept quiet. She hadn't worked with Das for long, but she'd learnt quickly that the woman didn't like to be interrupted when she was explaining something.

'So, I offered to send one of your team up there to speak to her. Problem is that she doesn't want to speak to somebody on your team. She wants to speak to you, Fletcher. I told her that you were on leave, but she said she'd wait. And, as you know, we can't wait.'

A pause. Kate wondered if this was the time to speak but Das sighed and continued.

'Look, Kate. I really don't think that these cases have anything to do with you, but it looks odd and I have to cover my back. If the chief super heard that I'd not acted when two connected murders were linked to one of my DIs, I'd never hear the end of it. I've looked into both cases and I'm satisfied that you have nothing to do with Margaret Whitaker, but the Gilruth case concerns me. You knew him and you found the body. How do you explain that?'

It seemed that a response was now required.

'Coincidence, ma'am. A bloody awful coincidence. I hadn't seen Chris Gilruth for over three years and I haven't heard from him or any member of his family since I moved back to Doncaster. I was on holiday with my... partner.' Kate struggled to find the correct word to describe her relationship with Nick. 'Boyfriend' seemed too casual, but 'partner' had a ring of permanence to it. And after last night, maybe 'ex' would be more appropriate. 'An elderly couple had spotted the body and I took charge. My training kicked in, that's all. I wasn't even certain it was Chris until Cumbria Constabulary confirmed it.'

'Okay,' Das didn't quite sound convinced but Maureen Gilruth's reluctance to talk had obviously backed her into a corner. 'I need to get the Gilruth woman to talk. If she'll only talk to you then I have to make that happen. I'm going to send Hollis round to your flat with a car. He'll text when he's there. Half an hour?'

'Of course, ma'am,' Kate said, wondering how the hell she was going to make herself presentable by the time Hollis arrived.

Two hours later Hollis turned off the A1 onto the A66. Kate had been going to suggest that they stop for coffee, but she didn't want the DC to have to face Scotch Corner services. The last time they'd both been there Hollis had received some devastating news that had almost broken him and could have cost him his career. She noticed that he'd not said much as they got closer to the junction, probably having similar thoughts. Whatever was on his mind, Kate didn't want to remind him of how he'd come close to a breakdown earlier in the year.

'Fancy a drink?' Hollis finally asked as the dual carriageway went down to a single winding lane. 'We've made good time for a Saturday. There's a café at a farm shop somewhere along here that's supposed to be good.'

Kate smiled to herself. She knew exactly what he'd been doing while he'd waited for her earlier. TripAdvisor.

'Sounds good,' she said. 'I could do with a coffee.'

'Thought you might be ready for more caffeine – and I wasn't going to stop at Scotch Corner for obvious reasons.'

Kate turned to look at him in surprise. He hadn't talked much about the previous summer and she'd decided to let him sort through it all at his own pace, so the reference to what had happened with his mother was unexpected.

'You doing okay with all that?' she asked, deliberately vague.

'Getting there,' Hollis admitted. 'Although, when Google Maps told me that this was the quickest route to Kendal I was tempted to ignore it and risk the M62.' He smiled to let her know that he was joking, at least partly.

'You know you can talk to me, if you need to,' Kate said.

Hollis nodded noncommittally.

'And you're welcome to buy me coffee any time,' she added, gesturing towards a sign for the farm shop.

The coffee was much better than Kate had expected and the millionaire's shortbread that Hollis brought back from the counter was a welcome addition considering she'd not eaten breakfast. The café was more like a restaurant, with high ceilings and discreetly spaced tables while the 'specials' board offering wood-fired pizzas and a range of flatbreads added to the upmarket atmosphere.

'Good find,' Kate said and was about to comment on the usual quality of their coffee spots when a group of women appeared from nowhere laughing and shouting. She immediately tensed expecting trouble, but Hollis just grinned.

'Hen party,' he mumbled, obviously sensing her change of mood.

He was right. Each of the women wore a pink T-shirt with a nickname on the back. 'Jackie Jockstrap Juggler' had a glass of rosé wine suspended from a cord around her neck suggesting that she might lose it if she put it down anywhere. 'Cunnilingus Cath' was wearing an enormous pair of fake breasts and 'Gabby Gobbler' was wearing antennae-like deely boppers with tiny pink penises on the end of each wire. She seemed the most drunk and the most embarrassed as she apologised to anybody who'd listen for having 'cocks on me head'.

Kate sipped her coffee and watched the other customers watching the women as they made their way to the toilets. Nobody seemed overly concerned or even particularly surprised that a group of drunk women had appeared out of nowhere high up in the middle of the Pennines.

'Wonder where they're off to?' she mused.

'Dunno. Blackpool maybe. They sound like Geordies so maybe they're heading to the west coast somewhere for a change.' Hollis didn't sound particularly interested. 'Can I ask you about this woman we're going to see?'

Kate had been expecting this. Her team knew that Dan could get away with more than any of the others when it came to asking Kate personal questions and she also knew that whatever she told him would be in confidence unless she said otherwise. 'What do you want to know?'

He stared into his coffee mug as though trying to work out how to ask a difficult question. 'Rumour is that you knew her son in a "more than friends" way.' He glanced up at her, something in his eyes suggesting that he thought he might have overstepped.

Kate thought about pulling rank to avoid the details, but Dan was a friend and he deserved better.

'I nearly had a relationship with him,' she admitted. 'But he was married and I was recently not married. Not the best basis for a lasting commitment. There's really not much else to say about it – we were friends before and after.'

'And that's why this woman wants to speak to you? Because you knew him?'

Kate didn't know how to answer because she had no idea why Maureen wouldn't speak to anybody else. The most likely explanation was that, having met Kate a few times, she wanted to tell her story to somebody who was familiar.

'Honestly? I don't know. It might be because I was there when his body was found. It might be because I knew Chris when he was alive. Maybe she thought it would be easier to speak to somebody that she'd had some previous contact with. I only met the woman a few times so it's hard to imagine what she might be thinking.'

Hollis nodded, clearly weighing up what Kate had told him.

'Can't be easy for her. Her son and her sister being killed within the space of a few weeks.'

'No,' Kate agreed. 'And I don't want to push her. She's grieving and she deserves our respect. We have to treat her gently. Understood?'

'Understood,' Hollis said, draining his coffee and standing up.

15

Sam scrolled slowly down the page 'Sheffield Road Juniors 1988 Reunion'. It had felt weird using Kate's login details, faintly stalkerish, even though she had the boss's permission. It was also strange using the identity 'Cathy Siddons' – a name which bore no resemblance to the one Kate used now. Sam had no idea what she was looking for, but she needed a break from looking at footage from traffic cameras around the nursing home from the date when Margaret had been signed out.

Contributors to the group hadn't just posted images from 1988. There were photographs of four-year-olds lined up in a school hall entitled 'First Day at School' and also 'Then and Now' shots showing how much – or little in some cases – a person had changed. The photographs from various school trips and sports days were mildly amusing – the strange fashions and odd haircuts seeming wildly outdated and poorly chosen. She scanned the class photographs, hovering the cursor over each face to see who had been tagged, making a note of anybody called Lee, Liam, Nick or Neil. No Liam or Nick had been tagged but in the comments beneath a 1985 class photo, Graham Atkinson had tried to name as many of the students as he could remember and there was a Lee in the first row and a Neil at the back – no surnames though. She continued her search and discovered that Lee and Neil appeared in three class photos together – her most likely candidates so far. She wished she had the name of the girl, it might have made her job easier if she could put three names together.

A folder of uploaded pictures caught her attention. Another school trip – 'Derbyshire Camping – July 1988'. Three images were displayed with '+15' on the final one. Sam clicked on the first one – a shot of two dark-haired girls outside a vivid orange tent labelled 'Angela and Vicky'. Both were wearing faded jeans and baggy T-shirts, one pale green, the other white. Neither girl looked especially happy to be having her photograph taken, and the two feet of space between them suggested that they weren't friends. There were other shots of pairs of children next to tents, each one labelled. The sixth photograph made Sam catch her breath. 'Lee and Neil'. Unlike Angela and Vicky, Lee and Neil had arms round each other's shoulders and were grinning at the camera, obviously the best of friends. Both boys looked in need of a haircut, their almost-mullets – one mid-brown and one very blond – had obviously not been combed for the camera in contrast to the girls' hair which looked recently groomed.

There were twelve tent photographs – five of girls and seven of boys – but no clues to who the third amigo might have been. Ten girls' names which meant absolutely nothing to Sam. The other photographs were shots of activities. One seemed to be a hike, one was raft building and the final one was a group shot around the scorched earth of a campfire simply labelled 'Last Morning at Camp'.

Sam zoomed in on the morning picture looking for Lee and Neil to see if they had a girl with them but was surprised to see that they were on opposite sides of the circle of children. And neither was smiling.

'Must've fallen out,' she muttered to herself.

She scrolled back to the raft-building picture which was focused on four boys wielding planks of wood but none of the boys was Lee or Neil. Just as she was about to go back to the image of the hike, something in the top corner of the raft photograph caught Sam's eye. She downloaded the image to her desktop and opened it with her own imaging software so she could enlarge it much further than Facebook allowed.

She was right. Behind the grinning foursome with their bits of wood was another group. Two boys and two girls – one of the girls was slightly apart from the other three children, sitting on an upturned plastic tub. She zoomed again and tried to enhance the portion of the image that showed the group she was interested in.

'Shit!' she cursed as the figures started to blur. She went back to the picture of Lee and Nick outside the tent and studied their clothing. Lee was wearing a yellow T-shirt with some sort of cartoon figure on the front and Neil had a Manchester United shirt on.

Checking again she could tell that the boys in the raft building picture were wearing yellow and red. She did the same thing with the girls, both dark haired, and decided that the most likely candidates were Angela and Vicky, with Angela being the one not taking part.

'Gotcha!' Sam exclaimed doing a mini fist pump and then immediately looking round to make sure that nobody had noticed.

She wrote the names Lee, Neil and Vicky on her notepad and then scrolled back to the 'Members' tab for the group. There was one Victoria, but she was a freckled red-head and extremely unlikely to be the adult version of dark-haired Vicky. There was also a Lee Bradley. Sam compared his profile picture with the boy next to the tent and couldn't rule him out. She scrawled his name on her notepad. Another member was Neil Grieveson who could very easily have been the boy in the Man United shirt in 1988. Energised, Sam scrolled through the photographs from the reunion in May. Lots of small groups with drinks raised and arms around each other. Smiles, flushed faces, rude hand gestures – everything she'd expect from a rowdy night out. She was hoping that somebody would have tagged the people that she was interested in, or at least added names underneath the photographs but she was disappointed; there was no mention of Lee or Neil or Vicky.

Then, in the background of a photograph of a man in his forties trying to breakdance, she spotted them. Three figures hunched around a small table; heads close together as though sharing secrets. She couldn't be certain, even after she'd enhanced the digital image, but one of the men looked like Lee Bradley and the woman could easily have been a grown-up version of Vicky. The photograph had been added by 'Sheffield Road Juniors 1988 Reunion' – obviously the group administrator. She clicked at the top of the page and found two people listed as admins – June Tuffrey and Danielle Forrester. Both had their privacy settings at the highest level.

Cautiously optimistic, Sam hit 'Message' on June Tuffrey's profile page. Even if the woman didn't know the real names of The Three Amigos, she might know somebody who did.

16

The woman who opened the door was exactly as Kate remembered her. Short – much shorter than Chris – with a cap of grey hair and shrewd blue eyes, Maureen Gilruth looked like the sort of woman anybody with any sense would wish for as their grandmother. She was smartly dressed in a dark blue skirt and white blouse and her make-up was subtle but expertly applied. Kate wondered if she'd been shopping or out with friends for the morning.

Having seen photographs of her sister it was clear that Maureen was the younger of the two by at least ten years and she seemed to be in full possession of her faculties as she gave Kate a sad smile and ushered her inside the house. Hollis introduced himself and shook hands with the woman, offering his condolences before accepting a seat on a tasteful mock-leather sofa which faced a huge picture window offering a view of the Kentmere fells.

'Lovely view,' he said. 'I'd never get anything done if I had that to look at all day.'

Maureen turned and looked out of the window seeming to get lost in her thoughts, her eyes fixed on the changing shapes of the clouds in the sky. 'It's never the same,' she said eventually. 'Not even minute by minute: it's always changing. You'd think I'd get tired of it having lived here for so long, but I haven't. It still sometimes catches me by surprise. After Duncan died and Chris got married, I thought about moving to a bungalow in Kendal, but I've lived in this village for too long to leave now.'

'It's beautiful,' Kate said. 'I've always liked Staveley.'

Maureen smiled at her gratefully. 'I bet you miss the fells, being down there.'

'Every day,' Kate conceded. She hadn't realised just how much she missed the shapes of the mountains against the clouds until her recent holiday with Nick. Now, looking up the valley towards the high fells, she wondered why she'd ever left. Her view across Town Fields didn't compare and the short sheep-less commute to work didn't seem as attractive as the winding route she used to take.

'Tea? Coffee?'

Kate dragged her eyes away from the window. 'Coffee please. With milk.'

Maureen turned to Hollis expectantly and he asked for the same.

Kate left Dan staring out of the window and followed the older woman into her kitchen. She watched as mugs and spoons were assembled on a worktop while the kettle hissed slowly to boiling point.

'How've you been?' Kate asked, quietly. 'This must have been a terrible shock. Chris and your sister.'

Maureen unscrewed the top of a jar of instant coffee and spooned it into the mugs with a trembling hand. 'I don't think it's really sunk in yet,' she admitted. 'Holly and the girls don't seem to know what to do without him and I'm not much help.'

Kate felt her cheeks start to warm at the mention of Chris's wife and children. 'If there's anything I can do...' she said, but Maureen waved away her offer.

'It'll just take time,' she said. 'I was the same when Duncan died, although Chris was grown up by then. It'll be hard on Lily and Sophie.' No mention of Margaret. She handed Kate a steaming mug of coffee and led the way back to the sitting room where Hollis was waiting with his notebook on his lap.

Maureen placed the other mug on a coaster on the table next to him and sat down opposite the two detectives.

'I'm sorry if it's caused you any problems, me asking to speak to you, but I know you and Chris were friends and I want somebody to listen without judgement. I thought you might be able to do that.'

'Of course,' Kate said. 'And anything you tell us today will only be used to help to catch whoever did this to Chris and Margaret.'

To her surprise, Maureen snorted disgustedly. 'Margaret. Haven't seen her for years. I bet most people who know me have no idea that I had a sister.'

'You weren't in touch?'

Maureen leaned back in her seat and crossed her arms defensively. 'I've not spoken to that woman since I took Chris off her when he was two weeks old. As far as I'm concerned, my sister's been dead for decades.'

'Why did she let you bring up Chris?' Kate asked, a suspicion starting to form in her mind.

Maureen's face reddened and she looked down at her lap. 'There's no easy way to explain that doesn't make me look bad. I blackmailed her. I couldn't have children and she didn't deserve them – not with that... that thing she married. How could she even think about bringing up a child in that house?'

'You mean David Whitaker?'

'I'd rather you didn't use his name in this house,' Maureen

hissed.

'You didn't approve of the marriage?'

A shake of the head.

'But you kept in touch with your sister?'

'At first. I always got a funny feeling about him, but I thought if he's good enough for Margaret then who am I to judge? He was kind to her. At first. Gave her expensive gifts, took her on holidays – nothing was too much for her. They'd been together about ten years when I got the sense that something was a bit off between them. I wondered if he was beating her or if it was that, what do they call it these days, coercive control? Then she told me what he was, and I turned on her – I couldn't help myself. I told her to go to the police, but she wouldn't. She said he'd told her that it was a one-off and that he was going to change, that he needed help.'

Kate noticed that Hollis had flipped open his notebook and was writing down Maureen's side of the conversation.

'What do you mean "what he was"? What was wrong with Dav... Margaret's husband?'

Maureen stared at her, a frown of anger creasing her forehead. 'You already know. You must do. He liked little kids. He was a pervert,' the word exploded out of her and she leaned forward, pointing a finger to emphasise her disgust.

'Margaret found out and she wanted to *help* him. Can you imagine – having sympathy with a man like that? He needed castrating not counselling. And then she fell pregnant – what sort of torture would he have put the child through? So, I told her – if she didn't let me have the baby, I'd go to the police myself. I was bluffing, of course, I had no evidence, but I'd seen what he was like with her, controlling everything. He'd have been the same with Chris – or worse. I'll never understand how she could even have thought about bringing a child into that relationship.'

Kate could see that beneath the woman's outrage was deep distress. She'd found out about the deaths of her son and her sister within a few days of each other and was obviously struggling.

'Maureen, I know this is difficult but...'

'It's not difficult, love, it's bloody agony. I can't believe that Chris is gone. Holly said that the police told her that he was stabbed, is that right? I don't know who'd do something like that.'

Kate hadn't been given authorisation to discuss the details of either case but there was nothing to be gained by holding back. Maureen had specifically asked for her and Kate felt an obligation to be honest with the woman. 'It looks like it, yes,' she said. 'At the moment Cumbria Constabulary are treating the case as a murder investigation.'

'And Margaret? I heard she'd been in a nursing home.'

'She had been, for some time. Her husband had her admitted when she developed dementia. Somebody claiming to be her niece had Margaret released into her care a couple of months ago. Her body was found last week in a storage facility in Doncaster. I'll give you more detail if you want to hear it but it's not pleasant.'

'And she was murdered as well? By this woman?'

'It looks that way,' Kate said. 'I'm sorry.'

'But it's not him? Not her husband?'

Kate shook her head. 'No. He's been in prison in Wakefield for the past five months. It can't have been him.'

'Prison? What for?'

Kate glanced at Hollis. She knew that she'd already told Maureen more than she should have but Whitaker's crimes would be a matter of public record. Hollis simply raised his eyebrows at her as if to say *You've come this far. What's a bit more information?*

'He was convicted on a number of counts involving grooming children,' Kate said. 'From what you've told us I doubt that'll come as much of a surprise.'

Maureen sighed and shook her head. 'Were there children hurt?'

'It was all internet-based,' Kate said. 'As far as I know, Whitaker was grooming and viewing but he didn't actually harm any children himself.'

'This time,' Maureen spat. 'He was a bloody teacher. How could they let somebody like that near kiddies? It doesn't make sense.'

Kate kept quiet. It didn't make sense, but she'd seen many cases where adults who had passed all the checks had been able to gain access to vulnerable children – the system wasn't perfect, but it was all that was available. And when Whitaker had started teaching the vetting system wouldn't have been anywhere near as rigorous as the current one. If he had no record of a conviction for child abuse on List 99 he'd have been able to undergo his teacher training – any other offences wouldn't have surfaced.

'I do appreciate you being straight with me, Kate. That's why I asked to see you. I know you and Chris were friends and I thought I could trust you to tell me the truth. And I wanted to tell somebody about how Chris ended up with me. He never knew that I wasn't his mum, you know. I thought about telling him, but I don't know what it would have achieved. If I'd told him about Margaret then I'd have had to tell him who his dad was as well, and I think he was better off not knowing.'

'Will you tell Holly?' Chris's wife's name felt odd in Kate's mouth, like the word was too big and didn't belong there.

'I don't know. It's the girls I worry about. What good will it do them to know about their grandfather? I really can't see any point in telling her now that Chris is gone.'

Kate could see her point. Why taint Holly's memories of Chris with the truth about his father?

'It's not my place to offer you advice,' Kate said. 'But the truth might come out because of Margaret's death. The connection's been made – DNA doesn't lie. If... when... we catch whoever did this then there'll be a trial and you won't be able to protect your daughter-in-law.'

Maureen nodded miserably. 'I hadn't really thought about that. You think the same person killed them both?'

'Honestly? I don't know at this stage.'

'But you will find him, or her?'

'We're doing everything we can,' Kate said, aware of how inadequate her assurances sounded. She glanced down at her untouched coffee. It would seem ungrateful not to drink it but she felt like the interview was over. They'd got what they came for and the decent thing to do now was to leave this woman alone with her grief.

'I can make you another,' Maureen said, obviously realising that Kate's drink had probably gone cold.

'It's fine,' Kate said, standing up. 'I really appreciate your time and I'll do my best to keep you updated on the investigation in Doncaster. I can't speak for the Cumbrian force but there are a lot of decent people there and they'll all go the extra mile for one of their own.'

The clichés were almost embarrassing, but she didn't have the words to reassure Chris's mother. She had no idea who had killed her son and her sister, or why. And she was worried that Das might deny her the opportunity to find out.

As they said their goodbyes, Kate took the car keys from Hollis. She couldn't face three more hours trapped inside her own head and driving would give her something else to think about.

17

Simon Charlton stared miserably through the side window of his car. He'd been waiting for nearly half an hour but there was still no sign of the person who'd e-mailed him three days ago.

He'd almost ignored the communication – it had been sitting in his junk mailbox with lots of other spam and a few important documents disguised to look like offers from drug companies or foreign banks. He knew the ones that were 'live'. The codes and references were obvious to anybody who was looking but, to a casual observer, they just looked like the usual scams and rubbish that everybody got. He saw that two had photographs attached and one had a video and he was trying to decide which to look at first. He knew that he'd enjoy the video most but sometimes the photographs could be very... stimulating.

As he hovered the mouse over the most promising subject line, he noticed a familiar place name towards the bottom of the list. He'd scrolled down and his breath caught in his throat. The sender was unknown to him, but the subject line was a taunt. *Camping: Derbyshire 1988.* Impossible. How could anybody possibly know the significance of that location in that year? The year it all began for him. The year he started to allow himself to be who he really was instead of a pale imitation of himself.

With a trembling hand he'd opened the e-mail and saw that it was blank; there was no message. His eyes were drawn to a series of attachments – all jpegs – and he clicked on the first one. It showed two girls standing next to a bright orange tent with woodland behind them. The next was similar but the girls were different. He continued to open the images – nine in all – and each one showed a pair or group of children, obviously on a camping holiday. He could tell from the clothes and the hairstyles that the year referenced in the subject line was probably correct – these photographs were from the late eighties so almost definitely from *that* camp.

He wondered if the other two had been targeted – Whitaker and Paulson – the one they called the sergeant major, with his dark moustache and full beard. Simon had encountered Whitaker many times over the years in chat rooms and on forums. He'd remembered him because he'd nicknamed himself Sir W, probably a reference to him being a teacher. He'd heard on the grapevine that Sir W was serving a few months in Wakefield – no sympathy there though if he'd been stupid enough to get caught. Charlton knew exactly what that was like.

Paulson had dropped off Simon's radar in the late nineties and he'd eventually heard through an acquaintance in a chat room that he'd been killed in a motorcycle crash in the Scottish Borders.

He'd checked the sender's address again 'Amigos31988', but it meant nothing to him. That had been three days ago. Since then he'd received three more messages. One simply said, '*I know what you did*'. The second claimed that Simon had 'fucked up' the sender's life and that he was a 'broken man' and the final one was a request to meet with a date, time and place so that the sender could get 'closure'.

Simon had been suspicious, but what choice did he have? If he didn't turn up, this man might go to the police and he was always hearing about historic sexual abuse cases on the news. If they talked, Simon thought, he might be able to make this stranger see reason and keep his mouth shut. If not, there was always money.

He was starting to feel a bit foolish though. Half an hour in a deserted car park waiting for somebody he wouldn't even recognise – what the hell was he doing? Even if this person did have some evidence of what had happened that summer it was unlikely to point to Simon. Whitaker was the ringleader – he always was, he liked to be in charge – and Whitaker was in prison. Unless this was all part of some sort of set-up to get him a lighter sentence. That didn't make sense though – Whitaker had been put away months ago. If he was going to broker some sort of deal, he'd have already done it.

'Bloody paranoid,' Charlton mumbled to himself, finally acknowledging the feeling of unease that had been plaguing him ever since he'd opened that first e-mail.

A figure appeared at the entrance to the car park and Simon sat up in his seat. Was this him? He watched as it approached and became clearer. A woman with a buggy, one of those three-wheeled, off-road jobs that cost almost as much as a small car. She passed him without a glance, and he watched in the rear-view mirror as she approached a car two rows behind him in the almost-deserted car park.

He heard the beep as she unlocked the doors and then he watched as she lifted the child into the back seat. He looked through the windscreen again, back to the entrance, vowing to give it another five minutes and then he'd go home.

Two minutes later and Simon realised that the woman with the kid hadn't driven off. He looked in his mirror and saw that she was still struggling with the buggy. She was trying to fold it up, but it seemed unwilling to collapse. He watched for a few seconds and was about to get out and help when the buggy seemed to fold of its own accord, trapping the woman's arm.

'Shit!' he hissed, leaping out of the car and reaching for his phone. He knew that the woman could easily have broken her arm or dislocated her shoulder – he'd read about the dangers of big buggies online in an article about transporting toddlers. As he approached, Simon could see the pain in the contortions of the woman's face. She was half bent over the boot of the car, clutching her forearm in the other, undamaged, hand.

'Here,' he said. 'Let me help.' He slipped his phone back into his pocket; there was no blood so probably no need for an ambulance. The woman held out her damaged arm and Simon saw her other hand disappear into her pocket. Before he could tell her that he knew first aid he felt an agonising jolt up his spine and his legs started to give way. The woman swung her supposedly damaged arm at him and used it to guide him towards the car boot. He couldn't stop her; couldn't move his legs or arms and he was fairly sure he'd pissed himself. The bitch had a Taser.

Simon didn't think he'd been fully unconscious, but he couldn't be sure. The movement of the car and the pain in his lower back both had a disorienting effect, but he gradually became aware that he was being driven away from the car park. As his muscles spasmed back into life he tried banging on the rear seats of the car.

'Hey! What the hell are you doing? What's going on?'

Silence from the driver. He tried to roll over so he could kick the back seats down, but the space was too confined, so he tried banging on the inside of the boot that was a few inches above his face. Again he shouted, but this time it was for help. If somebody on the street heard him they might get a registration number and call the police.

After what seemed like hours the car slowed to a stop and he heard the driver's door open and close. Bracing himself he tensed to attack whoever opened the boot. He waited, holding his breath. And waited. Nothing. Had he just been abandoned?

Trying to calm his breathing, Simon tilted his head so he could listen for footsteps either approaching or retreating but he couldn't hear anything. He gave in to the claustrophobia and started banging on the boot and shouting for help, not caring whether he attracted the attention of his assailant or of a passer-by – anybody who could get him out of there would be a blessing.

'Is somebody there?' A voice from outside.

'Yes! Oh God! Get me out.' Simon could hear the sob of relief in his own voice. The boot opened and a face peered in, followed by a rush of cold air. A young man wearing a baseball cap and a goatee.

'You okay, mate?'

'Do I look okay?' Simon asked, sitting up. 'Did you see the driver of this car? A woman with a kid?'

The man shook his head. 'Nobody around. I've just finished my shift at the pub and I heard you banging on the boot. Thought I'd better have a look.'

Simon eased himself up into a sitting position and swung his legs over the edge of the boot, ignoring the cramping sensation in his thighs. He appeared to be in a poorly lit car park next to a red-brick building.

'Where am I?'

'Thorpe,' the young man said, still peering at him intensely. 'You look like shit. Hang on.' He eased a small backpack off his shoulder and dug around inside.

'Here y'go,' he said, offering Simon a bottle of water.

Simon grabbed it and drank greedily.

'You wanna tell me what happened?'

Simon was only part way through his story when he started to feel woozy. At first he thought it might be the after-effects of being Tasered but, as his vision blurred he began to wonder about the water that he'd just drunk. 'Don't feel great,' he mumbled trying to stand up.

'It's okay,' the young man said. 'Let's get you over here and you can have a good long lie down.'

Simon made no protest as he allowed himself to be led down a narrow alley between high red-brick walls. He noticed that the man had something in his hand. Something that was catching the occasional flash of light from the street lamps. Something that looked very much like a blade.

And then it went black.

JULY 1988

The last day. Dusty lay on her side in her sleeping bag trying to decide what to do. Mr Whitaker had threatened them both with all kinds of punishments if either of them breathed a word about what had happened but what could he do, really? If she told her mum when they got back, then surely her mum would believe her and would go to the police. But what if nobody believed her? And what about the police? They'd ask her all sorts of questions about why she and Lucky had been wandering around in the middle of the night. They might ask her to describe what had happened and how could she do that? She didn't even want to think about it, despite the images that bombarded her mind every time she closed her eyes.

She knew that stuff like this happened – that some men liked to do things to children, but those men wore long coats and spoke in hushed voices. How could her teacher be one of those men? And who would believe that he was? Everybody said he was handsome and a decent man. It would be her word against his and who'd believe an eleven-year-old girl over a respected teacher?

She needed to talk to Lucky, but she wasn't sure if she could face him. He'd have seen what Whitaker did to her; he'd have seen her with her pants off. He'd know what happened and he'd know that she'd seen what that other man had done to him.

And then there was Ned. Mr Whitaker had taken him back to his tent to get changed and Ned had been different afterwards. Had the teacher done something to Ned as well? Dusty suspected that might be the case but she couldn't ask in case she was wrong. Or in case she was right.

'You've got to get up,' Angela said, poking her head through the unzipped doors of the tent. 'We're having a group photo before breakfast. Everybody has to be there.'

Dusty considered hurling a mouthful of swear words at the girl but, instead, she dragged her body out of the sleeping bag and struggled into her last clean T-shirt and a pair of denim shorts. As she crawled out of the tent she was assaulted by the sunlight – much too bright for a morning like this – she wanted rain and thunderclouds not blue skies and birds singing as though nothing had happened, nothing had changed.

Squinting against the brightness she scanned the clearing for her friends, but it looked like all the other kids had done as they were told as they were gathered round the ashes of last night's campfire. Heavy-legged, Dusty walked over to the group, still looking for Ned and Lucky. As she got closer, she realised why it had been difficult for her to spot them – they weren't together. Ned was at one side of the group and Lucky was at the other. Both looked utterly miserable. She gave Lucky a half smile as she walked past him to take up a position near the middle of the group, but he looked away, his eyes focused on a point in the middle distance. He looked tired, darkness beneath his eyes suggesting that he hadn't slept. Dusty supposed that she must look the same.

'Right!' the sergeant major barked. 'Everybody keep still and give us a big smile.' Dusty wanted to yell at him. To accuse him of... of what? The last time she'd seen him he was leaning against the door of the staff quarters, arms folded and a stupid grin on his face. He hadn't actually done anything, but he seemed to have enjoyed watching the other two men assault her and Lucky.

She couldn't manage a smile. She couldn't even pretend. Instead she stared at the ground waiting for it all to be over, waiting until she could go home where she was safe.

Breakfast was a rushed meal of cereal and juice and then it was time to start packing their things. Dusty ran back to her tent and stuffed her dirty clothes in her bag, throwing everything in as quickly as she could as if it would get her out of there faster.

'You okay?' A quiet voice from the doorway. Dusty turned, expecting it to be Ned or Lucky so she was disappointed to see Angela squinting at her with an expression of concern.

'I just want to go home,' Dusty said.

'You don't look well.'

'I'm fine. I just want to go home!' Dusty was aware that she was shouting but she didn't seem to be able to control the volume of her voice. 'So, bugger off and let me get on with my packing.'

Instead of following her instructions, Angela edged inside and zipped up the door flaps.

'Vicky, I'm so sorry.'

Dusty froze. Did Angela know? How could she know?

'I told Mr Whitaker that you lot were planning a midnight walk. I know I should have kept my mouth shut but I was worried that you'd get lost or fall in the stream or something. I didn't…' The girl's words were tumbling out in a rush, but they were lost on Dusty. She hadn't got past the first two. *I told…*

'You spragged on us? You told Mr Whitaker?'

Angela knelt at the foot of Dusty's sleeping bag, her eyes downcast.

'Oh my God! You know, don't you? You saw what happened – what they did to me and Lucky.'

Angela's cheeks flushed. 'I looked through the window but then I ran off.'

'And it's all your fault. If you'd kept your mouth shut, they wouldn't have caught us. They wouldn't have…'

Angela made a noise that was a cross between a hiccup and a sob.

'Come home with me and tell my mum and dad. They might believe it if you back me up.'

The other girl shook her head furiously. 'No. No way. They might come after me. I'm scared.' She edged away, one hand on the tent zip, her face suddenly pale in the strange orange light.

'Angela, what those men did was wrong. You know that. They told us that if we went to the police or to an adult they'd come after us and kill us. They said that nobody would believe us anyway.'

'I can't,' Angela whispered. 'I'm so sorry.' The zip whizzed up and she was gone, but Dusty wasn't finished. This girl was responsible for what had happened – she had to pay.

'You little shit!' she yelled, following Angela out into the clearing. 'I'll fucking kill you!'

At least ten pairs of eyes bored into her as she screamed her rage. 'You'd better stay away from me, Angela Fox, because if I ever get you alone, you're dead! Fucking dead! I'll get you – I don't care how long I have to wait. I'll fucking kill you! You'd better watch your back because I won't ever forget what you did!'

Dusty felt a hand on her arm and she swung round, fists clenched, ready to fight.

'Hey, calm down.' It was June Tuffrey staring at her as if she'd gone mad. 'What's she done?'

'I... she...' Dusty spluttered, unable to vocalise her hurt. 'She's a fucking bitch, that's all.'

June looked across the clearing and then back at Dusty. 'Can I help?'

Dusty shook her head. Movement from the boys' side caught her eye. Lucky staring at her as he eased his backpack onto his skinny shoulders.

'No,' she said. 'Nobody can help.'

18

Kate's phone rang just as she and Hollis were passing the turn for Wetherby. She hadn't bothered to connect it to the car's Bluetooth, so she passed it to Hollis after a quick glance at the screen.

'Get that for me. It's Das. And put it on speaker so I can hear what she wants.'

Hollis followed her instructions – holding the phone up to his mouth with the microphone close to his lips.

'DI Fletcher's phone, DC Hollis speaking.'

'Where's Kate?' Das snapped.

'She's driving, ma'am. She asked me to take the call and to put you on speaker.'

Kate smiled to herself at Hollis's subtle warning to Das that every word could be heard by both occupants of the car.

'How was the mother?'

'Distraught,' Hollis said before Kate could answer. 'But she gave us a lot of background.'

'Is there a connection?'

'Hard to say at this stage,' Kate said, raising her voice so that she could be heard above the sound of the engine. 'Maureen confirmed that Chris was David Whitaker's son. She adopted him when he was two weeks old.'

Hollis raised his eyebrows at her lie. Adoption was far too formal a word for such a loose arrangement – especially one based on blackmail.

'She hadn't seen her sister since,' Kate continued. 'To be honest she didn't seem too bothered about Margaret's death. She didn't want anything to do with her after Margaret told her about Whitaker.'

'Told her what?'

'That he's a pervert – Maureen's word – and that he was controlling during the marriage.'

There was a lengthy silence as Das appeared to be considering the implication of the information.

'How's the investigation going, ma'am?' Kate asked, prompting headshaking and a throat-cutting gesture from Hollis. Kate didn't care. It had been her case and she felt she had a right to know.

'That's why I'm ringing. A body's been found in Thorpe – in the school playground.'

'A child?'

'No. A man in his late fifties. ID was left in his pocket – Simon Charlton. Given the location I have to consider a connection between this and Margaret Whitaker. Her husband taught at the school – there might be a message here. O'Connor's there with Barratt but I'd like you to take a look. It's a bit of a grisly one so be prepared.'

Das hung up, leaving Kate baffled. 'Am I back on the case?' she asked Hollis.

He grinned at her. 'Looks like it.'

'Bloody hell! She could have said as much rather than talk to me like I'm doing her a favour. And what's with the warning? I've seen my share of "grisly" bodies.'

'Shall I ring Steve or Matt? They might tell me what's going on.'

Kate squinted as a blue road sign flew past the passenger side window. Judging by their current location they'd be in Thorpe in around forty-five minutes – if O'Connor and Barratt hadn't been told that she was on her way they might have finished with the scene by the time she got there. And it would be polite to let O'Connor know that she was back on the case. He wasn't a natural leader, but Hollis claimed that he'd been doing well with the organisation of the team and she didn't want to arrive unannounced and piss on his bonfire.

'Give Matt a buzz,' she said. 'Steve'll be busy overseeing the scene. But let them both know that we're on our way.'

She tried to concentrate on the traffic as Hollis made the call, but it was impossible to ignore his disbelieving 'What the fuck?' – Barratt must have divulged something especially juicy.

'Pre- or post-mortem?' Hollis asked and she saw him physically wince at the reply.

'Shit, that's rough.' He hung up. 'Do you want the gory bit first?'

'Go on. How bad is it?'

Hollis took a deep breath. 'Simon Charlton was discovered with his trousers round his ankles and his penis and testicles missing.'

'Nasty,' Kate said. 'Sounds like whoever did it had a grudge and it certainly links with Whitaker being a paedophile. Do they know anything about him beyond his ID? Where he was from, links to Whitaker or any other grooming gangs?'

'Not yet. Cooper's on the ID follow-up so I'd expect something quite soon. Matt said the pathologist's there at the moment so you might want to slow down a bit.'

Kate smiled. She'd locked horns on a few occasions with Suresh Kailisa, the pathologist based at the Doncaster Royal

Infirmary, but they also shared a mutual respect. Or Kate hoped they did. He didn't like it when she pushed him for answers too quickly and she found his methodical approach frustrating but he was thorough and thoughtful – qualities she admired in somebody who dealt with violent death every day.

'Y'know, I think I'll surprise him,' she said, pressing her foot down on the accelerator.

Floodlights had been erected in the playground of Thorpe Danum Academy by the time Kate pulled into the car park. The afternoon was rapidly becoming a dull November evening, damp and cold with dark, heavy clouds just above the tops of the buildings. She pulled her scarf more tightly round her neck and strode over to the cordon of blue and white tape surrounding a white crime scene tent.

'Talk to me,' she said, as Barratt approached, the hood of his overalls tight around his head and face.

'Body of a male, late fifties, well nourished. Driving licence IDs him as Simon Charlton. Left in a corner of the playground. The killer cut the lock on the gate – probably with a bolt cutter – and somehow got Charlton into this corner. I expect Dan told you about the mutilation?'

Kate nodded. 'Cause of death?'

'Exsanguination.'

'Sorry?'

'He bled to death – according to Kailisa. There's blood everywhere.'

'From having his bits cut off?'

Barratt shook his head and grimaced as he added detail. 'No. Whoever did this obviously decided that while they were busy in the groin area, they'd cut the femoral arteries as well. When I say "cut", the wounds look more like gouges.'

'Who found him?'

'School caretaker. He opens up every other Saturday afternoon for a local history group. Saw the padlock had been broken and assumed it was kids set on vandalism. Poor bugger got a real shock when he found this. Rang it in just after midday. The body was dumped in the angle of two walls – it's impossible to see it from the street or the car park despite the pool of blood.'

Barratt pulled down his hood and tried to smooth his hair down but the spiky style he'd recently adopted to cover the fact that he was prematurely balding didn't want to co-operate and stuck up at odd angles despite his efforts.

'Has Kailisa established time of death?' Kate asked, wincing in anticipation of one of the pathologist's harsh rebukes directed at her via Barratt.

'Judging by the pooling of the blood and the state of the wounds, he reckons last night, probably after midnight. There are wounds to his back and thighs consistent with a Taser and his trousers and underwear are wet, suggesting he lost control of his bladder. It seems likely that the device was used to subdue him and then his assailant mutilated him while he was still alive. If the electric charge had been high enough, he wouldn't have been able to put up a fight.'

'Killed here?'

Barratt nodded. 'Too much blood for the kill site to have been anywhere else. Kailisa thinks that he would have bled out in thirty to sixty minutes. Probably more like sixty as he'd have been in shock due to having his genitals cut off.'

Kate tried to reconstruct the murder. The scene was only a few yards from the car park – the two were connected by a narrow alley between two high Victorian brick walls which, Kate remembered, separated the original infant and junior schools. How was Charlton persuaded to get out of a car and walk to his death? Unless he was semi-conscious from a Taser assault and had been half carried here. Or he'd been drugged.

'I'm going to need to see the body,' she said, looking round for somebody who could provide her with protective overalls.

Barratt frowned and turned to look over his shoulder. 'With respect, Kate, Steve's in charge at the minute. I'm not sure he'll appreciate you taking over.'

Kate felt herself bristle at Barratt's insubordination and struggled to keep her tone neutral. Barratt was a stickler for rules and if O'Connor was representing Das at the scene then Kate really shouldn't step on his toes but, if she was back on the Margaret Whitaker case, she couldn't miss an opportunity to see if there was a connection.

'Matt,' she said as calmly as she could manage. Barratt's face fell and she could tell that he knew he wasn't going to like what she was going to say. 'I know O'Connor's in charge but Das has pulled me back onto the Whitaker case and, given the location of the kill site, I need to know if there's a connection.'

Barratt glanced over his shoulder again. 'Hang on.'

He disappeared inside the tent and came back thirty seconds later holding out a plastic bag containing a protective suit.

'Steve's waiting for you,' he said as he handed her the package. Kate struggled into the overalls and then ducked under the cordon tape as Barratt held it up for her. She could smell the blood as soon as she got close to the tent – a coppery smell that reminded her of wet pavements in the summer.

'DI Fletcher, what a lovely surprise.' Kailisa turned to smile at her, but Kate could tell from the way that the smile didn't reach his eyes that he wasn't pleased to see her. 'Has DC Barratt not given you enough information or is it just that you don't trust us to do a good job without your supervision?'

'Definitely the latter,' Kate said, with a grin at O'Connor to show she was joking. The DS was standing near the body's head and turned to peer over Kailisa's shoulder. He looked almost comical in overalls that were too small for his bulky frame and a surgical mask that covered his lower face.

'I know it's the body of a white male, we have an ID from a driving licence, probably killed here sometime last night. Cause of death exsanguination. Oh, and he's missing his genitals. Anything to add?'

'Not at the moment,' O'Connor said, still looking at the body. 'I've got Sam doing a trace on the ID – she'll let us know when she gets something. Barratt's organised a door-to-door of the houses around the school.'

'Do we think there's a link between this body and that of Margaret Whitaker?'

O'Connor sighed. 'Hard to say. There's evidence of Taser use here, which there wasn't with the woman's body. Different genders, different ages. The only connection is the school where her husband used to teach.'

'And the mutilation,' Kate reminded him. 'Parts of this body have been cut off and Margaret Whitaker's body was dismembered.'

'But, at first glance, the wounds indicate a different blade was used,' Kailisa interjected. 'The body in the storage locker was dismembered with a blade consistent with a meat saw and the flesh had been cut with something akin to a scalpel. The edges of this wound and the gouges to the thighs indicate a much bigger, less delicate blade.'

He pointed to the gaping red hole in the man's groin that Kate had been trying not to look at.

'The cuts to the femoral arteries suggest somebody with a basic knowledge of human anatomy. The blade has been twisted to ensure that there was no chance of the bleeding being stopped by any form of compression. Tourniquets may have stopped it but, by the time assistance arrived, he'd probably have bled out anyway.'

Kate looked round at the rest of the scene, trying not to breathe in too deeply. Yellow numbered markers were placed at three points at the edge of the dried pool of blood.

'What're they?' she asked O'Connor.

'Footprints. One approaching, two leaving.'

'You're joking? That's a bit careless. Anything from the tread patterns?'

'They're mostly smooth,' O'Connor said. 'Some stitching around the edge – possibly leather soles. Expensive – probably men's size six or seven so quite small. Could suggest a woman.'

'And hard to trace unless we can find the shoes and match the stitching.'

Kate stepped carefully over to the group of markers. One footprint was clearly pointing towards the body, the others were partials, but she could see from the heel shape that they were facing away.

'So, he or she left the body then came back. Maybe to check whether Charlton was still alive?'

'Possibly,' O'Connor agreed. 'Maybe he wanted to make sure that he'd done the job properly.'

'Or,' Kate said, suddenly struck by a grislier interpretation. 'He–'

A shout from the edge of the playground cut short her explanation.

19

'K ate! We've got something.' Hollis doubled over just outside the cordon to catch his breath.

'What is it?'

He shook his head. 'Just come on.'

Kate scrambled out of her coveralls and followed Hollis through the car park to the first in the row of terraced houses that buffered up against the school.

'I was following up on the door-to-door. Bloke next door to the school's been out all day so I gave him a knock just to check that he hadn't seen anything last night. Turns out he might have something interesting for us.'

Hollis tapped on the door and stood back as it was opened by an elderly man dressed in a faded dark suit holding a wriggling Staffordshire bull terrier puppy.

'Sshh, Pearl, it's just the policeman again,' he said, looking Kate up and down and then staring over her shoulder at Hollis.

Kate stepped forward, her ID extended. 'I'm Detective Inspector Kate Fletcher. I believe you have something to share with us that might be important.'

'Jack Williamson,' the man said, extending his free hand. 'I suppose you'll be wanting to come in?' He pushed the door open wider and stepped aside while Kate and Hollis pushed past him into a cramped hallway.

'Straight on,' Williamson said. 'Into the kitchen.'

They stood clustered around a small pine table, covered in the remains of breakfast – a dirty plate strewn with toast crusts, a slab of butter still in its wrapper, a jar of jam and a half-empty mug of tea.

'Tell DI Fletcher what you told me,' Hollis instructed. Williamson puffed out his chest and smiled faintly, obviously enjoying being the centre of attention.

'Well, last night Pearl started barking at about half one. I know what time it was because I checked when I put my bedroom light on. She's normally quiet at night unless she needs to go out, aren't you, lass?' He dipped his face to the dog who licked his nose enthusiastically.

'So, I came down and let her out into the yard for a wee. She ran round, sniffing and then started barking at the wall – the one that's next to the school playground. She was really agitated. It took me ages to get her back inside and, when I did, she was still whining to go out again. In the end I shut her in the kitchen and went back to bed. When I let her out this morning she was still sniffing up that wall, but she'd stopped barking.'

Kate tried to make sense of the information. It could have been anything. The dog was a puppy – she'd have barked at a cat, a fox, her own shadow if she'd caught it in the wrong light. She looked at Hollis, puzzled by his earlier excitement. The DC gave her an enigmatic smile as if to say *wait and see*.

'That's it? Did you find out what she was barking at?'

Williamson shook his head. 'I shone the light from my phone around the backyard, but I couldn't see anything and then, this morning I was in a rush to get out, so I just shouted her back in. There wasn't anything obvious. It might have been a cat or even kids messing about but nothing in the yard was damaged.'

He looked from Kate to Hollis and back again. 'I'd forgotten all about it to be honest until I saw all the police cars here when I got back this afternoon. Then this lad knocked on my door and we went out and had a proper look round.' He nodded to indicate that Hollis was 'this lad' and then glanced at the kitchen window fearfully, as though whatever was out there might somehow break in.

'You didn't think to ring the police last night?'

'What for?' Williamson asked, scornfully. 'It's not like they've got anything better to do than come out to see if there's a cat on my wall.'

He was right. There was no evidence of criminal activity at that point, but Kate couldn't help but wish that something had raised the man's suspicions. It would have made their job a lot easier.

'What's going on, anyway? I asked *him*,' another nod towards Hollis. 'But he's saying nothing. I thought somebody might have broken into the school but, from the look of the number of cars and vans, I'd say it's something a lot worse.'

'I'm afraid I can't talk about an ongoing investigation,' Kate said, and Williamson smiled at her.

'How many times a week do you say that? I suppose it'll have to do though. It'll be in the papers next week, I suppose.' He looked disappointed that he wasn't going to be privy to the details of the case and Kate wondered if his reference to the papers was a veiled threat to report whatever he'd found to the press.

'Not that I'll say owt,' he continued, as though he'd read her mind. 'No time for any of them these days. Full of lies and scandal.'

'If we could just go outside,' Kate said. 'I'm interested to see what DC Hollis found.'

'He didn't find it,' Williamson said. 'It was Pearl.' He thrust the dog towards her as though offering it for her to cuddle. Kate took a step back. She didn't mind dogs, but she had no desire to hold the puppy, especially when she felt that Williamson was stalling.

She looked round the kitchen again. There was nothing to suggest that he shared the house with anybody. No feminine touches such as oven gloves or a flowery apron. Kate suspected that the man was lonely and having the two of them in his house might have been the only company he'd had in days. 'Sir, please.'

His head jerked back and he gave her an offended frown. 'I was just saying that Pearl's the hero. Come on then.' He opened the back door and ushered Kate and Hollis out into a small yard surrounded by high red-brick walls on all three sides, the walls seeming to trap the gloom of late afternoon. A plastic chair and rickety wooden table stood in one corner and, on the other side, a tiny shed occupied the space between the house and the back wall. The boundary between the yard and the school playground was ivy-covered, the plant thick and green even in November. Battens had been screwed to the bricks forming a trellis for the ivy to climb, a job it had done with enthusiasm as stray stalks waved above the height of the wall.

'Needs cutting back,' Williamson said, apologetically. 'A bit high for me though.'

The dog was wriggling in his arms and sniffing the chilly air, her attention drawn to the ivy-covered wall. Hollis took out his phone and switched on the torch function. He walked over to the ivy and pointed the narrow beam to a point near the top of the wall.

'Here, look.'

Kate stepped closer and had to crane her neck to see where he was pointing. Hollis was at least a head taller than her and obviously had a better view.

'What is it?'

'I'm not certain, that's why I called you over before I got the SOCOs involved. There's something in the leaves. Come round here.'

He stepped sideways allowing Kate a better angle. He was right. There was something there. Something red and black.

'Mr Williamson, do you ever feed Pearl bones or raw meat?' Kate asked, the realisation of what she was looking at making her feel slightly sick.

'No. She's still a pup. Bones might choke her, and she likes tinned food.'

Kate nodded. It was possible that what she was seeing had been dropped by a passing crow – they ate carrion – but she wasn't convinced. The more she tried to make sense of the shape the more certain she was. It tied in with the footprints in the blood. The killer had walked over to this wall and then back to the body. She looked at the dog, still straining to get out of its owner's arms, and the killer's intent suddenly became obvious. He must have heard the dog barking in the house and decided to give her an early breakfast.

'Dan, get Kailisa and a couple of SOCOs over here.'

He pocketed his phone and pushed past her.

'Tell them that we might have found Simon Charlton's missing genitals.'

* * *

I *t gave me a jolt, seeing him in the flesh. He'd changed a lot in the*
last thirty years, but I could see it was him – still scrawny and
shifty looking. All he needed was a long mac to complete the image. I
could tell from his response to my e-mails that he had a deep vein of
paranoia just waiting to be tapped and exploited and I was happy to
try to take him closer to the edge. I didn't want to push him over
though. Where would be the fun in that? I didn't want him to run and
I certainly didn't want to cause him to harm himself. I wanted that
pleasure.

My idea was almost elegant in its simplicity. Lure him to some-
where out of the way and then Taser him so I could get him into the
car. After that... well... I could take my time, be creative. And I'm
getting good at that, aren't I?

When I approached the car park, I could see that his car was in
front of mine. Perfect. He'd definitely be watching to see who was
coming so he couldn't miss me. Hopefully he'd check his rear-view
mirror to see where I went and, if not, I'd planned to tap on his car
window and ask for help.

I must admit I felt a bit stupid pushing a buggy around with a doll
in it, but I'd done up the rain cover and I don't think anybody gave me

a second look. It was a great disguise. Who'd suspect anything sinister of a woman and a baby? The pantomime of putting the doll in the car and then wrestling with the buggy was kind of fun. I had no idea how much he saw but it was an award-winning performance and it obviously paid off because he leapt out of his car to help me.

He didn't see it coming. The first shot caught him at the back of his leg – straight through his jeans. He started to crumple so I guided him towards the car boot and then gave him another shot with the second Taser – close range this time – before I bundled him in.

I'd only been driving for ten minutes before I had to wind the window down. The stink of piss was awful. I couldn't help but hope that the papers would include that little detail – just a bit more humiliation for him. Not that he'd know – being dead.

I wasn't sure how conscious he might be, so I kept driving for an hour before heading to Thorpe. I thought that might have given him enough time to come round a bit.

A quick change, backpack retrieved from behind the passenger seat and I left him there.

For twenty minutes.

He was definitely conscious when I tiptoed back to the car after cutting the padlock on the playground gate and then standing a few yards away, waiting. He was thumping on the lid of the boot and I could hear muffled cries for help.

He didn't recognise me. I made sure by shining the light from my phone in his eyes, but I needn't have bothered, he had no idea. His face was red and puffy – he'd obviously been crying – and the smell was awful.

I sat him on the edge of the boot and listened to his story, telling him that I'd heard banging as I'd passed on my way home from a late shift in the pub kitchen. Where do I get this stuff from? I didn't even know I was going to say it until the words were out, hanging between us, waiting to be tested. He believed it completely.

I fished a bottle of water out of my bag and watched while he drank it, grateful for every mouthful, then we chatted for a while with me pretending to be concerned for his welfare and him trying to shrug it off.

The Rohypnol took effect quite quickly – it might have been due to the stress I'd put him under, or he might not have eaten for a few hours. Either way fifteen minutes after drinking the water he was starting to slur his words slightly. I gave it another ten minutes then eased him to his feet. He'd muttered something unintelligible, but he was compliant and seemed convinced when I told him that I was taking him home.

I dumped him in the darkest corner of the playground that I could find but there was still enough light from the street lights to allow me to do what I'd planned. He was almost completely unconscious when I'd pulled down his sodden jeans and pants. Almost but not quite. He watched with slitted eyes as I took the knife out and squatted down next to him. I thought he'd scream or yell, but his pain seemed to take him beyond vocalisation. Instead, his mouth opened wide, silently protesting before his eyes rolled back in his head.

To finish the job, I dug into his thighs, hard, and twisted the knife. There wasn't as much blood as I'd been expecting but then something in him seemed to spring to life and the black-red fluid came pumping out. I watched for a few seconds and then remembered what I was holding in my gloved left hand.

What to do with his junk?

I'd heard a dog earlier as I'd cut through the padlock and that gave me an idea. I wondered if Rover might enjoy a tasty breakfast when his owner let him out in the morning. As quietly as possible I crept over to the wall that separated the yard of the house from the playground, stood on tiptoe and dropped the bloody bundle over.

I strolled back to Charlton and waited for him to die.

Can you recover DNA from dog shit?

20

K ate slid a latte onto Sam Cooper's desk and gave her a big grin. 'You deserve that. Come on. Briefing in two minutes.'

Cooper picked up the cup, took a huge swig and sighed. 'Not sure about deserve but I certainly need it.'

Kate knew that Sam had been working all weekend, desperately trying to find a link between David Whitaker and Simon Charlton. She'd also been looking for the identities of The Three Amigos after following a series of leads from Kate's new Facebook account and it looked like they were close.

'Can I skip the briefing?' Cooper asked. 'There're still a couple of things I want to check.'

'Not a chance,' Kate said. 'You've found a lot of important information and I want you there to take credit for it.'

'But, I...'

'No buts. Come on, Sam, let's get it over with.'

Kate felt a bit mean for pushing the DC, but she'd seen Cooper isolate herself before when she became immersed in her work and she knew it wasn't healthy. The two of them had worked through Sunday, Kate in a bid to avoid having to talk to

Nick, but Cooper had hardly spoken and she needed a prod to get her back into the land of the living.

The other members of the team were all hunched over their own coffees when Kate and Sam entered the meeting room, and Kate was surprised to see Priya Das sitting next to O'Connor. This wasn't part of the arrangement – she was supposed to see Das later.

The DCI obviously saw Kate's look of confusion and held up her hands as though in apology or submission. 'Don't mind me. I'm just eager to hear what progress you've all made, and I didn't want to wait for our meeting, Kate. Hope that's okay?'

Kate nodded and logged on to the laptop that was connected to the projector at one end of the room, wondering what Das was really up to. It was out of character for her to interfere so either she was genuinely interested and couldn't wait, or she was checking up on Kate after the revelation about Chris Gilruth.

'Right,' Kate began. 'Simon Charlton.' She displayed an image of the man's body on the screen and saw O'Connor and Barratt flinch even though they'd seen it *in situ*.

'Found in the playground of Thorpe Danum Academy on Saturday afternoon. Cause of death exsanguination from wounds to both femoral arteries. Mutilation to the genital area – penis and testicles recovered from a second site.'

Das raised a finger to interrupt. 'Is the ID confirmed?'

'The body hasn't been formally identified but the image on the driving licence is of the same man. His house was locked when uniformed officers visited and neighbours don't know where he is. The house is under surveillance pending a warrant for us to search the premises – which I'm hoping will be granted today.'

Das nodded and gestured for Kate to continue.

'Charlton's record shows two convictions. One for driving whilst under the influence of alcohol, fifteen years ago. He was fined and he lost his licence for eighteen months.' Kate paused and scanned the attentive faces of her team. The next revelation was a biggie.

'In 2013, he was arrested for exposure at a playground. He served three months and was placed on the sex offenders list. Needless to say, his victims were children, hence the custodial sentence.'

Barratt and Hollis's hands were both in the air, but Kate waved them down. 'I know. The obvious conclusion is that Charlton is somehow connected to David Whitaker – another known sex offender. Given the location of the kill site it was impossible to ignore that possibility. So, Cooper's been doing some digging.'

Kate sat down, allowing Cooper to take the floor. She fumbled a USB drive into the laptop and tapped the trackpad until an image of a group of children appeared.

'Okay,' she began. '1988. This is an image of a school trip. The fourth years at Sheffield Road Junior School, Thorpe. The figure on the right-hand side, at the back, is David Whitaker, now David Wallace. He was a teacher at the school, and he was responsible for the end-of-year trip.'

She tapped and another photograph appeared – it was obviously quite old, but the identity of the subject was obvious. A much younger Simon Charlton.

'For three years, between 1986 and 1989, Simon Charlton worked as an outdoor instructor at Clough Farm Activity Centre in Derbyshire. The same activity centre that David Whitaker used for the school trip.'

Kate noticed Das lean forward in her seat, her eyes scanning the photograph. 'So, we've got a connection?' she asked.

'Probably, but not conclusively. There are a number of photographs from the '88 trip but none show Charlton. Without staff logs for the time, it's impossible to know whether Charlton was on duty when Whitaker took kids to the centre. Unless we can find somebody who was on one of the trips.'

Sam quickly flicked through the images that she'd downloaded from Facebook showing the children paired in front of tents.

'These are all from 1988 which is the year that a group of kids calling themselves The Three Amigos went to the activity centre. Obviously – given the aliases that our killer has used – we want to find out who these three are. The head teacher of Thorpe Danum remembers two boys and a girl and I think I've worked out who the lads were based on his thoughts about their names.'

Sam pointed at the image showing on the screen. 'Lee Bradley and Neil Grieveson.'

She went back to an image of two girls. 'These two are Angela and Vicky. Looking at some of the photos of the activities, I think Vicky is the third amigo.'

Silence as the rest of the team digested what Sam had found out.

'So, your working hypothesis is that Whitaker and Charlton abused these kids and now one or all of them are exacting their revenge? It's all a bit *I Spit on Your Grave,* isn't it?' Das said.

Kate noted the baffled looks from three members of the group. 'It's a video nasty from the seventies or eighties. A woman is raped and then seeks revenge on her attackers. I haven't seen it but there's a famous scene where she chops off the genitals of one of her attackers,' she explained.

She smiled as O'Connor crossed his legs with theatrical precision.

'So, we're looking for a gang of vigilante film buffs?' Hollis asked.

'To be honest, I don't know who we're looking for,' Kate admitted. 'But there's a clear connection between the three murders – David Whitaker. His wife and son both killed and then somebody who he may have known, mutilated and dumped at his former workplace. The only names we have are connected to a 1980s comedy, but we do know that a group of children called themselves The Three Amigos and those kids were on that trip with Whitaker and, potentially, Charlton. We need to find them. Sam?'

Cooper tapped on the laptop and brought up images from a dingy-looking pub – obviously much more recent than the camping pictures.

'These were taken at a school reunion earlier this year. This is Lee Bradley.' She pointed to the middle figure in a group of three sitting at a table in the background of a group portrait. 'This is Neil Grieveson.' Another gesture with her fingers. 'And this,' she tapped the face of the woman sitting on the right, 'this is probably Vicky. Calvin Russell said that he thought the person who rented the storage unit may have been transgender – it could easily have been a woman in disguise. The footprints at the school scene were quite small for a man and it was definitely a woman who collected Margaret from the care home. I'd think finding Vicky would be our priority.'

'So, what?' O'Connor said. 'You think they got together at this reunion and decided to exact their revenge for abuse that happened thirty years ago? It's a bit of a leap. Isn't it possible that Whitaker abused or attacked somebody else during all this time and that person is out to get him? Maybe Charlton was involved as well. You know what that type are like – they hunt in packs.'

'A perfectly reasonable theory,' Sam said with a smile. 'But what about the names? Martin Short? Stephanie Martin? Coincidence?'

O'Connor shrugged.

'Do we know it's the same killer?' Das interjected. 'We've got three bodies and three potential suspects. Could they have done one each?'

Kate thought about it. It would make some sense – a sort of poetic justice – that each victim of abuse was, in turn, responsible for an act of revenge. She didn't have enough evidence for the theory, but she also couldn't confirm a single killer. She'd asked Kailisa to contact the pathologist in Cumbria about the weapon used to kill Chris Gilruth, but she hadn't heard from him – hardly surprising considering it was still 9am on a dreary Monday morning.

'It's possible,' Kate conceded. 'If we can place the three of them together at the reunion then it's possible that they planned this together and possibly more than one of them is involved in the actual murders.'

'Next steps?'

Kate had thought hard about what to do next. They needed to confirm the identity of The Three Amigos and then ascertain their movements on the day of Charlton's murder and that of Chris Gilruth. They had no conclusive time frame for the death of Margaret Whitaker so it would be impossible to either establish or disprove an alibi, but it might be possible to connect one of them to her removal from the nursing home.

'I think Barratt and O'Connor should attend the PM on Charlton as they were first at the scene.'

Neither man looked very impressed with her suggestion, but she pressed on.

'Sam's in contact with the woman who helped to organise the reunion – a June Tuffrey – she's arranged an interview to try to get more information, especially about Vicky. Sam used my

Facebook ID so I'm going to conduct the interview. I don't think we can approach Bradley or Grieveson separately in case they alert the others. We need all three questioned simultaneously as soon as we can locate the third member of the group. If we can't find her then we talk to Grieveson and Bradley.'

'We don't have a lot of time,' Das said.

'Sorry?'

'Look. The connection here is David Whitaker, yes?'

Kate nodded.

'So, he's a potential victim if we don't track down who's responsible for these murders?'

'Yes, but–'

'Then we need to act quickly. David Whitaker is due for release next week.'

21

'God, I hate this time of year,' Hollis complained as he and Kate stood shivering on June Tuffrey's doorstep, jacket collars raised against a light but relentless drizzle.

'I hate this bloody estate,' Kate countered, folding her arms more tightly and easing her shoulders up towards her ears in a pointless attempt to keep warm. 'Every case we work seems to end up here. It's like something from the *Twilight Zone*. Every time I turn a corner, no matter which direction I'm going in, I end up back here.'

Hollis looked like he was about to say something but the door in front of them opened and Kate's attention was drawn to the woman who stood on the threshold. If she hadn't known that she was in her early forties, Kate would have thought June Tuffrey was much older. Her shoulder-length hair was shot through with streaks of grey and her face was lined and pale. She was a few inches smaller than Kate and accentuated her diminutive size with a slight stoop. Only her clothes – a pink hoodie and dark leggings – suggested that she wasn't approaching her sixties.

'June Tuffrey?' Kate asked, holding out her ID.

The woman nodded. 'Come in. It's June Palmer now though. Tuffrey's my maiden name. I used it on Facebook so people might remember me.'

She showed them into a bright living room which seemed to contain a memory of summer in its pale-yellow walls and understated floral fabrics. Kate felt warmer than she had all morning and she didn't think it was just the central heating.

'Have a seat,' June said, indicating the sofa. Hollis sat and immediately took out his notebook.

'You're going to write down what I say?'

'Only if that's okay with you,' Kate said. 'It's important that we have a record for our enquiry.' She plonked herself next to Hollis in the hope that she'd be less intimidating if she was sitting down and was relieved when June nodded and took a seat opposite them.

'June, is it okay to call you June?' The woman nodded so Kate continued. 'We're trying to gather some information about a group of people that you were at junior school with.'

'Are you the one who used to live round here?' June asked.

Kate smiled. 'I was brought up on the estate and then we moved away. I've been in Doncaster for the last couple of years now. I was just saying to my colleague that I always seem to end up on Crosslands.'

'So, you went to Sheffield Road School?'

Kate nodded and June continued. 'It was a funny place. I suppose all schools are though. Friendship groups forming and then splitting up. It was really strange to see everybody at the reunion, well, those that turned up.' Kate thought that she detected an edge of bitterness in the woman's tone. Had she expected more people? Did she not think her efforts were appreciated?

'It looked like a good crowd, judging by the photographs.'

'Aye. Well, I got a bit of stick as well as support. Some people thought it would have been better to have it in the summer, but the pub gets booked up for weddings and that. Besides, it was dirt cheap just after Christmas. Tony, the landlord, did me a good rate because it's their quietest time. But it was a good night.' Her sad smile contradicted her words.

'June, I'm trying to track down three people in particular. They were friends at school and you might have known them. I think we've worked out who two of them might be, but we'd really like to find out the identity of the third.'

June nodded; her eyes fixed on Kate's.

'They called themselves The Three Amigos.'

'Oh, aye. I haven't heard that in a while. The Three Amigos. They named themselves after a film, you know. Thought it was funny. Ned, Lucky and Dusty.'

'You remember them?'

''Course I do. Lee, Neil and Vicky. They were at the reunion.'

'This would be Lee Barlow and Neil Grieveson?' Hollis interrupted. June nodded and he made a note.

'They were really close friends, but they all went to separate schools when we left the juniors. Sad really. But they got together again at the reunion. Spent all night talking.'

'Were there any former teachers there? At the reunion?' Kate didn't expect there to have been, but it was worth a try. Perhaps seeing Whitaker again after so long had been the catalyst for the murders.

'Only one. Mrs Dalston. I thought she'd have died years ago but there she was. Still walked with a limp.'

Kate was puzzled. 'How come? She didn't limp when I was at the school.'

June shook her head as though she couldn't quite believe what she was about to say. 'Broke her ankle on a school trip. I was there. We were abseiling from a bridge and she misjudged the drop. Fell the last few feet and did her ankle in. Shame really. She missed the last night of the trip.'

'What about Mr Whitaker. Did he turn up to the reunion?'

'No chance!' June spat. 'I'd have called the police if he did.'

'Why?'

June's eyes narrowed. 'He wasn't right, that one. He always was a bit weird – everybody said so. He had to move away from here and the rumour was that it was something to do with little kids.' She paused to let the implication sink in even though it was clear to Kate what she meant.

'And you knew this when you were at school? Did something happen?'

'We never knew. But kids get a feeling sometimes, don't they, if something's not right. I never trusted him.'

Kate couldn't help but wonder how much of this was hindsight. It seemed unlikely that children that age would think about their teachers in those terms, but she didn't question June's account.

'He was on that trip, wasn't he? Whitaker? The trip where Mrs Dalston broke her ankle.'

June nodded. 'He organised it every year. We talked about nothing else for weeks before we went. It was like a goodbye to our friends and the school, I suppose. It was even more of a goodbye for me because I didn't go back for the last few days. My dad had rented a caravan at Bridlington, so we went the next day. No more junior school.'

Kate could see that Hollis was making notes but, so far, there wasn't much that was useful. They needed names.

'June, can we get back to The Three Amigos. They were definitely Lee Bradley, Neil Grieveson and Vicky?'

June nodded. 'Lee was Lucky and Neil was Ned – because of the initials of their first names.'

'What about Vicky?' Kate knew that the third character was called Dusty – it didn't match with the others.

'That was the one that they thought was really funny,' June said with a tight-lipped grin. 'Vicky was Dusty because her surname was Rhodes – Dusty Rhodes? She thought it was hysterical, but then she always was a bit strange.'

Hollis sat up a bit straighter. 'Strange in what way?'

June's eyes drifted to the wall above Kate's head for a few seconds. 'Intense, I suppose. A bit quiet when she wasn't with the other two. She was clever as well. Probably the cleverest in our year. I bet she went to university.'

Kate took out her phone and showed June the image of two girls outside a tent – the one of Vicky and Angela.

'June, is that Vicky on the right?'

The other woman took the phone and used two fingers to expand the photograph, frowning in concentration.

'Yes. That's Vicky with Angela Fox. I remember she didn't want to share a tent with Angela, but she couldn't share with the lads, could she? God, I'd forgotten how much she hated Angela.'

'Vicky and Angela didn't get on very well?' Kate asked, taking back her phone and texting *Vicky Rhodes* to Cooper. 'Do you know why?'

June shrugged. 'I thought they were getting on okay, but the last time I saw Vicky Rhodes she was threatening to kill Angela Fox. And I think she really meant it.'

22

Linda Mitchell was just putting away her shopping when the doorbell rang. She shuffled to her walking frame and began the long trek to the front door cursing the delivery driver. What had he forgotten this time? She didn't know how the supermarkets recruited these people but the last three had all either given her the wrong items or they'd forgotten something essential.

'Hold your horses,' she shouted. 'I'm not as quick as I used to be.'

Breathing heavily from the exertion she peered through the spyhole expecting the delivery driver to be standing there with an apologetic look on his face. Instead she saw a well-built woman with short dark hair.

'Who are *you*?' she asked, opening the door. Her irritation with the supposed delivery driver had carried forward into her greeting, but she didn't feel any need to apologise.

'My name's Stacey Duffy,' the woman said, holding out a business card. 'I'm with the *South Yorkshire Post*.'

Linda snorted. 'You must've got the wrong house, love. I've not done anything interesting and it's pretty quiet round here.'

The young woman – Stacey – smiled. 'I'm not accusing you of anything, Mrs Mitchell. I'd just like a quick word. It's about your upstairs neighbour.'

Linda glanced at the ceiling of the hallway as though he was up there now. She knew he wasn't though. She knew exactly where he was. 'What's he done? I thought he'd been put away.'

Stacey nodded. 'He's still in prison, Mrs Mitchell. I'd like to talk to you about his release. If I could just come in for a few minutes?'

Linda quickly weighed up her options. The woman's ID looked official and there was nothing threatening or suspicious in her tone. Besides, Linda always wore a panic button round her neck. Social services would have somebody round in minutes if they thought she was in some sort of trouble. They'd told her that it was in case she had a fall, but she'd have no compunction about using it to summon help if she was being attacked.

'Come on in then. I'm a bit busy so you'll have to excuse the mess.' She tottered down the hall, her recently repaired hip aching with every step. She needed to sit down and rest for a few minutes.

'In here,' she said, leading the way into the kitchen and collapsing thankfully onto one of the wooden chairs that flanked the table. She saw the journalist's eyes flicking round and sensed her judgement. So what if she still had tins and packets everywhere? And she hadn't had the home help in for a few days so there was a bit of muck on the floor and the sink could do with a scrub.

'You look worn out,' Stacey observed with a smile. 'Shall I make you a cup of tea?'

She was forward, this one. But it was tempting. Linda had been planning on putting her feet up with a cuppa for an hour or so and she was parched after trying to sort out the shopping and then having to attend to this young woman. How bad could it be to allow somebody else to take care of her for five minutes?

'Go on then,' she said. 'Teabags are in the cupboard next to the sink, mugs are in the next one along and, well, you can see where the kettle is. Milk's in the fridge. Use the one on the left – it's older.'

Linda watched carefully as the woman made the tea, nodding her approval as she removed the teabag before adding the milk. Nothing worse than leaving the bag in with the milk, it made the tea weak and creamy-tasting.

'Right then,' Stacey said, passing a mug across the table and taking a seat as though this were *her* home and Linda was the guest. 'Let's have a little chat.'

Linda took a sip of her tea. She couldn't work out what this was about, but she wasn't entirely sure that the journalist could be trusted.

'How long has David Wallace lived upstairs?'

That took a bit of thinking about. It had been since Ian had died because Linda remembered hammering on the door of her upstairs neighbour when she'd found her husband slumped over the bed. Tony and Sheila had been up there then. They'd been good neighbours, quiet and friendly. Ian had been gone for four years in February.

'Three years or so,' Linda decided.

'And how have you found him as a neighbour?'

'Quiet,' she answered, truthfully. She barely knew he was there most of the time. She'd hear his footsteps or the occasional flush of the toilet but that was it. No loud music. No telly turned up full.

'So, you were shocked when you heard he'd been arrested?'

The honest answer was yes but Linda didn't want to give the impression that she'd been taken in by one of *that* sort. 'Not really,' she said. 'It's always the quiet ones, isn't it? I must admit I was a bit shocked that it was kiddies though. I could tell that he was a bit secretive. Shifty he was. Never really made eye contact. I thought there might have been something dodgy about him. Glad he's been put away.'

'So, you're aware of his offences?'

Linda nodded.

'Are you also aware that he's due for release?'

'That can't be right!' Ever since David Wallace had been arrested, Linda couldn't help but think about her grandchildren. Her son, Mark, didn't bring them round often but at least now there was nothing to worry about. She hated to think of them being here with that monster upstairs, but she was certain that they'd never been alone with him. In fact, she wasn't even sure if they'd met Wallace. But now that was a possibility that she couldn't even contemplate. 'How long has he been in jail?' she asked.

'Nearly six months.'

That didn't seem like long enough. Linda thought that they threw away the key with kiddie fiddlers these days. 'Are you sure? That can't be right after what he did.'

The journalist just nodded, her mouth a thin line as though she didn't trust herself to speak.

'When?' Linda asked.

'Not long. Couple of weeks.'

Linda drained her teacup. Two weeks and then he'd be free. 'Is that why you've come? To warn me?'

Stacey nodded. 'And to ask for your help.'

'Help?'

The woman leaned across the table and lowered her voice. 'We can't get access to a release date. The authorities won't allow it. Rehabilitation of offenders and all that.'

Linda nodded, even though she wasn't quite sure what the woman meant.

'So, I thought you might be willing to let us – me – know when he gets back. You could listen out for him. It's in the public interest for us to let people know that he's at large again as soon as possible. God knows what could happen if he got his hands on a child. If we expose his whereabouts the council will probably have to move him.' Stacey sat back again, looking at Linda as though daring her to disagree.

'I could do that,' Linda said, a thought creeping into her mind. Information could be valuable. 'But what's in it for me.'

Stacey smiled broadly. 'The newspaper would see that you were appropriately remunerated,' she said. Linda translated the statement as *money*. She'd get paid for keeping people safe. And he might get moved away from the area if others kicked up a fuss.

'Of course I'll help,' she said. 'It'd be a pleasure to get rid of a monster like that.'

Stacey stood up and placed a business card on the table. 'There's my mobile number. Call any time, day or night. I want to know as soon as he's back.'

Linda picked up the card.

'Will do,' she said. 'The minute I hear anything.'

'You won't regret it,' Stacey said. 'I'll see myself out. Hope to be in touch soon.'

Linda listened to the woman's footsteps receding down the hallway and then the opening and closing of the front door. Humming to herself, she ran a finger across the glossy surface of Stacey's card.

She'd be ready.

'Right, we've got a name,' Kate said, securing her seat belt and tapping the screen of her phone. 'I'm going to task Sam with finding Angela Fox as well. If Vicky really did have it in for her thirty years ago it's possible that she might be in danger.'

'Do you think so?' Hollis's tone was sceptical. 'It's a long time ago and kids fall out over anything. I threatened to kill my best mate at least twice a week when I was that age.'

'But we're dealing with a potential murder suspect, not a child.'

Hollis nodded. Point taken.

As they drove through the estate, Kate contemplated the grey streets. Dan was right, November was awful, and it was especially awful in the north of England on a drizzly morning. They passed the house where Kate had grown up, one more red-brick box in a row of red-brick boxes. She remembered days like this when she was a child. She'd look out of her bedroom window to see if it was raining before deciding what to wear for the day. She had a fool-proof method for assessing the weather. The roof of the house behind theirs was tiled, like the rest of the houses, with shiny, red clay tiles. On a wet day the chimney was reflected in the slick surface. The tiles dried erratically so on a less wet day the roof was a patchwork, and on a sunny day there was no reflection at all. Every house they passed on their way off the estate had a roof that showed a reflection of the chimney.

'Kate, you're going to want to see this,' Cooper said as soon as Kate stepped back into the office. She'd sent Hollis up to the canteen for refreshments to give her a chance to check her text messages. She'd had one from Nick on the drive back to Doncaster, but she hadn't wanted to open it in case the DC saw it and asked about the relationship. It was short – trite, almost: *we need to talk*. She'd ignored it, deciding to deal with it later, and now Cooper was about to distract her.

'What've you found?' she asked, pulling a chair up to Sam's desk and sitting next to her. On the screen was a black-and-white image which was clearly a still from CCTV footage. It showed a wide view of a car park at night, probably from a camera placed high up on a telegraph pole or lamp post.

'Charlton's car,' Cooper said. 'It was found this morning in a car park just off Thorne Road, near the hospital. Unlocked but no keys.'

'The keys were on the body,' Kate said.

Sam ignored her. 'So, I requested CCTV and it must be my lucky day because I got the files ten minutes ago. I've only just started but I've found Charlton pulling into the car park at around 7.30pm. He then just seems to be waiting.'

'Meeting somebody?'

'Could be. As I said, this is as far as I've got. He's in the dark hatchback, bottom left.' Cooper tapped a key, but the image remained the same.

'Is it playing?' Kate asked.

'Yep. Not much happening though. Oh, here's a cat.'

They watched as a black feline eased itself off the wall at the back of the car park and slowly wandered out of the range of the camera. Charlton's car still hadn't moved.

Cooper sighed and sped up the image until a figure appeared at the top of the screen.

'Who's that?'

Cooper shook her head. 'No idea. Can't make out any features but it looks like a woman and, not being one for stereotypes, it's pushing a buggy, so odds are it's female.'

The figure approached a saloon car two rows behind Charlton's, removed the child from the buggy and bent over, presumably strapping it into a car seat. She then opened the car's boot and appeared to be grappling with the buggy which looked like it didn't want to fold up.

'Here we go,' Cooper whispered as, on the screen, Charlton got out of his car and approached the struggling woman. It was impossible to tell if anything was said but he took the buggy from her and turned his back as he tried to collapse it.

'Whoa!' Cooper exclaimed as Charlton collapsed, with the buggy, onto the ground. They watched as he struggled to his feet only to be met with an outstretched arm from his attacker. He went down again, this time half inside the open car boot. The woman calmly tipped him in and threw the buggy into the back seat before getting in the car and driving off.

Kate checked the time code. The whole encounter had taken just over two minutes.

'Taser?'

'Taser,' Cooper confirmed, rewinding and freezing on the outstretched arm. 'You can just about make out the wires. And here, she scoops it all up with him when she stuffs him in the boot. It looks like she might have had two, but it's a bit hard to make out. One shock probably wouldn't have been enough to subdue him completely but if she got him twice and left the electrodes in him, he'd have been helpless for about half a minute. Plenty of time to stuff him in the boot. And combine that with the first shock – his muscles would have been like jelly for a good twenty minutes or so.'

That tied in with the marks that Kailisa had found on the body. But Charlton would have recovered from the electric shock reasonably quickly. If Kailisa was right about time of death, what happened between Charlton being put in the car and him being killed in the playground?

'Can we see the car's reg plate?'

Sam rewound and watched the footage again.

'Nope. It's in shadow when she's parked and blurred when she leaves. I'll try to enhance it but it's doubtful. Makes me wonder if she'd smeared something on it to make it hard for the camera to pick up. Can't make out what type of car it is either. Could be an Audi or a Toyota maybe. Saloon cars aren't as popular as hatchbacks so I might be able to work out what model it is if I look on a few car makers' websites. Trouble is, it's hard to tell if it's a new model or something older.'

'What about CCTV near the school?'

'There's nothing close – I checked. The nearest is on Doncaster Road. I can have a look but there are a lot of smaller roads into Thorpe. If I was intending to kill somebody I'd want to avoid being seen for as long as possible.'

'But she had to know there were cameras in the car park. It's a huge risk.'

'What's a huge risk?' Hollis had arrived with coffees and, while Sam filled him in and showed him the footage, Kate tried to make sense of what they'd discovered. If this was the woman who had kidnapped and killed Margaret Whitaker, she seemed supremely confident, arrogant almost. There were other cars in the car park. Somebody could have turned up at any point during her encounter with Charlton. And then what?

'Hang on,' she said. 'What about the baby? Who'd kidnap somebody when they've got a kid in the car?'

'There was no baby,' Sam said. 'Look'

She played a two second clip of the footage. 'Look at its head when she gets it out of the buggy.'

Kate watched as the unknown woman lifted the child free of the straps and turned to put it in the car. Its head lolled at an unnatural angle as she leaned down to place it on the back seat.

'It's a doll. Window dressing to make her act more credible.'

'Jesus,' Kate whispered. 'She's bloody good.'

Kate watched again as the figure turned to Charlton as he approached, thinking he was doing the decent thing, trying to help – he obviously didn't perceive any threat from this woman.

'He was expecting a man,' Kate said. 'Otherwise he wouldn't have got out of the car to help. He'd have been much more suspicious. She played him.'

'What about the Taser?' Hollis asked. 'We could try to trace it, or them. If she bought it here, O'Connor might have a contact who might be able to help.'

'That's a big if,' Kate said. Most Tasers that were recovered from crime scenes had been purchased abroad – directed through a PO box or some other anonymised address in case customs picked them up. If this woman had bought hers online, she could have got it from Germany or the US as easily as ordering a book or a CD. It wasn't in the exporter's interests to be worried about the laws in the country that they were posting the item to. Let the buyer worry about that. The only risk was that it would be picked up and confiscated by UK customs as it entered the country and, Kate knew, a lot still got through.

'It's probably a dead end,' she said. 'But I'll get Steve to ask around. If she did buy it locally, he might be able to jog somebody's memory. My hunch is that she's much too clever for that, though. Sam, did you have any luck with either of the names I gave you?'

Cooper shook her head. 'I've got Vicky at York University in 1996, she studied law, and then again at a firm of solicitors in Manchester until 2005. Nothing after that so far. She's not on the current electoral role under that name and I can't find any record of a marriage. Nothing for Angela Fox but, you only texted me forty-five minutes ago.' She gave Kate a cheeky grin which made her look like a naughty school kid. 'I think I've done pretty well considering.'

Kate gave her shoulder a light slap. Cooper had taken a long time to come round to the fact that it was okay to joke with the others, including Kate, and it was still refreshing to see her in a light-hearted mood. When Kate had first joined the team, Cooper had tried calling her *ma'am* which had lasted all of ten minutes. After that she'd spent a few months avoiding calling her boss anything at all until she finally managed to adapt to the use of her first name. Kate interchanged surnames and first names for all the others but, after O'Connor's first tentative *Fletch*, she'd been Kate. It wasn't out of some high-blown notion of egalitarianism or an attempt to convey herself as 'one of the boys', she just preferred using her first name to her former husband's surname, and she had no desire to go back to being Cathy Siddons.

'Okay, smartarse,' she said. 'Keep looking. Dan'll help out.'

Hollis sighed. He hated being stuck behind a desk but he was good at digging around in the virtual world. Not as good as Cooper but not bad.

'If we can't get an address for Vicky Rhodes today, I think we need to talk to the other two, one of them might be able to tell us where she is. Das is right, we can't wait until Whitaker's released.' Her phone vibrated in her pocket. An e-mail from Barratt headed *PM*.

Opening it, Kate scanned through. There wasn't much more than Kailisa had said at the scene. Time of death was still esti-mated to have been between 11pm and 2am, cause of death was exsanguination. The marks that the pathologist had spotted were consistent with a Taser, as was the fact that Charlton had voided his bladder sometime before he was mutilated. Crucially there was no physical evidence linking this murder with that of Margaret Whitaker. The blades used were different and there was no DNA. Kailisa had obviously spent some time explaining the type of blade used and Barratt, in his sponge-like way, had absorbed all the details and passed them on to Kate. The blade was consistent with a large kitchen knife, sharpened along one edge and blunt on the other and it was 3.4 centimetres wide at its widest point.

There might not be a physical link to Margaret's murder, but the knife could link to Chris's. Kate stepped away from her colleagues, switched her phone to the keypad and dialled a number. Time to call in a favour.

Don't you just hate waiting around? I've always been the sort of person that likes to get things done so, once I start something, I like to get it finished. I've been watching the local news in the hope that they'll start speculating about the two murders in South Yorkshire, but nobody seems to be joining the dots. Can people really not see the link? I didn't think the police were that dim, but you just never know. I hope he's heard though. Tucked away in his little cell playing with himself. I hope he's terrified of what's going to happen when he gets out.

He should be. What I did to Charlton is nothing compared to what

I've got planned for him. He's got to suffer for what he did and for what I've been through for the last thirty years. He'll pay for the life I could have had and for the other lives he's ruined.

I know when he's due to be released and I've got his downstairs neighbour primed to let me know the minute he sets foot in his flat. I've known since he was sent down that I'd be waiting for him and I've planned everything to lead up to the big event. It's like the others were the supporting acts and he's the massive finale. The one everybody's been waiting for. I hope I hear the crowd cheering in my head when I finally do it – chanting my name, crying out for more.

But I'm getting ahead of myself, aren't I? Everything I've done so far has taken so much planning and I can't let that go to waste. If I'm going to finish this then I need to be careful, thoughtful and thorough. It's got me this far.

I just wish I didn't have to wait.

24

Kate's meeting with Das had gone as well as she could have expected. The DCI wasn't keen to link the two murders because the implications were uncomfortable, especially with the Cumbria case thrown in, but she had been convinced that David Whitaker might be in danger. Despite her scepticism about The Three Amigos theory she'd given the go-ahead for Bradley and Grieveson to be interviewed and Kate had co-ordinated her team so that the interviews were to be conducted simultaneously. Barratt and O'Connor, white-faced from the PM, had been dispatched to Lee Bradley's workplace in Doncaster, while she and Hollis were en route to Neil Grieveson's home in Sheffield.

Kate's phone rang just as they turned off the Parkway and she recognised the number immediately. Her former boss in Penrith. 'DCI Bland, thanks for ringing me back.'

'Fletcher, you always were the unorthodox one. To be honest, I wasn't surprised when I got your message.'

His strong Cumbrian accent, with its associations of mountains and open spaces, made Kate smile as she asked, 'And you checked for me?'

It hadn't been an easy decision, but Kate felt like she was working without a key part of the puzzle and she knew somebody who could provide her with the piece that she needed. She'd left a message for her former DCI, Colin Bland, and asked if he could confirm that the murder weapon in the Gilruth case was consistent with what they knew about the knife used to emasculate and murder Simon Charlton.

A sigh at the other end of the phone. 'I checked.'

Kate had known he would. Bland was an old-fashioned policeman with a strong sense of loyalty. She knew that he felt partly responsible for her moving away from Cumbria to seek promotion and she'd bargained on that sense of guilt working in her favour.

'Without a direct comparison it's impossible to tell if the knives used were the same. But, there's nothing to suggest that they weren't. Your description of your knife matches with the one from Chris's PM report. Same width of blade. They might not be the same but there's nothing conclusive to suggest that they aren't.'

It wasn't much but at least Kate knew that Chris wasn't murdered with a completely different sort of knife. It *could* have been the same killer with the same weapon.

She exchanged a few pleasantries with Bland about the differences in weather between the west and east of the country, before thanking him and hanging up.

'Potential link between Chris Gilruth's and Simon Charlton's murders.' She explained the details to Hollis who looked less than impressed.

'So, they weren't necessarily killed with the same weapon, but they also weren't killed with completely different weapons? It's a bit thin.'

'Better hold on to it,' Kate said with a tight grin. 'Because it might be all we've got to link these murders.'

Hollis pulled the car into a bus stop in front of a row of shops in Crookes and turned off the engine.

'This it?' Kate asked, scanning the buildings. There was a betting shop, a pizza takeaway, a chemist which looked like it might have been recently renovated and an old-fashioned hardware shop. None of the windows were boarded up and most of the paintwork on display was clean, if a little dated in places.

'According to our records Grieveson lives over the bookies.'

'No job?'

'He works from home. As far as Sam could find out it looks like he has some sort of internet business buying and selling collectibles.'

'What sort of collectibles?'

Hollis shrugged. 'No idea. Probably something geeky. Sci-fi or *Game of Thrones* memorabilia I expect.'

Kate led the way down an alley between two rows of shops and round into a small yard. The back door of the betting shop was open despite the cold and she could hear the droning commentary of a race coming from a radio or television. There was another door, set back in an alcove, with 4B stencilled onto the flaking green paint. Kate pressed the bell next to the door and heard it ringing inside the flat. A few seconds later there were footsteps on the stairs inside and the door was opened by a tall, skinny man in a dark grey T-shirt and torn jeans. His eyes were bloodshot as they looked at Kate and then Hollis, and the hand on the door jamb was unsteady.

'Neil Grieveson?' Kate asked before the man could ask who they were. He nodded in confirmation, his eyes unable to settle anywhere.

Kate introduced herself and Hollis and asked if they could come up to the flat.

'What's this about?' Grieveson asked, his voice low pitched and with the slight hoarseness of a habitual smoker.

'I'd rather we talked inside,' Kate said.

Grieveson nodded and opened the door to allow them to pass.

'After you,' Hollis said with a grin. Kate knew that he wasn't being polite – he didn't want to give Grieveson the opportunity to abscond while they were on the stairs. Grieveson grinned back as though reading Hollis's mind and understanding that he'd been outsmarted before turning and heading up the stairs.

The flat looked like something out of a Channel 5 documentary about hoarders. There were cardboard boxes on the stairs, boxes in the narrow hallway and even more boxes in the small living room that Grieveson led them into. A dining table nestled beneath the only window in the room and was the only piece of furniture not strewn with cardboard and assorted packaging material. It housed a laptop, an array of mugs and glasses and a half-empty vodka bottle.

'Business good?' Hollis asked, looking round.

'Not bad,' Grieveson said, clearing a space on the dingy sofa and indicating that they could sit down. Kate studied his face, looking for the boy that she'd seen in the photographs that Sam had found. If she didn't know how old Neil Grieveson was, she'd have had difficulty ageing him. His lean figure and the way he was dressed suggested twenties to early thirties but the bald scalp and dark lines around his eyes made him seem much older. She sat down and waited for Hollis to decide where to position himself. She knew that he wouldn't sit – too difficult to respond if Grieveson made an unexpected move – she predicted either standing by the door or perched on the edge of the table.

'What's this about?' Grieveson asked again, turning to Hollis who was leaning in the doorway.

'We think you might be able to help us with an investigation,' Kate said, deliberately vague.

'What sort of investigation?'

'It involves somebody that we think you might know.'

Grieveson pulled out a dining chair, sat down and reached a shaky hand out to a packet of cigarettes. He pulled one out and inserted it between his chapped lips. 'Who?' The cigarette jittered in his mouth as he spoke.

'Does "The Three Amigos" mean anything to you?'

'The what?' Grieveson had managed to light his cigarette. He took a drag and puffed out smoke towards the off-white ceiling.

'You and two of your friends called yourselves The Three Amigos when you were at junior school. Correct?'

'Christ, that was thirty years ago. How am I supposed to remember?'

'Let me help. Lee Bradley and Vicky Rhodes. They were the other two.' Kate watched him closely as he looked out of the window and then down at the screen of his laptop. He couldn't look at her or Hollis.

'What about another name? David Whitaker. Mr Whitaker was a teacher at Sheffield Road Juniors when you were there.'

'Doesn't ring any bells,' Grieveson said, shaking his head.

'Neil,' Hollis said from the doorway. 'We know that you were friends with Lee and Vicky. We've got photographs showing the three of you on a camping trip to Derbyshire. A trip led by David Whitaker.'

Grieveson visibly paled. 'Like I said, that was years ago. We all went to different secondary schools and that was the end of our friendship.'

'Until January this year,' Hollis continued. 'When you met up in Thorpe at a school reunion. And the three of you came up with a plan to get revenge on Whitaker.'

Grieveson shook his head. 'I have no idea what you're talking about.'

Kate sighed heavily, more for effect than out of any real sense of frustration. 'Okay, then let me spell it out for you. David Whitaker is a convicted paedophile currently serving a six-month sentence for grooming a minor. We know that Whitaker taught at Sheffield Road Junior School when you and your friends were there. We also know that he was on a camping trip in 1988 which the three of you also attended. We believe that, since the reunion in January, the three of you have conspired against David Whitaker in an act of revenge. As we speak two other members of my team are interviewing Lee Bradley. And we're close to tracking down Vicky Rhodes as well.'

Grieveson gave a sound between a snort and a laugh. 'Tracking down Vicky? Why would you need to track her down? She lives in the Canaries – it's not like she's hiding or on the run or something. I'll give you her phone number if you want. She's not been back to South Yorkshire since January. She had nothing to do with this.'

'Nothing to do with what?' Hollis jumped in.

Grieveson stubbed out his cigarette and reached for the bottle of vodka. 'I suppose I always knew somebody would work it out,' he said, pouring a large measure of the spirit into one of the mugs on the table. 'It was only a matter of time. But, before I say anything else, you need to know that it was me and Lee. Vicky wasn't involved even though it was her idea in the first place. She couldn't risk her job but me and Lee, well,' he gestured to the piles of boxes around the room, 'it's not like I had a lot to lose and Lee's in a poxy office job that he hates. We both knew it would be worth doing time if we got to see that bastard suffer.'

Hollis pulled out the other dining chair and sat opposite Grieveson at the table, notebook in one hand, pencil in the other.

'Okay, Neil,' he said, gently. 'Start from the beginning.'

25

'D o you believe him?' Kate asked as soon as they were back in the car.

'I think there's too much detail not to,' Hollis responded. 'We can easily check the case in the files and see if it matches what he told us.'

Kate wanted to punch the dashboard in frustration. Grieveson had admitted his part in David Whitaker's suffering, but it had nothing to do with the murders. He'd confessed to entrapment and, given the circumstances, Kate doubted that there would be much appetite from the CPS for pursuing prosecution. Apparently, Grieveson and Bradley had read online about a group of men in the north east who were actively engaged in vigilante activity against known and suspected paedophiles. They used social media to trap them and then turned the evidence over to their local police. Lee and Neil had done the same with Whitaker, but they'd submitted everything anonymously, gambling on there being enough evidence in a search of Whitaker's house to get a conviction. And it had worked.

A tearful Grieveson had explained the abuse he'd suffered on the camping trip and how he, Lee and Vicky had finally been able to talk about it to each other at the reunion. Their meeting had been the catalyst for the plot against Whitaker – the catharsis of finally being able to be open about what had happened had turned to thoughts of revenge and the three of them had formulated a plan. Bradley and Grieveson had set up a fake Facebook profile and posed as a minor online. They'd trapped Whitaker into meeting 'Jamie' and then sent the evidence to the police anonymously.

Grieveson had been keen to point out that, although it had been Vicky's idea, the woman had nothing to do with the details. She worked as a lawyer in Tenerife and it would have been career suicide for her to have taken an active part in the plan. She'd been keeping tabs on Whitaker and knew about his change of name, taking it as further evidence that he was still an active paedophile and needed to hide his true identity. Grieveson also claimed that Vicky Rhodes had been out of the country since January – but he only had her word for it. Kate hoped that somebody at immigration might know otherwise.

She took her phone out of her pocket and dialled the number that Grieveson had given her for Vicky in Tenerife. No answer. It was a mobile number but, if Vicky was with a client, she wouldn't have answered anyway so Kate left a message asking Vicky to ring her back.

A text came in from Cooper.

Angela Fox. Works at DRI. Colleagues say she's on holiday. Lives in Tickhill. No answer at home or mobile. No sign of her car.

'Shit!' Kate hissed.
'What's up?'

'Sam's found contact details for Angela Fox but she's not there. Her workmates at the hospital think she's on holiday. No reply on her mobile though.'

'Doesn't mean anything,' Hollis said, his tone betraying his lack of conviction. 'She might be in a poor signal area or she might have turned her phone off as she's on holiday.'

'Or she might be the next victim and we might be too late. I want to get over to the DRI and talk to her colleagues. Somebody might know something.'

~

Entering the hospital inevitably made Kate think of Nick and how she'd responded to his brief text with an equally terse *Fine*. The chances of bumping into him were tiny but, as she strode up to the main reception desk, she felt a prickle at the back of her neck as though he might be watching her.

Kate flashed her ID and asked for directions to the admin office where Angela Fox worked. She wasn't surprised to be directed downstairs into the bowels of the sprawling 1960s monstrosity of a building; in her limited experience of the DRI most of the structure housed wards and laboratories – she'd never seen anything resembling office space.

'Through there.' Hollis pointed to a sign on the wall indicating that 'Administration' was further down the dingy corridor. He pushed open a door and Kate followed him into an open-plan office divided into groups of four desks, each one separated from its neighbour by a blue or grey partition. The egg box-like effect was enhanced by the low ceiling and the lack of natural light.

Just inside the door was a single desk and its occupant looked up as they entered.

'Can I help you?' the woman peered over reading glasses that were so small Kate wondered if they could have any effect on her vision. Her fair hair was tied back in a neat ponytail and she wore a plain, pale blue blouse open at the neck to reveal a discreet gold cross.

'Detective Inspector Fletcher and DC Hollis,' Kate said. 'I believe one of my colleagues rang earlier about Angela Fox.'

The woman stared at her for a second and then nodded enthusiastically, making her ponytail bounce on her back. 'Of course. I couldn't tell her much except that Angela is on holiday. I don't understand what else you could want.'

Kate wasn't sure herself, but she felt a need to find out as much as possible about the woman if they were to have any chance of protecting her. 'Is there anybody that Angela is particularly close to? Somebody she might confide in?'

The woman gave Kate a wry smile. 'Have a look around, detective inspector. The workspace isn't exactly conducive to socialising. And, to be honest, it's not encouraged.'

'But you must have coffee breaks, cigarette breaks, that sort of thing.'

The woman sighed. 'Try Dylan, third desk on the right at the back. He probably spends the most time with Angela.'

Kate followed her directions and wasn't surprised to see over a dozen heads turn to watch as she and Hollis crossed the office – it didn't feel like a place where very much of interest happened. Dylan had already turned his seat round and he smiled at Kate as she approached.

'Dylan?'

'Is this about Angela? Somebody rang earlier and I said that she was on holiday. Has something happened to her?' He looked intrigued rather than upset, his slightly breathless questions suggesting that he wasn't an especially close colleague.

'Why do you ask?' Hollis wanted to know.

Dylan smoothed his over-gelled blond hair back from his forehead and looked at Hollis with steady blue eyes. 'Because it seems a bit unlikely that the police are making enquiries about Angela unless she's in some sort of trouble or something's happened to her. I don't know her well, but I know enough to think it's more likely to be option B.'

He folded his arms across his chest, creasing his immaculate white shirt and rumpling his navy-blue tie.

'You don't know her well?' Kate wondered why she'd been sent to this particular desk.

'Well, we're not BFFs but we chat a bit. We're the only two smokers in the office. Well, vapers now. We try to have our breaks at the same time otherwise it can get a bit lonely out in the smoking shelter.'

Kate looked round. 'What is this place? I know it's admin but what sort? Patient records?'

Dylan gave her a patronising smile. 'If the manager is to be believed, we're much more than records, we're the beating heart of the hospital. Over there we have appointments admin,' he said, indicating a section of the office near the front. 'To the left is records, over there is something mysterious that nobody understands to do with programming the MRI scanners and our section is mainly general IT support.'

'And Angela's role?'

'As I said, mainly IT support.'

'Can we go somewhere a bit less... exposed?' Kate asked. 'I'm hoping you might be able to give us some information to help us to track Angela down.'

'Track her down? No need,' Dylan said with a grin. 'She's in Scotland. Mull to be exact. She's renting a cottage up there for two weeks. She should be back next week – she's been away for nearly a week already.'

'In November?' Hollis's voice squeaked with surprise. It did seem unlikely. Who'd choose to head so far north at this time of year?

'She likes the solitude. It's a regular thing before the Christmas season. She likes to get away for a while.'

'You're extra busy at Christmas?'

'Not here. Angela's in an AmDram group and they start planning their spring production at the beginning of December as well as having pantomime rehearsals.'

'Do you know the name of the group?' Hollis asked, taking his notebook out of his breast pocket.

'Christchurch Players. They're based in the old cinema in town.'

'And Angela acts?'

Dylan shook his head and smiled. 'If you met her, you'd know how ridiculous that sounds. She does stuff behind the scenes. She's far too shy to get up on stage. She doesn't even like having her name in the programme.'

'Is she married? Boyfriend? Girlfriend?'

'Don't think so,' Dylan responded. 'She's never mentioned a significant other. Straight though, I'd guess, but she's never shown much interest in romance.'

'And she lives alone?'

'Again, I can't be sure but I'm fairly certain that she lives in a village somewhere, in her parents' house. She said that they were dead so I assume she inherited it – I can barely afford my shoebox of a flat on what we get paid.'

'And you've not heard from her since she left for her holiday?'

'No. But I wouldn't expect to. As I said, we're not that close, we just chat on our breaks.'

Kate thanked him for his time and they left the oppressive underground space.

As they were crossing the car park Kate's mobile rang. She

glanced at the screen, expecting an update from Cooper or one of the others but the number wasn't familiar.

'Fletcher,' she snapped, expecting sales or a PPI scam.

'Detective Inspector Fletcher? This is Vicky Rhodes. I believe you wanted to talk to me about something?'

26

'Thanks for getting back to me,' Kate said, her tone genial even as her mind was racing. Had Vicky Rhodes, once known as Dusty, spoken to Grieveson? Did she know that he'd confessed to setting up Whitaker? 'Would it be possible for me to ring you back in a few minutes?'

'That won't work for me,' said the woman at the other end of the line. 'I'm on a brief break between clients. I'm free later if that's any good. We could Skype or FaceTime if it's easier?'

Kate was grateful for the suggestion. She wanted to be able to see Vicky's reactions when she was asked a range of questions and a video link would be as close to face-to-face as they could get. They could even record it, with Vicky's consent, in order to properly assess her responses.

'Vicky Rhodes?' Hollis asked, as Kate ended the call, even though he'd clearly heard both sides of the conversation. 'That's a surprise.'

'I know,' Kate agreed. 'I want to be back at base when we Skype. I'm sure Sam's got some useful software to help us to get the most out of the interview.'

A text pinged into Kate's message service. Vicky Rhodes's Skype details.

'At least we might be able to tell if she really is in Tenerife,' Hollis said. 'We can get her to pan round with the camera and see if it's sunny.' Kate wasn't sure if he was joking but it was a thought that had already crossed her mind.

Kate's team were already assembled by the time she and Hollis got back to Doncaster Central. O'Connor was sitting at the head of the conference table swinging back on his chair and chatting to Barratt who had both hands wrapped round a mug of coffee. Cooper was watching something on her laptop and, from the way she kept tapping her keyboard every few seconds, Kate guessed it was CCTV footage from somewhere.

'Right,' Kate said as Hollis slipped into a seat next to Barratt. 'I want a full progress report – I'm assuming you've all had a busy day – who's first?'

Sam looked up from her computer but made no move to speak while Barratt and O'Connor looked at each other.

'As Matt said in his e-mail, PM on Charlton didn't reveal much that we didn't already know,' O'Connor began. 'Preliminary ID confirmed from the photo on his driving licence in the absence of information about next of kin. Wounds to his back and the backs of his thigh look like Taser burns, no sign that he was restrained, no ligature marks. Kailisa suspects that he was drugged to enable his killer to keep him compliant and get him to the kill site – obviously bloods have been sent away to check for the usual suspects. Cause of death exsanguination. Preliminary examination of the genitals suggests that they're definitely his as the excision pattern of the wound and the missing flesh match up.'

'Would've been a bit unlikely to find somebody else's bits at the scene,' Hollis muttered.

'True,' O'Connor said. 'Just being thorough. Obviously, we'll have to wait for toxicology and DNA but Kailisa isn't especially hopeful about the latter.'

'Anything to link this murder to that of Margaret Whitaker?'

O'Connor shook his head. 'Bugger all.'

Kate was tempted to share what she'd heard from Colin Bland, but it was too tenuous a link to Charlton's murder to risk Das finding out that she'd got information through slightly underhand means. Instead she moved on to the second part of Barratt and O'Connor's day.

'We've got Neil Grieveson confessing to setting David Whitaker up and he names Lee Bradley as an accomplice. What's Bradley got to say for himself?' Kate asked, turning to Barratt.

The DC shook his head. 'He denies all knowledge of anything to do with Whitaker. Says he met Grieveson and Rhodes at the reunion and they finally spoke about the abuse but that's as far as it went. He confirms Vicky Rhodes's ID as the third amigo and told us that she lives on Tenerife – her job's something to do with property. He doesn't know where Grieveson lives and hasn't spoken to either of them since the reunion.'

'That's bollocks,' Hollis interjected.

'You believed Grieveson?' Kate asked.

'I can't believe that Grieveson cooked it up on his own. He was terrified when we turned up – I'll bet that Bradley took charge and now he's letting his mate take the fall. I think we should get him in here and tell him what Grieveson told us.'

Kate thought about it. Was there really any point? There was no evidence linking either man with the murders and there would be little mileage in pursuing a prosecution for the entrapment of a known paedophile. Especially as Whitaker had been convicted on solid evidence found at his home.

'Let's leave it for now,' she said. 'Matt, contact Bradley and let him know what his 'friend' told us. I'm happy for you to give the impression that we don't know what to believe and that we're keeping an open mind at the moment. I expect Grieveson will already have been in touch with him anyway. Right, Sam?'

Cooper looked up at Kate and then back at her laptop. 'I've been thinking about the car that was used to abduct Simon Charlton. How many of us drive saloon cars these days?'

Blank looks and head shakes all round.

'They're not that common and most of them are high end. It seemed a bit unlikely that our kidnapper just happened to have one at his or her disposal so I've been looking at car hire companies in the local area. It looks like only the big nationals have saloon cars for hire so I've rung the branches in Doncaster, Rotherham and Sheffield. Two of them rent out Skoda Octavias and one only had BMW saloons. I've tried to enhance the CCTV footage, but the car doesn't look like a recent model. So, that leaves second-hand car dealers. I did a search and then rang around a few to see if they'd sold a dark saloon car in recent weeks. JB Motors on Balby Road sold a 2003 Skoda Fabia saloon three weeks ago.'

Kate felt a frisson of electricity run round her team. This could be it.

'I got a name. But that's where it starts to turn to crap,' Cooper admitted. 'The client was a woman. She paid with a credit card in the name Stephanie Martin. The same name as Margaret Wallace's "niece" who took her out of the nursing home. I asked for a description. Shortish, blondeish, fortyish, attractive.'

'Could be Vicky Rhodes,' Kate said. 'She's dark haired but hair colour is the easiest thing to change. Or it could have been a wig.' She sighed in frustration. It seemed like this woman was always one step ahead of them – if it was a woman – and they were playing catch-up all the time.

'Got a date and time?' she asked Cooper.

'Three weeks ago. On a Friday afternoon. The salesman says she didn't even take it for a test drive. Put a deposit on her card and picked it up on the Saturday.'

'And no doubt dumped it somewhere after she'd killed Charlton.'

At least Cooper had a description and an index number for the car. If it turned up in the area it could be tested for DNA, but Kate was willing to bet that it had been left on one of the estates in Doncaster with the keys in and would be a burnt-out wreck by now. It did tell them more about their suspect though. She had money. A second-hand car of that age wouldn't have been expensive but not many people had a few hundred pounds to throw away.

'Nice work, Sam,' Kate said. 'We'll need to look at the credit card. Barratt, I need you to get round there to take a formal statement. You never know, the salesman might remember something else. Take a photo of Vicky as well, just to be certain it's not her.'

'Speaking of which,' Hollis said, tapping his watch. 'We need to set up that Skype call.'

Kate nodded.

'Anything else?'

Cooper blushed, obviously she had something to add. 'Simon Charlton's house has been searched and I've got access to his laptop. I'm going to see if I can find how contact was made between him and his killer.'

'How did you get that so quickly,' O'Connor asked, suspicion clear in his tone.

Cooper's blush deepened. 'I know somebody in digital forensics. She owed me a favour.'

Barratt smiled to himself and Kate could see where this was heading; she just wasn't sure whether Cooper could handle it.

'Oh, that tall brunette you used to hang around with – Judy... Jenny? I wonder what you did to get her in your debt.' O'Connor was grinning as he teased his colleague, no malice in his tone but Kate knew how sensitive Cooper could be about her private life.

'I'd tell you, Steve, but I really don't think you'd understand. And I *know* you could never do the same.'

Kate watched as Barratt's jaw dropped open. Cooper was finally standing up for herself. She'd had plenty of teasing from O'Connor about her 'preferences' and her 'conquests' – most of it good-natured – but she'd chosen to ignore most of it; until now.

'Better not let Abby know,' O'Connor continued, referring to Sam's partner – despite the recent wedding, Sam refused to refer to Abby as her wife.

'What makes you think Abby wasn't in on it?' Cooper said, picking up her laptop and heading for the door. 'It was a *really* big favour Jenny owed me.'

27

Kate glanced at the time in the corner of the screen and mentally added an hour. Vicky Rhodes should be home from work now and, hopefully, ready to chat. Looking over to the opposite desk, Kate checked that Cooper was ready if Rhodes gave them the go-ahead to record the conversation and then she tapped the call icon and waited for it to connect. An image of herself appeared in the top right-hand corner of the screen. She looked tired, her blonde hair in need of a touch-up at the roots and her foundation not doing its job very effectively. Turning fifty earlier in the year hadn't been as much of a shock as she'd expected but her reflection or a candid photograph could still take her by surprise.

'Detective Inspector Fletcher.' Vicky Rhodes's voice was warm as though she was greeting an old friend, but the screen remained blank.

'Good evening, Vicky. I'm afraid we might have a technical hitch. I don't seem to be able to see you.'

Kate flicked Cooper a quick glance and the DC responded with a shrug. Not their end then.

'Hang on,' Rhodes was saying. 'This laptop has a mind of its own. That any better?'

A female face appeared on screen, her expression somewhere between concern and amusement and Kate recognised Vicky Rhodes from the Facebook photos of the reunion. Her dark hair was slicked back from her flushed face and Kate assumed that she had just got out of the shower. She was wearing a long-sleeved white blouse which accentuated her deeply tanned skin.

'That's great, thanks,' she said, noticing that her own image was smiling. Kate hated this kind of communication. She could never remember to look at the webcam when she spoke, and neither could most people she spoke to. They usually seemed to be staring at each other's chins or looking off to one side as though disinterested.

'So, what can I help you with? I understand that you've spoken to Neil and Lee.'

She *had* been in touch with the other two. Hardly surprising but a little bit annoying that Kate wouldn't have the element of surprise.

'Before we carry on, would you mind if we record this call?'

Vicky frowned. 'For what purpose?'

'I'd like to be able to share it with the rest of my team at a later date.'

The other woman shook her head. 'I don't think I can agree to that. As far as I'm concerned, my speaking to you is a courtesy. If our conversation were to be recorded, then it would put the whole interview on a more formal footing, and I'd be entitled to have legal representation present. Which I don't. I suggest you make notes.'

The smile was still there but there was something steely around Vicky Rhodes's eyes. This might have been couched as a 'chat', but her legal training was ensuring that she wasn't going to be tricked or caught unawares.

'I completely understand,' Kate said, reaching for her notebook and a pen. 'Let's start with a few basics. Can you confirm your name and current address?'

Rhodes did, giving her middle name as Elizabeth and her address as a flat in Santa Cruz, Tenerife's principal city. She'd lived there for the past seven years and worked for a law firm that helped expats to buy property across the Canary Islands.

'I'd have thought, with your contacts, you'd be able to get a good deal on a nice little villa somewhere,' Kate said.

'I like the city,' Vicky responded. 'There's a good selection of bars and restaurants close by and it's a two-minute walk to my office. And it's not very touristy.'

'Sounds ideal,' Kate said, aware that she was making small talk. 'And is that where you are now?'

The image on the screen swayed and Vicky Rhodes disappeared completely. After a dizzying half second Kate's computer display was filled with a view from high up looking across a busy port to a sea that was turning deep blue in the evening light.

'Santa Cruz de Tenerife,' Vicky's voice informed her. 'The view from my balcony. If you look closely enough, I'm sure you can make out that some of the signage around the port is in Spanish.' There was a hint of sarcasm in her tone that made Kate uncomfortable. Was this staged, prepared?

She scribbled a note and passed it across to Cooper asking her to check flights in and out of Tenerife from all airports in the north of England. Could Vicky have been in Thorpe in the early hours of Saturday morning and managed to get back to her home in time for work on Monday?

The scene shifted again and Vicky Rhodes was back in shot.

'Thanks for the tour,' Kate said. 'Just what I need to see at the back end of November while I'm stuck in Doncaster.'

Vicky smiled. 'I know somebody who can help you buy a nice apartment out here. If you get in soon, before Brexit that is.'

'I'll keep it in mind. You said you'd talked to Mr Bradley and Mr Grieveson? What was that about?'

If Kate had managed to wrong-foot her, Rhodes certainly didn't show it.

'I spoke to Lee. He said that the police wanted to know about his involvement with David Whitaker. Neil had been in touch and had been less than tight-lipped.'

'You knew about the entrapment?'

'I've heard two versions of events from two different people. If you want to give me yours I'm willing to listen, but none of this has anything to do with me.'

'So, you don't know David Whitaker, or David Wallace as he now calls himself?'

'I *knew* him. When I was eleven years old. He was my teacher. I don't know him now and I don't want to.'

'Why's that?'

For a second, Kate thought the screen had frozen. Vicky Rhodes's expressionless face gazed out at her, eyes fixed firmly on her own. And then she smiled faintly. 'DI Fletcher, I know what Neil Grieveson told you. And I know what effect it's had on his life. We hadn't spoken for thirty years so when we met up in January I was expecting him to have changed, everybody does, but I was shocked. He was a happy kid with a wicked sense of humour. He was witty, clever and had a real talent for art. Now he sells crap that nobody really wants on the internet and rarely goes out of his flat. That's what Whitaker did to him.'

'And what did Whitaker do to you?'

The screen went black.

'What's going on?' Cooper asked as Kate tapped randomly on her keyboard.

'Lost the connection. Shit.'

Cooper got up and leaned over Kate's shoulder, peering at the blank screen.

'You've not lost the connection. She's muted the conversation from her end. But she's not disconnected. Maybe give her a few minutes.'

Cooper slid a piece of paper onto Kate's desk, obviously unwilling to discuss the contents in case Vicky Rhodes could still hear them.

Sunday 12.05 from Newcastle. Arrived Tenerife South 16.25.

Kate scanned it and nodded. Rhodes could have easily been in South Yorkshire on Saturday night and Sunday morning and managed to get back.

Kate scribbled a note instructing Sam to contact Border Force to see if Rhodes's passport had been used. Even if it hadn't it was entirely possible that she had a fake. She was just about to pass the note over the desk when the screen flickered back into life.

'Sorry about that,' Rhodes was smiling but she looked shaken. 'I just needed one of these if I'm going to tell that story.' She raised a glass of clear liquid, ice cubes rattling metallically as she shook it gently. 'Gin and tonic. I considered a beer, but the stronger stuff is best for this kind of conversation. Shame you can't join me.'

Kate silently agreed. A stiff drink would go down well after the day she'd had.

'So, what do you want to know?' Rhodes took a big gulp of her drink.

'July 1988. You went on a school trip to Derbyshire with your classmates and, specifically, your two friends. You called your-selves The Three Amigos after the film of the same name. At some point during the trip at least one of your friends was sexually abused by Whitaker. I think you were too.'

Rhodes nodded.

'You were?'

Another nod.

Kate lowered her voice. 'What happened to you, Vicky?'

'I'm not going to give you the details. You must have an idea of what grown men do to children to satisfy their perversions.' She spat the last word and took another sip of her gin and tonic.

'Okay. What happened afterwards? Did you tell anybody?'

'Of course not. Who was I going to tell? I was eleven. And, besides, they threatened us. Told us that they knew where we lived and that they'd come and get us if we told anybody. We were kids. We believed it.'

'They? Who was with Whitaker?'

Another large gulp of G and T.

'There were three of them. One we called the sergeant major because he was huge and strict. The other one worked for the outdoor centre. I don't remember his name. I'm not even sure if I knew it at the time.'

It tied in with what Neil Grieveson had told Kate and Hollis. He'd said that Whitaker had assaulted him in his tent under the pretext of helping him to change out of his wet clothes. Grieveson explained that his two friends had gone out for a night walk, but he hadn't wanted to after his encounter with his teacher. He'd known something was wrong when Lee got back but they didn't speak about it, instead falling out with each other over something trivial. They hadn't spoken about it until the reunion.

'I'm sorry,' Kate said. Even if Vicky Rhodes was connected to the murders, she'd obviously suffered horribly at the hands of somebody she was supposed to be able to trust and Kate felt uncomfortable asking her to relive the trauma. 'Can you tell me what happened at the reunion? Why did you decide it was time to talk about what had happened?'

Vicky stared down for a few seconds. 'It was when I saw Neil. Me and Lee, we're doing all right for ourselves. Lee's married and I'm happily single but Neil... Neil's really fucked up. I thought opening up about what had happened to us might help but all he could talk about was revenge. He wanted to get back at Whitaker and it sounds like he did.'

'He says it was your idea.'

'It was. Kind of. At least, I mentioned the group that Neil and Lee copied.'

'But you were safely out here. Beyond suspicion.'

Vicky smiled. 'You must have done a background check on me. You know I'm a lawyer. It would be professional suicide to be involved in something like that.'

Kate's sympathy dissipated. The woman from a minute ago had turned into a self-absorbed, self-serving coward. She was the puppet mistress, pulling the strings of her friends while she sat in the sun out of harm's way. It was uncharitable, Kate knew, to think of Vicky Rhodes like that but Kate had met Neil Grieveson and seen how easy he'd be to manipulate. He had barely any personality and no self-esteem.

'I need to ask you where you were on Saturday. And on a number of other dates this year.'

Rhodes took another swig of her drink. 'I was here on Saturday. At my flat. I'd had a busy week so I caught up on some Netflix.'

'What about Sunday morning?'

'I went for a swim. Then I had an early lunch in one of the local cafés.'

'Alone?'

Vicky nodded.

No alibi then. Kate gave the date of Margaret Whitaker's

removal from the nursing home and the probable weekend of Chris Gilruth's murder, but Rhodes had no specific memory of either date.

'What about Angela Fox? Do you remember her?'

'Of course I remember her.'

'Was she another of Whitaker's victims?'

'Not that I'm aware of. Even if she was, I doubt she'd talk to me about it.'

'Why's that?'

'We weren't friends. Not at school and not afterwards.'

There was something strained and unnatural about Vicky's voice. She sounded like she was telling a story that she knew well to an unfamiliar audience.

'I heard that you threatened to kill her.'

Vicky smiled slowly. 'When was this?'

She knew that Kate had nothing to back up her accusation.

'When you were eleven,' Kate admitted. 'At the end of the camping trip. You said that if you ever got your hands on her you'd kill her.'

The smile got wider. 'And you never threatened anybody when you were a child? Somebody pinched your usual seat on the school bus? Somebody stole a boyfriend? It was what we said. How many times did you tell your friends that your mum or dad would kill you if you were home late?'

She was right. Kate could list at least three different occasions when she'd threatened to kill her sister and meant every word. Once for eating Kate's half of a KitKat.

'When did you last see Angela? Was she at the reunion?'

Vicky answered without hesitation. 'Not that I recall. If she was, I didn't see her or speak to her. Have you asked her?'

'Not yet,' Kate said. She didn't want Vicky to know that they couldn't find Angela or that there was some concern for her well-being. If Angela was in danger for her role in what had happened to Vicky and her friends, then Kate certainly didn't want to alert one of their main suspects.

After asking Vicky to check her diary for the dates she'd given, Kate ended the call.

'What did you make of her?' Kate asked Cooper, who'd been listening to the conversation.

Cooper thought for a few seconds. 'I don't doubt that she went through something horrendous when she was a child, but I certainly didn't warm to the adult. The way she planted a seed in the minds of her friends and then stood back to see what would happen... that's cold. And her lack of alibi. If she'd wanted to prove her innocence she'd have been falling over herself to suggest people who might have seen her but she didn't care. Either she's confident that we can't find out where she was on Saturday or she was watching Netflix at home and has absolutely nothing to hide.'

'Great,' Kate said. 'Now what?'

Cooper grimaced and turned a shade paler. 'Now, I'm going to go through Simon Charlton's digital record and I think you should go home. Can you pass me a bucket on your way out? I think I might need it.'

28

The gap in the fence around the old quarry site didn't look recent. Kate didn't believe that it had been caused by whoever had driven the car that was now a burnt-out wreck onto the muddy grassland. It was a place she knew well. When she'd been growing up in Thorpe, Kate and her friends had played in the quarry, dodging the lorries that brought their loads of waste from the steelworks of Sheffield to dump there. In its heyday it had been one of the largest clay quarries in Europe but as the material ran out, the brickworks closed down and the buildings were demolished, along with the huge chimney that must have dominated the Thorpe skyline for decades before Kate was born. Then the rush had begun to fill in the site, made all the more urgent when a girl had died, drowned during a summer downpour, in one of the air shafts that had served the main furnace.

The car was sitting on an island of scorched grass, its front wheels lodged in a muddy furrow. It was easy to imagine the scene – exuberant joy riders spotting the gap in the fence, racing through and then becoming stuck in a deep rut. Abandoning the car would have been second nature – torching it may have been a bonus.

'Who found it?' Kate asked Hollis who'd been on the scene since first light.

The DC pointed to a young woman standing next to the fence drinking something from a paper cup. She had a blanket draped around her shoulders and, even from this distance, Kate could see that her face was unnaturally pale. It seemed a bit of an overreaction to finding a burnt-out car.

'What's up with her?' Kate asked. 'It's just a car.'

'It's not the car, it's what's inside it,' Hollis said cryptically. 'Come and have a look.'

They both donned paper protective suits and bootees before approaching the car via the step plates that had been set in place by the scene of crime officers who were now bustling around the burnt-out wreck.

'In there,' Hollis said, pointing to one of the rear windows.

Kate bent and peered through the gap left when the glass had exploded due to the heat of the fire and took in a sharp breath. She'd seen the CCTV footage of the woman who'd bundled Simon Charlton into the car but, even knowing that what she could see wasn't real, she felt a jolt of disbelief. A child seat was still in place and a shapeless form slumped forwards as though trying to break free from the restraining straps. Even though it was blackened and partially melted, Kate could see how easily the doll might have been mistaken for a dead infant.

'Christ, that'd give anybody a shock,' she said. 'SOCOs found anything yet?'

'Not a thing. Index plate matches the one bought from JB Motors by Stephanie Martin. It's the right make and model. Keys were still in, but the fire will have destroyed all the trace evidence.'

'She knew exactly what she was doing,' Kate said. 'She'll

have left it somewhere obvious to tempt teenage joyriders and they've done her cleaning up. Now we've got a location for the car, see if we can get CCTV or ANPR camera footage from the area. I doubt she dumped the car at the school, but we might be able to trace it from here backwards. Although most of the usual joy riders probably know where the cameras are these days and won't have risked being spotted.'

Hollis made a note in his daybook and took out his phone.

'I'll get Sam onto it straight away.'

'No,' Kate put up a hand to stop him from dialling. 'Ask Barratt. Sam might be feeling a bit rough this morning. She started looking at the contents of Charlton's laptop last night – leave her alone for a bit.'

Hollis grimaced and scrolled though his contacts. 'Can't say I envy her that,' he said as he turned his back and spoke quietly to Barratt.

Cooper was much more up-beat than Kate had expected. She'd already finished looking through Charlton's hard drive and obviously had something that she wanted to share as she beckoned for Kate to pull up a seat next to her.

'You okay?' Kate asked, a little puzzled by her exuberant mood.

'Fine. I've been through most of Charlton's dodgy stuff. It's not nice but I've seen worse. Apparently, there's more on a flash drive that the SOCOs found under one of the stair risers. Can't believe anybody would use that as a hiding place – I've seen it on at least three cop shows this year. I don't think I'll be able to get hold of it, but I can't say I'm bothered.'

'What else have you got? You wouldn't be this hyper if you'd spent the morning looking at kiddie porn – I know you, Sam, you'd be ready for a large drink.'

'I'm always ready for a large drink these days,' Cooper joked. 'But, to answer your question, my contact managed to get me access to Charlton's e-mails. Have a look at this.'

She tapped a few keys and an e-mail inbox appeared on her screen. 'Look at the second one down.'

Kate followed Sam's instruction and saw an e-mail from *Amigos31988*. There were two more further down the list.

'I take it you've had a look at these?'

'Better. I've printed them out. They're in the order that Charlton received them.'

She handed Kate three sheets of paper and sat back in her chair, waiting expectantly as Kate scanned through the information.

One was a series of images which were familiar to Kate. They were the same photographs she'd seen on Facebook – the camping trip from 1988, pairs of children outside identical orange tents. The second e-mail contained five words: *I know what you did*. The final one explained how the sender had been left a 'broken man' after the abuse that he'd suffered at the hands of Charlton and 'another' and a demand that they meet up to allow the sender 'closure'. The final e-mail also hinted at consequences if Charlton didn't turn up at the stated time and place.

'That's where he was kidnapped,' Kate said, noting the location of the car park where the CCTV footage had shown Charlton being bundled into the car that Kate had seen earlier. 'He was lured there. And whoever did it knew all about his past.'

'That's what it looks like,' Cooper agreed. 'It must be somebody who was there in 1988 or somebody who knows what happened.'

Which narrowed down their search considerably. There

were around two dozen students, two teachers and some staff from the outdoor centre involved in the trip. Kate started making notes and organising her priorities. She needed to put names to all the children in the photographs and she needed to find out about the staff from the outdoor centre as a matter of urgency. She knew that David Whitaker and Liz Dalston had been the teachers in attendance and, while she knew exactly where to find Whitaker, she might need some help in tracking down Mrs Dalston.

'Where are Barratt and O'Connor?' Kate asked Sam.

'Matt's finishing up the search of Charlton's house and I think Steve's here somewhere. I saw him at his desk a little while ago.'

'Right. I'm going to get everybody together. We need to start getting organised. These e-mails change everything. Our killer has to be somebody who was on that trip – nothing else makes sense. My money's still on one of our three amigos but they're bloody clever.'

'*Strangers on a Train*?'

'What?'

'That film,' Sam explained. 'Two people meet up and agree to kill each other's partners so they'll each have an alibi for the time of the crime.'

'You think we've got three different killers? I'm not convinced. And wasn't the premise of the film that the two murderers had no connection with each other? That was the beauty of their plan.'

'Well, it was just a thought,' Cooper said. 'I've not seen anything to convince me that this is the work of a single killer despite the connection between the victims.'

Nor had Kate. That was part of the problem.

29

Kate was impressed by the speed with which her team responded to her summons. Within an hour they were assembled in the briefing room – a sense of urgency starting to build. She'd found O'Connor in the staff canteen when she'd gone up for coffee and had been prepared to jokingly admonish him for slacking – she knew he'd have been working on something – when he'd turned so that she could see that he was on the phone and raised a finger to ask her to wait. He hadn't looked especially animated, so she'd got her drink and left him to it.

'Dan, anything from the burnt-out car?'

Hollis shook his head. 'Not so far. There was a lot of damage, but the boot space was mostly intact. It was probably closed when they set the car alight. One of the SOCOs was fairly hopeful about recovering some trace from the carpet.'

Kate nodded. It was a bit of a long shot. Any trace evidence from the boot would probably link to Simon Charlton but the killer might have been careless. They had to hope.

'Matt? Charlton's house? Any link to Whitaker or to our three main suspects?'

'Nothing,' Barratt said. 'It looks like he was careful after he'd been caught out once before. The laptop and USB stick are our best hope but, from what I can gather, it was all pretty standard stuff.'

'Right,' Kate said, raising the remote control to turn on the projector. 'That leads us nicely into this morning's latest discovery. Sam's managed to get into Charlton's e-mail, and she found these.'

Kate scrolled through the three messages, showing the order that they'd been received. 'We can see from the address that we have a link to our three main suspects and the images in the second e-mail are the same ones that Sam found on Facebook. Everything seems to take us back to that camping trip in 1988.'

'So, we're still looking at Grieveson, Bradley and Rhodes?' Barratt asked.

'Among others,' Kate said. 'There were over twenty kids on that trip and one other teacher. There were also at least two members of the outdoor centre staff. I think Charlton was there and there was the large man in the group picture.' Kate displayed the image on the screen. 'We know from June Tuffrey that the other teacher, Liz Dalston, wasn't there for the last night of the trip as she'd injured her ankle earlier in the day. We also know that Grieveson, Bradley and Rhodes were abused, probably that day. But, were they the only ones? Did anybody else know what was going on or did anybody else suffer at the hands of Whitaker and Charlton?'

Silence as the others assessed the implications of what Kate was saying.

'We need to track down and interview everybody who was on that trip.'

'Including Whitaker?' Hollis asked.

'Including Whitaker. But we leave him for now. I want as much information as possible before we confront him with what we know. I got the impression from his sister-in-law that he's clever and manipulative.'

The others nodded their agreement. There was no use allowing Whitaker to wriggle out of his responsibility for recent events.

'Right. I've been having a think about priorities and I think we need to start chasing up people who were on that trip and at the reunion. June Tuffrey seems to be our best contact so, Matt, can you get on to that? And Sam, work on it from Facebook.'

The two DCs nodded.

'We also need to find Liz Dalston – I think she might still be alive despite having taught me back in the Stone Age.' Polite sniggers all round.

'I've found her,' Sam said. 'Had a look while you were getting coffee. She lives in Warmsworth.'

Kate laughed. 'I don't believe it. She's still on the main road next to the traffic lights?'

Sam started to say something, but Kate cut her off. 'She used to tell us that she could see the lights changing behind her bedroom curtains. When I was little, I thought it must be a really exotic place to live. I always used to look for her when we went past on the bus on the way to Doncaster.'

Kate looked up to see each member of her team staring at her. As one, they looked away as though embarrassed. It wasn't like Kate to talk about herself or her past even, though they all knew that she'd grown up in Thorpe and knew the area better than any of them.

'Anyway,' she continued after a deep breath. 'Good work, Sam. Hollis – with me to interview Mrs Dalston. We also need to find Angela Fox. At the moment I'm working on the premise that she's a potential victim. I don't know what happened between her and Vicky Rhodes, but something went badly wrong there and I'm not at all convinced by Rhodes's explanation that it was just a childish expression. We need to track her down and make sure she's not in danger.'

'Already on it,' O'Connor said. 'I've spent a good part of the morning ringing holiday companies that let cottages on Mull. So far, I've drawn a blank, but I'll keep on it. Trouble is, if she's rented from a friend or from somebody who lets out their cottage on an informal basis then I might not find her.'

'If she's there,' Hollis added ominously.

He was right to be concerned. Kate was deeply troubled by their inability to track down Angela Fox. If the woman had set off for Mull, it would have been easy for the killer to intercept her or to meet her on the island and attack her. She might not have even left the area – the killer could have met her at home.

'Okay. Steve – keep ringing round. Sam's got details of Fox's car – I doubt there's much in the way of ANPR coverage up there, but it might help to identify her. And check her house in Tickhill. If she doesn't turn up, we might have to get a warrant to search the premises. I'll give you the contact details for the colleague we spoke to at the DRI, he might have heard from her or he might be able to give a specific date for when she left or when she's due back. He was a bit vague when we spoke to him, but you might be able to jog his memory.'

Kate smiled to herself at the thought of O'Connor grilling Dylan. The DS was an intimidating figure at the best of times with his stocky build that never seemed to be fully contained within his clothes and his dark red, biker-style facial hair. Couple that with his warrant card and she was willing to bet that Angela's colleague would quickly buckle if he knew anything.

30

Liz Dalston's bungalow was exactly where Kate remembered. A 1950s prefabricated building, it sat at the crossroads of the main Thorpe to Doncaster Road and two more minor routes to outlying villages. The traffic lights were still there, although the bungalow's garden was screened by tall hedges of dark green leylandii – possibly as a defence against traffic noise and the ever-changing red, amber and green.

Kate opened the small gate in the hedge and led the way to the front door, trying to control the flood of memories that bombarded her as she thought about seeing her former teacher for the first time in over thirty years. Mrs Dalston had been Kate's teacher the year her mother died, and she'd been kind and thoughtful, especially when Kate's friends were less than considerate. Kate knew that the woman would be in her seventies now – when they'd spoken on the phone, she'd heard the tremor in the older woman's voice but it was still familiar and strangely reassuring. She'd given her rank and name but hadn't disclosed her former identity, unwilling to prejudice the interview or distract either of them from the details of the school trip.

As soon as the door opened though, Kate saw that her subterfuge had been pointless.

'Cathy Siddons! What a surprise after all these years.'

The woman holding the door open bore little resemblance to the teacher that Kate remembered, apart from the intelligent blue eyes which now nestled within a web of wrinkles. The auburn hair that Mrs Dalston had worn in a long ponytail was now short and wispy, turning the woman's head into a dandelion clock of grey and white.

'You can't possibly recognise me,' Kate said.

'I'd like to pretend that my memory's that good,' Mrs Dalston said with a broad grin. 'The truth is I've seen you in the papers. That child killer case a couple of years ago? They mentioned that you'd grown up in the area and what your maiden name was. And then that supposed mercy killing in Thorpe. You're making quite a name for yourself.'

As Kate was struggling for an appropriate response, Mrs Dalston ushered them into a small living room at the front of the house, leaning heavily on a walking stick as she hobbled down the hallway. It was gloomy despite the hour – obviously the shade from the large hedge – but at least the traffic lights were out of sight. Sparsely furnished with a fifties-style three-piece suite which could have been original or might have been an IKEA copy and a dark wood coffee table, there was little in the room that reflected the personality of the woman who lived in the house. There were no photographs, very few ornaments apart from a wooden Buddha on the windowsill, and no television. The wall opposite the window was shelved and each shelf was stuffed with books which had obviously been crammed into any and every available space. The only concession to life in the twenty-first century was a digital radio placed on a small side table within easy reach of one of the armchairs.

After refusing hot drinks, Kate and Hollis settled themselves on the sofa while Mrs Dalston eased herself into one of the armchairs. She studied Kate with a faint smile which deepened her wrinkles. 'I do remember you, you know. I'd only been teaching for a couple of years when you were in my class. I'm not surprised you've made something of yourself. Really bright, this one.' The last comment was directed at Hollis who smiled, clearly uncomfortable with this insight into his boss's past.

'But I'm sure you're not here to talk about all that. What can I do for you both?'

Kate allowed Hollis to outline the reason for the visit and their interest in the camping trip while she studied her former teacher – lost in memories. She remembered returning to school after her mother's funeral and all her friends having difficulty talking to her. It was Mrs Dalston who had explained that it didn't mean that they weren't bothered – they just didn't know what to say or how to help. Now, as an adult, Kate dealt with grief on a regular basis and she suddenly realised that her teacher had probably been basing her insight on her own experience. She looked around the room again and wondered what had happened to Mr Dalston. Was the loss of a husband the event that allowed the woman in front of her to make such a difference to Kate's life?

'So, you remember the trip well?' Hollis was asking.

'Hard to forget,' Mrs Dalston said, patting the walking stick that she'd propped against the arm of her chair. 'Haven't been able to walk properly since. Though, to be honest, it wasn't so bad until I hit my sixties. It's all downhill after that.'

'What happened?' Kate asked.

Mrs Dalston smiled and glanced down at her foot. 'I broke my ankle. Stupid really but we all do daft things when we're young. On the last day of the trip we all went abseiling off Millers Dale Bridge. I was a bit nervous. I've never been especially fond of heights. I was one of the last to go. One of the instructors was showing my colleague how to guide the rope so that it didn't allow the person on the end to drop too quickly but he hadn't quite got the hang of it and he lost me about eight feet from the ground. I was lucky it was just my ankle really – could have been a lot worse.'

'So, it was an accident?'

'Of course. It's not like he let me go on purpose.'

'Who was holding the rope?' Kate asked, even though she thought she knew the answer.

'David Whitaker. It was his trip really. He organised it every year and it was the first time I'd been.' Kate noticed a subtle shift in her tone and a slight hardening around her mouth. She might not believe Whitaker had intentionally harmed her, but Mrs Dalston didn't like the man.

'And it was a popular trip? With the children.'

Mrs Dalston nodded. 'Oh, they loved it. It was the highlight of their last year at Sheffield Road. Some of them started planning what they'd do when they were still in the year below. A lot of children went on to Thorpe Comp but there were quite a few who went to other schools, so it was good for them to be able to say a last goodbye to their friends.'

Kate watched as Hollis made notes. The next few questions were crucial, and she needed to ask them in the correct order to avoid leading Mrs Dalston in any way.

'Do you remember a group of kids who called themselves The Three Amigos?'

Another smile – much broader this time. 'Of course. They were all in my class when they were in third year, or year five as it became. Named themselves after some daft film. I suggested The Three Musketeers might be more appropriate, but they didn't know what I was talking about.'

'Do you remember their names?'

'I might if you gave me a couple of hours. They named themselves after the main characters and I think each name might have connected to their real names in some way. Their initials possibly.'

'Lee Bradley, Vicky Rhodes and Neil Grieveson,' Hollis said.

'That sounds about right. Vicky Rhodes. Another exceptionally bright girl.' Mrs Dalston smiled at Kate and she heard Hollis, next to her, snigger softly.

'They were on the camping trip when you got injured,' Hollis continued.

'Were they? I must admit, after a while the years blur together. I'll have to take your word for that.'

So far, the interview had added very little to what they already knew apart from Kate's sense that her former teacher hadn't liked David Whitaker. They needed to try to pin down details. Kate slipped her mobile phone out of her pocket and flicked to the photographs of the camping trip.

'We're trying to put names to the people in these photographs and to establish who else was on the trip – especially adults. We've got a few student names; the three we've given plus Angela Fox and June Tuffrey. We'd really like to know about the outdoor centre staff. This man in particular.'

Kate scrolled to the photograph of the final day and pointed to the burly man on the back row.

'The sergeant major,' Mrs Dalston said softly. 'That's what the kids called him. He was a bit brusque.'

'Real name?'

The former teacher closed her eyes in concentration. 'Paul something? Or maybe that was his surname, Paulson, Pawson? I'm sorry, I can't remember.'

'What about this man? Was he there?' She showed Mrs Dalston a scan of a photograph that had been found in Charlton's house. A much younger Charlton in army fatigues, smiling for the camera. Sam thought it would have been taken when he was around twenty – in 1988.

'That's Simon,' Mrs Dalston said without hesitation. 'He took me to the hospital when I hurt my ankle. A lovely young man. He was very kind. Didn't want to leave me there overnight but there was nothing he could do for me other than wait and that seemed a bit pointless. He reminded me a lot of my husband, Barry, when he was younger.'

A shadow crossed the woman's face and Kate suddenly understood the full reason for her teacher's empathy all those years ago. Her husband had died, leaving her a young widow.

'I don't suppose you remember his last name?'

'I think I'm doing quite well remembering any of this, but no, sorry.'

It didn't matter. They'd got a positive identification for Simon Charlton. He *had* been on that trip. One more piece fell into place. Kate took a breath. The questions were about to get a bit more difficult and she was worried that she might cause offence if she suggested that Mrs Dalston knew anything about Whitaker's character.

'David Whitaker,' Kate said. 'You worked with him for a few years?'

'Six or seven.'

'Did you know him very well?'

'Not really.' The brief responses were defensive. This woman knew something.

'Did you leave the school first or did he?'

'He did.'

'Do you know where he went. Did he move to another school?'

'I don't remember. I'm sorry.'

'But you heard the rumours?'

The woman seemed to sag in her seat as though all the air

had been sucked from her lungs and she reached out for her walking stick as though she needed the reassurance of something steady. 'I heard *some* rumours,' she said, her tone defeated rather than defensive. 'There was never any evidence but, in a case like that, there's usually no smoke without fire.'

'I'm sorry to have to ask this, Mrs Dalston, but is it possible that David Whitaker may have harmed some of the children on the camping trip?'

The woman looked frightened, cornered as though she was being accused of neglecting her duty. 'I told you, I was in hospital for the last night. I didn't see or suspect anything up to that point. It was after the trip that the rumours started. As I said, there was nothing concrete but that was the last Derbyshire trip. The head said it was due to budget cuts but a few of us wondered if he thought Whitaker couldn't be trusted.'

She looked at Kate, obviously expecting more questions and then her eyes widened. 'Do you think he deliberately let me fall? To get rid of me? Do you *know* that something happened on that trip?'

Kate sighed and nodded. 'It seems likely. We know of three people who claim to have been abused by Whitaker in Derbyshire in 1988. We think that there may be a link between that abuse and a recent series of crimes.'

'What sort of crimes?'

Kate shook her head.

'Of course, you can't say. Look, there were never any complaints made but the whispers were obviously strong enough to drive Whitaker away. I only hope that he didn't carry on working with children. Oh, were those other two men involved? Not Simon, surely?'

'We really can't say, but your confirmation that Simon was there is a very significant piece of evidence.'

Mrs Dalston hung her head, one of her hands gripping the

arm of the chair so tightly that her knuckles turned white. Her breathing was fast and shallow, and Kate could see her shoulders trembling.

'Are you all right?' she asked, leaning forward and putting a hand on the older woman's knee.

'Not really. It's the worst thing, for a teacher. We're supposed to protect children. If I'd been there it might not have happened.'

'It's not your fault,' Hollis said, his voice low and shaky. 'You were hurt. There's nothing you could have done. And you didn't know about it until today.'

The woman looked up at him, her eyes bright with tears. 'I know, but it still feels like it's my responsibility.'

'That's the teacher in you,' Kate said. 'Never off duty. You were such a help to me when my mum died and I'm sure that you helped lots of other lost and broken kids. This isn't your fault. It's David Whitaker's fault and, one way or another, he'll be made to pay.'

Even as Kate said the words, she realised that she wasn't sure whether she meant that Whitaker would face justice from the courts or from whoever was killing the people around him. The awful thing was, watching this decent woman try to shoulder a burden that wasn't hers to carry, Kate didn't think she cared either way, as long as Whitaker paid for his actions.

* * *

They'll have found Simon Charlton by now. Probably worked out who he is as well – it's not like I was careful about hiding his identity. I wonder if they're starting to put it all together. I know I could spot the link from outer space but that's because I'm involved, in the know. What must it look like to an outsider?

He'll be out soon. There's a big part of me that can't wait and another part that doesn't want this to be over. It's been fun. Does that sound awful? Not the killing per se – cutting up that old woman was just about the worst thing I've ever had to do – but the planning, the disguises, the endless need to be one step ahead. It's been exhilarating.

Do you want to know the best part? I've done it all without guilt. That horrible feeling that's been hanging over me for years has finally gone. That tells me that I'm doing the right thing – or at least the wrong thing for the right reasons.

And now there's only him left. I wish I had more time, but I know it has to be done soon. Nearly everything's in place. Even if the police haven't pieced everything together, he definitely will have and he'll know why I've chosen that place. They'll all know why I've chosen that place. But only once it's too late.

31

HMP Wakefield always reminded Kate of the Doncaster Royal Infirmary. They both had the same grey, utilitarian façade, both seemed like they were brooding, keeping secrets. At least, Kate knew, there was some hope in the DRI, but the prison always made her feel lost and depressed. She believed in rehabilitation, of course, she'd seen many examples, but the reality of day-to-day prison life was so grim and dreary that she wasn't sure how any sort of redemption ever came about.

She peered through the drizzle, looking for a parking space in the visitors' section.

'Twenty-four more sleeps,' Hollis said, apropos of nothing.

'What?' Kate snapped. She thought she'd found a spot but, as she'd got closer, it had turned out to be occupied by one of those smug Smart cars.

'It's the first of December. Twenty-four more sleeps till Christmas.'

'Yay.'

'Not a fan?' Hollis asked, clearly reading the sarcasm in her voice.

'Not really. And not this year.'

'Problems?'

Kate didn't respond. She saw reversing lights ahead and manoeuvred herself into position behind a driver who was leaving.

'I'd have thought you'd have been looking forward to seeing Ben.'

Kate had no idea what Hollis imagined her Christmases were like, but he obviously thought that it was a time for family. He didn't know that she hadn't seen her son for months. Nobody had – except his colleagues and his girlfriend, Emma.

'Ben's in China.'

Hollis turned to look at her as she eased into the recently vacated parking space. 'Seriously?'

'Seriously. It's part of his master's research. He and Emma are studying the impact of deforestation on something or other.'

'Oh.' Hollis looked nonplussed. 'Well, I'm sure you and Nick will manage to eat drink and be merry.'

Kate considered telling him that she and Nick weren't on the best of terms, but she didn't want to have to fend off a barrage of questions that she didn't know the answers to. They'd texted each other a few more times after Nick's initial contact and Nick had rung, but she'd been working and missed his call. The argument was starting to feel like an overreaction and Kate really didn't want the embarrassment of having to explain it to Hollis. Especially as she thought it might make her look like the villain.

'Probably,' she mumbled, shrugging off her seat belt and opening the car door. Being outside in the rain was better than having to spend any more time exploring her feelings about her relationship with Nick.

The visitation order had come through the previous day and Kate had been tempted to put the names of each member of her team into a hat and draw one out. Nobody enjoyed interviewing prisoners and she knew that a visit to a known paedophile was probably at the bottom of anybody's list of fun ways to spend the day. In the end, she'd had no choice but to bring Hollis. Sam was still working on identifying people who'd been on the Derbyshire trip, with help from June Tuffrey, while O'Connor and Barratt were still trying to track down Angela Fox. Nobody they'd spoken to on Mull knew her or knew of her whereabouts and O'Connor had asked one of the three local uniformed officers on the island to keep a look out for her and her car. He'd also re-interviewed Dylan, Angela's colleague, but he'd had nothing of importance to add.

Barratt had been to Tickhill but there was nobody at Angela's address and her neighbours were clueless. Das had applied for a warrant to search the premises on the basis that Angela's life may be in danger – she just hoped that they wouldn't find another body when they finally got into the house. A text buzzed into her mobile as they approached the prison entrance. Barratt. The warrant to gain access to Angela Fox's house had come through. Kate texted back for him to action it. They needed somebody in there as quickly as possible.

'Nice place,' Hollis observed as Kate pressed the buzzer next to the entrance to the prison's reception.

'If you like grey,' Kate said. Everything in her eyeline was monochrome. Grey brick walls, grey concrete, black tarmac made slickly reflective by the increasingly heavy rain.

'Do you think that's why they give the prisoners such bright uniforms?' Hollis joked. 'To make up for the lack of colour everywhere else.'

Wakefield's prison uniform was probably the most striking that Kate had seen. Green and yellow stripes on trousers and jackets ensured that prisoners stood out from the guards and the visitors. It wasn't a uniform that an escapee would get far in.

'I think it's so they don't have to dress up and make an effort for Christmas. They already look like bloody Christmas elves.'

Hollis smiled and seemed about to say something when the door clicked open and a tall male prison officer in a dark uniform ushered them inside.

The reception area was where the similarity to the DRI ended for Kate. At the hospital, visitors were funnelled through a bright atrium decorated with plants and helpful signage: here, a sour-faced woman sat behind a low wooden desk surrounded by plain, pale green walls and a single poster informing those who wanted to go any further what they were and were not allowed to take with them. 'Can I help you?' the woman asked without looking up from her keyboard.

Kate took out her ID and gestured for Hollis to do the same. 'We're from South Yorkshire Police,' she said. 'We've got a visitation order for today.'

The woman stared at her, green eyes giving nothing away, and then directed her gaze at Hollis. Her expression turned vaguely predatory as she took in Hollis's smartly cut blond hair and freshly shaved cheeks and chin. 'Who are you here to see?' she asked, eyes still on Hollis.

'David Wallace.'

She turned back to her keyboard and typed something so quickly that Kate got the impression that she might have been hitting keys at random.

'Wallace?'

'He's been here since June. Cat B prisoner.'

'Wallace,' the woman murmured as she wiggled the mouse and tapped another key. 'Got him.'

'And is there a visitor order on his file?'

'Nope.'

'No? But we were told yesterday. You should have had notification.'

The woman stared at Kate. 'There's no visitor order on his file for today.'

For a second Kate had the feeling that she was in a comedy sketch and that the woman was going to tell her *the computer says no.*

'There must be some sort of admin error,' Kate said, automatically reaching for her phone. Somebody somewhere must be able to sort this out.

'There's no error,' the woman said. 'You can't see Mr Wallace today. Not even if you've got written permission from the Home Office.'

'But that's ridiculous. What's the problem? Why can't we see him?'

The woman smiled slowly as though about to deliver a punchline to an especially clever joke. 'You can't see Mr Wallace because he's not here. He was released earlier today.'

32

O'Connor didn't like Tickhill. He didn't trust the place. There was something unsettling about a town that, on the surface, was so perfect. It wasn't just the duck pond nestled beneath the walls of the mysterious castle that only opened its gates to the public for one afternoon a year. It wasn't the sympathetic mix of old and new houses grouped around the lanes leading to the church. It was something to do with the feel of the place. O'Connor would have put good money on there being a thriving dogging scene or a popular swingers' club. It was just too *Stepford Wives* to be real.

Angela Fox's house only contributed to the feeling. Halfway up a narrow street in the shadow of the church it was the middle of a short row of identical terraced houses. Each had a black door, a slightly bowed downstairs window and a spotless brick façade. Even in the grey drizzle of a December morning, the houses looked attractive and bright.

A team of SOCOs waited in their van parked outside the pub while O'Connor and Barratt approached the house accompanied by a uniformed officer whose walk was slightly off balance due to the weight of the small battering ram that he carried.

'We knock front and back before we use the big red key,' Barratt said. 'And, if any of the neighbours appear, we deal with them first. This isn't a drugs raid so be sensitive.'

A single nod from the man in uniform.

O'Connor marched up to the front door and knocked loudly with his fist, ignoring the brass knocker that stood out against the black paint. They waited a few seconds and then he knocked again.

'Right, round the back.' Barratt led the way down an alley until they reached the back gate of the property. The walls bounding the back gardens were only around three feet high, so the small group was clearly visible to the occupants of all the properties in the row. O'Connor didn't care. He wasn't bothered about being discreet, but he allowed Barratt to take the lead and open the back gate slowly and carefully.

The back garden was tiny but perfectly maintained. A small square of lawn was bordered by knee-high shrubs and two rose bushes that had been pruned for the winter. Two more knocks established that there was nobody at home, so O'Connor leaned into the window, using his hand to cut the glare from the feeble winter sun that was threatening to make an appearance, and looked inside. No sign of life. He could make out a pine table and various appliances crammed into a small space. On the draining board, directly in front of him was a single mug and two plates. He had no way of knowing how long they'd been there.

'Nobody home,' he said to his companions. 'Looks like we're going to have to make a bit of noise.'

The uniformed officer slipped on his safety helmet and lowered the visor before taking a practised swing with the battering ram at the side of the door just above the handle. The wood splintered but held. One more thud and they were inside.

'Wait there,' O'Connor instructed the man. 'I'll shout if we need you.'

He stepped over the threshold and slipped on a pair of nitrile gloves, looking behind him to check that Barratt had done the same. He placed one gloved hand against the kitchen radiator. Stone cold. Not that it meant anything – Angela Fox may have been frugal with her living expenses and kept central heating use to a minimum. He turned to the sink and removed the cloth hanging over the taps. Bone dry – he could tell even through his gloves. If the occupant *had* gone on holiday it certainly wasn't in the last couple of days.

'Let's split up,' he said to Barratt. 'I'll take downstairs; you have a look in the bedrooms.' Barratt nodded and opened the door to the hallway.

The living room was tidy to the point of obsession. A cream sofa contrasted with the chocolate brown carpet and a light wood coffee table sat on a white rug in the middle of the room. The alcoves next to the fireplace contained bookshelves – their contents organised by size and not a single book out of place. There were a couple of framed prints on the walls – one of Tickhill Castle and the other of the duck pond – and a photograph of an elderly couple was perched on the windowsill.

In one corner of the room a small television shared a stand with a digital radio. O'Connor moved closer and noted the dust on the surfaces of both objects. The person who'd organised this room didn't seem the type to allow dust to gather.

O'Connor went back into the hallway and moved to the front door in two strides. A small pile of envelopes and brightly coloured flyers advertising takeaways and supermarket deals was scattered across the doormat. He crouched on his haunches and stirred the papers with one finger. Three white envelopes were addressed to Angela Fox – one was embossed with the AA logo – probably insurance, one was from HMRC and the third had the address of a charity on the rear. Nothing especially personal – nothing to offer any clues to Angela's whereabouts.

Straightening up, O'Connor glanced up at the gloomy staircase. There was nothing useful on the ground floor – the best use of his time was to help Barratt upstairs. He plodded up to the landing listening for the DC and identified his footsteps in the bedroom that faced onto the street.

'Caught you,' he said, pushing the door open.

'Nothing to catch,' Barratt said with a rueful smile. 'There's bugger-all here. The wardrobe looks like there might be a few gaps and two of the drawers in that chest look like they might have had stuff removed but it's hard to tell – everything's so bloody neat and tidy. I've looked on top of the wardrobe and under the bed and there's no sign of any luggage which suggests that she might have gone away. I checked the bathroom – no toothbrush or toothpaste and the soap's all dry and cracked.'

'What about the other room?'

'Study,' Barratt said. 'A couple of bookshelves, desk and chair, a printer.'

'No computer?'

'Nope. No charger either. If she uses a laptop, she's taken it with her.'

O'Connor stuck his head round the door of the smaller room just to be sure, but he had no reason to doubt Barratt's assessment. If there was one word he'd use to describe Matt Barratt it would be *thorough*.

'Now what?' he asked as Barratt joined him on the landing.

'Have you checked that cupboard?'

There was a door at the top of the stairs which looked older than the others, the panels a slightly different configuration and the paintwork wasn't as pristine. O'Connor wondered if it was original to the house and had proved difficult to replace. The doorknob was also different, a round Bakelite globe somewhere between the size of a golf ball and a tennis ball. A bolt was attached just below an ancient-looking keyhole with no key.

'If something jumps out, I don't want to hear you scream like a girl,' O'Connor teased, his hand on the bolt.

'Can't promise,' Barratt said.

It wasn't a cupboard. The door opened onto a second set of stairs, narrower and more cramped than the main staircase.

'Wasn't expecting that,' Barratt said. 'Attic room. I hadn't noticed a window in the roof.'

'Probably hard to see unless you're standing well back. After you.' O'Connor gestured for Barratt to go up first. Barratt looked dubious but did as he was told, bowing to the DS's seniority.

'What's up there?' O'Connor said, craning his neck until he could just make out the top of the short flight of stairs. 'Matt? What can you see?'

Barratt didn't respond and O'Connor could hear footsteps above his head as his colleague stepped further into the attic space. 'Matt? What's up there?'

Two seconds later Barratt's pale face appeared in the square of light at the top of the stairs.

'I think we need to call the boss. Now!'

33

David Wallace dumped the small parcel of belongings in the hallway of his dingy flat and went straight through to the kitchen. Six months. Six months since he'd been here, and everything was exactly the same. He opened the fridge. Same tins of luncheon meat and corned beef, same jar of olives, same tube of tomato puree. The place even smelt the same – faintly musty with a hint of lemon air freshener.

He opened the cupboard above the sink and removed a mug and a jar of instant coffee before filling and emptying the kettle then filling it again. No milk. He'd briefly considered asking the taxi driver to stop at Lidl so he could stock up on a few basics, but the man had made it clear by his silence that he wasn't the type to be sympathetic to somebody he'd picked up outside Wakefield Prison with only a brown paper parcel and a handful of ten pound notes.

Mug in hand Wallace made his way through to the sitting room, switching on the central heating from the switch in the hallway as he passed. He plonked himself in his favourite chair, the arms worn smooth where his hands rested and a dip in the back where his head settled automatically. He could see out of the window, through the greying net curtain, and spent a few minutes watching as a car slowed down in the small cul-de-sac where he lived and then turned and left. It was a quiet spot. Three blocks of flats, four flats per block – two up and two down. The greenery surrounding them was well kept by the housing association but responsibility for the interior of the flats was left to the residents and Wallace knew that he probably wasn't the cleanest or tidiest tenant.

He took a sip of his coffee. Too hot, so he placed it on the dust covered surface of the table next to his chair. The television remote nestled near his hand and he considered turning it on and losing himself in some awful quiz show, but he knew he wouldn't be able to relax. He was too angry.

Six months.

It had passed slowly. More so because he knew that it was unfair. Wallace had no illusions about what he was – he'd accepted his nature a long time ago. But he'd always been careful. He'd moved on from Thorpe when things had got a little too uncomfortable and he'd changed his name – forcing Margaret to do the same.

Margaret.

Poor cow. He'd asked if he could be let out for a morning to identify her body; to say his goodbyes. Laid it on a bit too thick possibly. The answer was no. They'd managed with dental records and the counsellor had seemed to take some sort of pleasure in confirming the identity. Wallace had felt nothing. She'd been in that home for her own good and he'd felt no guilt in putting her there. He hadn't bothered to visit because there was no point. She hadn't recognised him for over a year and that was unlikely to change.

He knew that her murder was a message. Just like his imprisonment. Somebody was out to get him. Somebody had set him up and cost him six months of his life. And, if they thought they could get away with it, they were wrong. He didn't know who it was, but he was going to find out and he'd make them pay. What had happened to him in prison was nothing compared to what he'd do to whoever had tricked him.

A tap at the door almost made him knock his drink over. He looked at his watch. An hour and a half had passed – he'd been lost in his thoughts for ninety minutes. How could that have happened?

He peered round the net curtains trying to add some detail to the figure that stood below him, looking up at his living room window. It was nearly dark outside, the short December day drawing to a close. His visitor looked like a woman, smallish and dark haired. Nobody he knew.

Wallace considered just waiting for her to go away but, if she was there in some sort of official capacity, it would be another black mark against him.

He stomped down the stairs and threw open the door. 'Yes?' he snapped.

'Mr Wallace?'

He nodded in confirmation.

The woman held up an ID card that was suspended from her neck on a bright blue lanyard. 'I'm from social services. Have you got a minute?'

'No.'

'Mr Wallace, I need to speak to you about your benefits and what happens now that you've been released. It's in your best interests to co-operate.'

'Fine,' Wallace grunted. 'Come in then.'

He followed her up the stairs. 'On the left,' he said, directing her into the kitchen. It was the least comfortable room in the flat. He didn't want to encourage her to stay any longer than necessary and, if he didn't offer a drink, she wasn't going to hang around.

She sat at the table and rummaged in her handbag while he stood near the window, watching the street lights flicker to life as night descended.

'I just need to find the correct forms for you to fill in and then we can make a start on processing any claim you might have,' the woman said. Wallace studied her. In her early- to mid-forties she was quite well built with short dark hair, shaved around her neck. Despite the chill she wore a dress, some sort of flowery pattern not at all suited to a December afternoon that was growing darker by the minute. Wallace had decided that she was probably a lesbian when, as she straightened up, he noticed the prominent bulge of a pregnancy. Still, that meant nothing these days.

'Right,' she said, breathless after her exertions. 'I think this is everything.' She straightened a pile of papers on the kitchen table and put a hand on her belly. 'Do you think I could have drink of water? Everything seems to be such an effort at the minute.'

Wallace sighed and reached up into a cupboard to get a glass. It felt a bit greasy, but he wasn't going to apologise – it wasn't like this woman was an invited guest.

'How long will this take?' he asked. 'Only I've–'

He didn't get a chance to finish his sentence. Pain seared up from the small of his back to the base of his skull and he collapsed in front of the sink. He vaguely registered the woman kicking the glass away from his hand and pulling something out from under her dress. It wasn't a baby, it was a small rucksack.

'What the–?'

She put a finger to her lips as though shushing a noisy child and then clamped a hand across his mouth. He considered biting her, he even thought he might have tried, but the hand was holding something. A cloth? The smell was awful and he started to gag but then he felt his muscles relax and, with one final breath, he felt himself slide into unconsciousness.

34

Google Maps said it would take fifty-five minutes from HMP Wakefield to Tickhill. Hollis made it in under forty. Kate wasn't sure whether Hollis was driving so fast to get them to their destination or to escape her rage. She was furious. Somebody must have known that Wallace was being released, but nobody had thought to let her know. Instead they'd had a wasted journey and were having to play catch-up again.

Kate had called Das to request that a car be sent to Bentley to check David Wallace's flat. The DCI hadn't been keen, suggesting that, as Kate hadn't known, there was no way that the murderer could have found out about the premature release. She'd defended the prison staff, citing policies that allowed for the early release of offenders who may be vulnerable to excessive press interest or vigilante attacks, but Kate hadn't been interested. It was done and now she had to try to limit the potential fallout. It had taken all her powers of persuasion but, eventually, Das conceded that there may be a danger to Wallace's life and that she'd be remiss in her duty if she didn't follow Kate's suggestion.

Kate's second phone call had been to Cooper to update her

regarding Barratt and O'Connor's discovery in the house in Tickhill. Sam had been busy chasing up former pupils of Sheffield Road School, but she'd not found anything useful. She'd also checked up on Vicky Rhodes's alibis for the murders and they seemed to be genuine, which hadn't been a huge surprise to Kate after their online conversation.

'Pull in here,' she instructed Hollis as he turned up a side street aiming for Tickhill church. 'Steve said the street's narrow and the forensics team have already parked their van outside the house.'

Hollis followed her instructions and they walked the 200 yards to where Angela Fox lived.

Kate flashed her ID at the uniformed officer standing next to the back door and pushed past him into the kitchen. 'Steve? Matt? Where is it?'

She heard footsteps on the stairs and Barratt appeared in the hallway wearing a white paper overall with the hood up.

'Attic room. SOCOs are busy in the bathroom at the moment so you should be able to have a look. You'll need to cover up. O'Connor's declared it a crime scene.'

Kate struggled into a protective suit, wrestled her sweating hands into rubber gloves and slid paper bootees over her shoes. Next to her, Hollis did the same.

'Shit,' she whispered, as she took in the attic room. 'Bloody hell.'

'Bit of a surprise, eh?' O'Connor smiled at her, but Kate could see the strain in the lines around his eyes and the tightness in his mouth. He'd done a good job in securing the scene and directing the forensic investigation, but he'd have had to make some tough decisions in her absence.

Kate stood in the middle of the floor and turned 360 degrees so she could look at the walls of the room. Each one was covered with paper. News articles about Wallace's arrest – local and national – photographs, maps. Some she recognised – orange tents and pairs of children, stills from the recent reunion, an OS map of part of the Peak District – others obviously had meaning for Angela, but they would need examining and analysing before they made sense to Kate's team.

'What's in there?' she asked, pointing to a wardrobe that took up most of one wall.

O'Connor opened both doors – one was backed by a full-length mirror, the other had more papers tacked to its inside. One half was shelved while the second half had hanging room for clothes. The shelves caught Kate's attention. Boxes and pallets of stage make-up, packets of 'fake facial hair' and two mannequin heads designed to hold wigs. The clothes were nearly all masculine – tracksuits, trousers, a couple of jackets and two beautifully ironed shirts.

'She did costume and make-up for her theatre group,' Kate said. 'One of her colleagues told us. But this is all very specific.' She pulled a baseball cap from one of the shelves and turned it around in her gloved hands, remembering Calvin Russell's description of the young man who'd rented the storage unit where Margaret's body had been hidden.

'We found a butcher's saw in one of the kitchen drawers. Tested positive for blood,' O'Connor said. 'Not sure whether it's human or not.'

'Maybe she'd been butchering her own meat,' Kate offered, her attention still gripped by the contents of the wardrobe

O'Connor shook his head. 'A bit unlikely. It's been bagged and tagged to check for DNA. The SOCOs are swabbing the bathroom and using UV to check for blood in there. It's the most obvious place to cut up a body.'

Kate took a step closer to the wall opposite the dormer window. A section of map had caught her attention. This one wasn't Derbyshire – she recognised the names. It was the Lakes.

She leaned closer and could make a faint line in pencil tracing a route – a route that would have taken a walker to within a few yards of the crags above the spot where Chris Gilruth had been found.

'I can't believe we thought she was in danger when it was her all along,' Kate said.

'It's still all circumstantial at the moment,' O'Connor said. 'Until something turns up that positively links her with any of the murders, this could all be explained away. Maybe she's transgender and figuring out her identity. She likes to walk in the Lakes. She has fond memories of her school trip to Derbyshire.'

'Why do you think she's done all this?' Kate asked. 'Was she another of Whitaker's victims?'

O'Connor shrugged. 'Probably.'

'Then why kill Charlton? And if it was Charlton who abused her, why kill Chris and Margaret? We're missing something.'

Her train of thought was interrupted by a shout from the bathroom. Hollis.

'Kate? You're going to want to see this.'

She dashed down the steep stairs, nearly losing her footing as she reached the bottom step. Hollis was standing just outside the bathroom door.

'Go in and have a look. One of the SOCOs is in there.'

Kate stepped inside and was surprised to find herself in almost total darkness when Hollis closed the door behind her. The small window had been covered with thick black paper and the light was turned off. Kate turned to ask Hollis what the hell was going on when the forensic investigator switched on a UV light source.

'Over there,' he said, splashing violet light across a section of tiles just above the level of the bath.

As the light settled Kate could see quite clearly the silhouette of a hand.

'There's more.'

The light moved, this time to the toilet cistern. Again, on the tiles, was a dark mark which Kate identified as a thumb print.

'And here.'

This time the light was directed at the vinyl flooring next to the bath. Another partial handprint.

'Nice work,' Kate said as she opened the door. So much for Angela butchering her own meat. However, O'Connor was right – until they had DNA evidence, everything else was circumstantial. It *was* very compelling though. The only thing missing in Kate's mind was a clear motive. If Angela was another victim, then why hadn't she simply gone after her abuser? Unless both men had been involved.

Kate's phone rang. Das.

'Ma'am?'

'Just got a report back from the officer sent round to check on David Wallace's house – or are we calling him David Whitaker now? No sign of life. Lights are off. Neighbours haven't seen anything. Downstairs neighbour is out but we'll get some sort of follow-up as soon as she's home.'

'So, we've no idea where he is? Isn't he tagged?'

'No. He'd served his full term. The magistrate didn't think tagging was appropriate, that's why he was given a custodial sentence.'

'Does he have access to a vehicle? Does he have friends or family nearby?'

'Everything's being checked. Nothing so far. There's no vehicle registered in his name and no known family or acquaintance in a ten-mile radius.'

'She's got to him, hasn't she?' Kate said, more to herself than to the DCI.

'Who?'

'Can we force entry into his flat?' Kate asked, already

knowing what the answer would be, but she felt compelled to ask in case Das knew of a loophole or a precedent that Kate hadn't heard of.

'There's nothing to suggest danger to life – he might have been at the shops or the cinema. We'll need a warrant and I doubt we'd be able to get one until tomorrow morning.'

'Then let's do it,' Kate said. It was a long time to wait when somebody's life was in danger but there wasn't much else they could do. And, by tomorrow morning, David Whitaker would be dead – Kate was convinced.

***

I was a bit worried that I'd given him too much chloroform, but he seemed to be breathing quite well and mumbling a bit as though he was just having a nap. I kept holding the rag over his nose and mouth every twenty minutes or so, just to keep him under until I could get him out of there. It was horrible being so close to him, knowing what he'd done. He barely resembled the teacher that I remembered – he'd been so handsome, so full of himself when I was at school, but this man was a shell, broken and hollow. I was glad that his life had turned to crap.

The doorbell rang once, followed by a knock. I gave him another lungful and crept as close to the living room window as I dared. Police car. I wasn't sure whether a nosy neighbour had called them or whether it was something to do with his release conditions, but I just sat tight and waited. They couldn't possibly know that I was here. I'd been staying in a B&B in Rotherham for the past few days, my car in an underground car park in the town centre. They couldn't have pieced it all together and worked out where I was that quickly. I could hear the police officer knocking on other doors and, two short conversations later, he was gone.

It still wasn't quite late enough though, so I amused myself by allowing him to come nearly to consciousness – just enough to realise that his hands were tied and he was in some sort of danger – before putting him under again. I know it was a form of torture, but he deserved it. While he was able to hear me, I kept telling him what he'd done, what he was, and then he'd drift away again for ten or fifteen minutes.

He had no idea who I was or why I was there. But he was going to find out. I waited until it was fully dark before bringing my car round to the front of the block of flats. Then I dragged him to the top of the stairs and let him go. He was weak and floppy from the drug and just slid down, landing in a puddle between the bottom step and the door. It didn't look like it hurt at all – which was disappointing.

The most dangerous part was getting him out to the car, but I'd been watching the cul-de-sac and there was very little activity after around 6pm. Most of the old folk seemed settled by then – not much to do on a grim winter's evening. Even if somebody did see me, by the time they'd called the police I'd be on my way and it would be too late. I hauled him to his feet and opened the door, letting him lean on me but use his legs as I guided him outside. I was whispering that it was all going to be all right, that he was fine, and he seemed to go along with me.

I plonked him in the front seat and fastened the belt around him before driving to the industrial estate on the outskirts of Doncaster. I pulled in behind a warehouse and transferred my passenger to the boot, giving him a hefty hit of chloroform before I started my final journey.

35

The phone rang for what seemed like an eternity before Vicky Rhodes answered. Kate had gone over every possible scenario in her mind and it came back to the solicitor. Why had she threatened to kill Angela Fox? And had she really manipulated her two childhood friends into framing Whitaker? She'd claimed to have planted the seed but was there more to it than that? What, if anything, had she said to Angela at the reunion?

'DI Fletcher,' Vicky said as she answered. She'd obviously stored Kate's number in her phone. Had she been expecting further contact?

'Tell me about Angela Fox,' Kate said, not bothering with a greeting.

'What about her?'

'What happened between the two of you on that camping trip? I know you said your threat to kill her was just a childish expression, but I don't believe you. I have at least one witness who says you were furious and that if you could have got your hands on Angela you may well have carried out your threat.'

A chuckle at the other end. 'I told you. I was angry, but it was just kid's stuff. What's this about, detective inspector?'

Kate ignored the question. 'She did something that links to the abuse that you suffered. I think that you hold her responsible in some way – whether you actually told her that or not.'

'I haven't seen Angela Fox for thirty years. How could I have told her anything?'

'What about the reunion?'

'What about it?'

'Didn't you see Angela there?'

'I've already told you that I didn't.'

Kate didn't believe her. She needed something to link the two women together.

'Okay. You knew Angela when you were children. Did she have any special places that she liked? Somewhere that she might have gone on holiday?'

'We weren't friends. I shared a tent with her for a few nights but that wasn't my choice. How would I know where she went on holiday?'

'Who were her friends? Who did she knock about with?'

A pause on the other end of the line. 'Honestly? I have no idea. She was barely on my radar at school.'

'And yet you hated her enough to threaten to kill her. In a manner that concerned at least one other child. In my experience, that depth of emotion comes from long acquaintance or from a very serious offence against you.'

Silence.

'You have no idea where she might go if she was in trouble?'

'Not a clue,' Vicky said, her tone completely unconcerned.

Kate hung up, half tempted to throw her phone at the wall in frustration. Instead she texted Cooper and told her to ask anybody who was at the reunion for their photographs. If

Rhodes and Fox had met that night, there might be photographic evidence on somebody's phone.

Kate stomped back upstairs to the attic room. 'Barratt, Hollis, get yourselves up here!' The answer might be in this room, somewhere amongst the strange collection of costumes and documents, and she needed her team to help her to find it.

Two sets of footsteps on the stairs preceded the entrance of the two DCs, both clad in protective overalls, gloves and bootees.

'Have a good look at all this crap,' Kate snapped. 'The answer's here somewhere. Where has Angela Fox taken Whitaker?'

Barratt scanned the wall opposite the window while Hollis contemplated the contents of the wardrobe. O'Connor, standing at the top of the stairs, seemed to have found something interesting on his phone.

'What about the school?' Barratt suggested. 'It's where we found Charlton.'

'Not sure she'd use the same location twice,' Kate said. 'But it's worth a look.' The thought had already occurred to her, but it didn't feel right.

'How do we know she's not at Whitaker's flat?' Hollis asked.

'We don't. But we can't knock the door down without something more concrete than a hunch. I've asked Das to hunt down a warrant for the morning.'

'We need to go back to the past,' O'Connor said, pointing at the pictures from the camping trip. 'Everything started on that trip and the reunion was some sort of catalyst. If she was abused by Whitaker and/or Charlton, why wait thirty years to exact her revenge? She either saw somebody or something was said to spark this off.'

'Like Bradley and Grieveson,' Kate said. 'Rhodes planted a seed and they ran with it and got Whitaker put away.'

'You think Vicky Rhodes might be behind this as well?' Barratt asked, his tone doubtful.

'Not a clue,' Kate said. 'Rhodes claims that there was no contact between herself and Fox at the reunion. We have no evidence to the contrary. Come on, what do we know about Angela Fox? What do her friends and colleagues say?'

'Quiet?' Hollis suggested. 'We know she liked theatre but only behind the scenes. She chose isolated locations for her holidays. I got the impression that Dylan felt a bit sorry for her.'

'Loner,' Barratt added. 'Nobody close to her. Maybe childhood abuse has prevented her from forming relationships – she might find it hard to trust people. That's not uncommon. This could be revenge for what Whitaker did to her. We could include Charlton in that as well – the ritualistic elements of his murder suggest retribution,' Barratt suggested. 'Maybe she was Whitaker's victim, but she knew that Charlton had assaulted one or more of her friends. Or vice versa.'

'But why would she do that? Why would she kill as revenge for somebody *else's* abuse?' Kate asked, trying to create a scenario where Barratt's suggestion made sense.

'She might just see Whitaker and Charlton as guilty of the same thing if she and her friends were hurt at the same time.'

'Which brings us back to why *now*? There's something else. Something that we're missing. And we still don't know where she's taken Whitaker.'

Blank looks from the two DCs.

'O'Connor, will you put your bloody phone down? We could do with your input here.'

The DS gave Kate a lazy grin and held up his phone. 'Millers Dale Bridge. You can still do abseiling from the top. It's close to where the kids camped, and we know that they went here. Didn't you say that the other teacher got injured there and had to go to the hospital? We keep saying that everything leads back to that camping trip – then I think that's where she might have taken him.'

Kate looked at the papers Sellotaped to the walls around her. The pictures of happy kids, the map of part of Derbyshire and the image of the bridge. It did make a certain sense that Angela would finish this where it had started.

'Right, Matt, to the school. Take a couple of uniforms with you. Dan, Steve, you're coming with me to Derbyshire. I'll call the local DCI or chief super or anybody else who can get us some warm bodies on that bridge. If we're wrong, I want you both there to share the embarrassment – this was your call, Steve.'

'And if I'm right?' O'Connor asked, already halfway down the stairs.

'I owe you a pint,' Kate said. 'Maybe even two.'

36

I t was nearly 10pm when Kate and Hollis pulled up in the Millers Dale car park. A full moon was high in the sky illuminating a section of the Monsal Trail – a former railway which had been converted into a popular hiking and cycling route. Kate had contacted Derbyshire Police and they had confirmed that a dark blue Citroen C4 had been spotted nearby – carefully parked and unoccupied. Just before they'd turned off the A623, ten minutes previously, another phone call had confirmed that there were two figures on Millers Dale Bridge. Kate had advised caution but knew that she and Hollis might arrive too late to intervene.

Hollis leapt out of the car as soon as he'd put on the handbrake, shrugging himself into a padded high-vis jacket. Kate did the same. O'Connor was somewhere behind them – having been held up at traffic lights somewhere round Sheffield – but Kate couldn't wait for him. David Whitaker might be dead already.

'Which way?' Hollis asked, switching on his torch and playing the light across the grey gravel of the parking area, catching the reflective markings on two police cars parked either side of a dark hatchback.

Kate tried to remember the map she'd studied as they'd sped through the Derbyshire countryside. 'Left past the old station and left again onto the trail. The bridge is a couple of hundred yards further up.'

They'd only gone a few steps when a figure seemed to materialise out of the darkness.

'DI Fletcher?' The deep voice indicated a male, but Kate couldn't see beyond the blinding beam of his high-intensity torch.

'Who's asking?'

'PC Ollie Gould. I've been told to wait here. They're expecting you.'

'They?'

'DI Sophia Hall and a uniformed sergeant – Damian Leese, I think. They've got eyes on the suspect and another person – male, sixties or seventies, slight build.'

It sounded like Fox had managed to get Whitaker out onto the bridge.

'Advice is to approach with caution.'

Kate managed to refrain from telling the PC that he was simply repeating her own advice back to her and set off past him at a slow jog. Hollis switched off his torch as they reached the flat expanse of the disused railway. The surface was the same fine, grey gravel as the car park and the moonlight lit up every dip and puddle. Ahead, Kate could see high-powered torch beams and a collection of silhouettes, but she couldn't make out who was who. She slowed to a steady walk, Hollis falling into step beside her, and squinted against the harsh lights, trying to add detail to the shapes in the darkness. She could clearly make out a tall female and a male in high-vis about fifty yards ahead of her but the people at the edge of the trail were a complex mix of shadow and dark clothing.

A beam of light suddenly flicked towards Kate and Hollis.

'Who's that?' The woman's voice was authoritative, leaving no room for hesitation.

'DI Kate Fletcher, DC Dan Hollis – South Yorkshire Police. I'm the one who called this in,' Kate said, slowing her pace further as she moved closer to the other two police officers. For a few seconds all she could hear was her own laboured breathing and the crunch of gravel as she and Hollis approached their Derbyshire colleagues.

'What's happening?' Kate asked as she got closer.

'Hard to say,' the woman – Hall – answered. As she trained the torch on the two people on the bridge, Kate was able to get a closer look at her counterpart. Tall, probably close to six feet and dressed in dark clothes, she was a formidable figure. Short dark hair topped a pale face which was half swaddled in a thick scarf that snuggled beneath the collar of a high-vis jacket like the ones Kate and Hollis wore. 'There's a man and woman out on the bridge. The man is tied up in some way and he's on the wrong side of the railings. Looks to me like the woman hauled the man over and then tied his hands to the top rail.'

'Have you spoken to either of them?'

'They know we're here, that's about it. The woman warned us to keep away. I think she was tying the rope when we arrived but it's hard to be sure.'

'Whoa, something's happening,' the sergeant said, straightening his torch. Kate looked across to the edge of the bridge, straining to make out any details in the darkness. The two figures were suddenly lit up sharply as Hollis lifted his torch to add to the illumination.

'That better?' he asked. Kate gave him a nod that he wouldn't be able to see as she concentrated on Angela Fox and David Whitaker. With the extra light it was easier to see what Fox had done. She'd got Whitaker over the railings and had tied his bound hands to the top rail with nylon climbing rope that flickered in the light, obviously run through with some kind of reflective thread. There seemed to be a narrow parapet below the iron work, on which Whitaker was standing, his body leaning forwards. The only thing stopping him from toppling to his probable death was the rope around his hands.

'What's below the bridge?' Kate asked Hall.

'The river. It's shallow and not very wide.'

'How much of a drop?'

'Eighty feet. I've got people down there.'

Eighty feet. Enough for serious injury but not certain death. What was Fox up to?

'Stay back!' Fox was holding something in the air, waving it above her head. It caught the light, arcing white beams up into the night sky. A knife.

Hall immediately lifted her airwave radio. The weapon changed things. If the suspect was armed, they were all in danger and Kate knew that Hall had no choice. She listened as the Derbyshire DI requested backup from an authorised firearms officer. But how long would that take? Kate's training and instincts were screaming at her to do anything possible to prevent the loss of David Whitaker's life and she knew that the time to act may have already passed. She shouted to Hollis to send O'Connor into position with the police officers below the bridge and then took a deep breath.

'Angela?' Kate stepped towards the two figures.

'What the fuck, Fletcher?' Hall hissed. Kate ignored her and took another step forward.

'Angela, my name's Kate. I'm with the police. Can we talk?'

Kate could make out some kind of movement and, for a split second, she thought she'd misjudged the situation. Then a torch beam caught Fox and Whitaker full on and Kate understood what the ropes and the knife meant. Whitaker had rope round his wrists and his neck. One swipe from Fox's blade and she'd cut through the bindings on his hands, leaving the man to plummet to the length of the rope and hang. There was no way he'd be able to manoeuvre his arms so that he could cling on to the railings behind him. Even if that were a possibility, he looked woozy, as though he'd been drugged.

'Angela,' Kate tried again. 'You don't need to do this. Just talk to me.'

'Go away.'

It was a start. Fox had acknowledged Kate's presence; had engaged with her.

'We've been looking for you, Angela. We're here to help.'

'Go away. You can't help.'

'Angela, I know who he is. I know what he did. This isn't the way. We can prosecute him. There are always historic abuse cases coming to light. He'll pay for what he did to you.'

A flash of light as the blade moved.

'What he did to me?'

'We know that David Whitaker is a paedophile. We know he assaulted some of your classmates on a school trip. They've spoken out. You can do the same.'

'You have no idea.' The tone had changed. Fox was sullen, sarcastic. 'He did nothing to me. David Whitaker never touched me.'

Kate was confused. She'd been convinced that Fox was another of Whitaker's victims hence the attempt to destroy his entire family. Was it Charlton then?

'What happened, Angela? Tell me what happened on that trip. You can trust me. If you kill him, you'll spend a long time in jail but if you show some mercy it will go in your favour.' Kate was making it up as she went along but she could see that the knife was close to Whitaker's hands again.

'I don't care,' the other woman said. 'It doesn't matter what happens to me. It's all my fault. I deserve everything that's coming to me. I destroyed their lives.'

'Whose lives? Whose lives did you destroy, Angela?'

Silence. At first Kate thought that Fox wasn't going to answer but then she heard a loud sniff. She was crying.

'Angela?'

'It's all my fault and I don't know what to do anymore. If I can do this last thing then it might put things right.'

'What things?'

'It's my fault he hurt them.'

'Who? Who did he hurt?' Kate knew the answer, but she was desperate to keep Angela talking; to keep the knife away from Whitaker.

'Vicky and Lee. I was there. I saw what happened. I saw what Whitaker and Charlton were doing. They were just little kids. How could they do that to little kids?'

Kate kept quiet, willing Angela to fill the silence.

'I told Mr Whitaker what they were planning. I didn't think they should be wandering around the campsite at night, so I told. And then they got caught and those men... those men attacked them. It's my fault. I've had to live with this for thirty years. But no more. It's nearly over.'

Suddenly it all made sense. Angela Fox wasn't a victim; she felt that she'd been complicit in the abuse. But why act now? The answer was obvious. The reunion. It had sparked her memories and fed her guilt until she couldn't bear it any longer.

Kate heard a car close by and then footsteps on the gravel track, but she didn't dare turn round. If she lost Fox's attention now Whitaker would die – she was certain.

'Angela,' she tried again, ignoring the metallic voice on the radio behind her. 'Angela, what happened isn't your fault. Men like this don't do these things on the spur of the moment. They're meticulous. They plan. Nothing you did would have changed the outcome.'

She could make out Angela's face, pale in the torchlight as she nodded. 'I thought that, for a long time. I told myself that what I did wasn't the root cause of the abuse. But it's not true. I know it's my fault and I'm prepared to face the consequences. I have to put this right – for them. For Lee and Vicky.'

'I've spoken to Vicky,' Kate said. 'She doesn't blame you. She didn't even mention you. She has a good life. She's moved on. You don't have to do this.'

'DI Fletcher!' Hall's voice. Kate closed her eyes, willing her to hold on for a few more seconds. 'DI Fletcher, there is an authorised firearms officer next to me. Please inform the suspect that she is in the line of fire.'

'The suspect heard it for herself,' Angela Fox shouted back, her voice defiant. 'And the suspect doesn't care.'

A blur of movement and then there was a single figure on the bridge. Kate took a step forwards as Angela Fox fell to her knees, hands entwined across the top of her head in surrender. But Whitaker was gone.

Kate rushed to the railings where the climbing rope strained against the weight of the body on the other end. Grabbing a handful, Kate pulled, desperately trying to haul Whitaker back to the bridge. Shouts from below, one of them sounded like O'Connor. There were other police officers down there, obviously waiting in case the rope wasn't tied properly or something else happened to cause Whitaker to fall unchecked.

And then she saw him, like a child's swing in a light breeze, swaying lazily left to right, midway between the bridge and the black ribbon of the river.

There would be no rescue for David Whitaker.

37

Kate scanned the wine list, trying to decide if she actually wanted a drink. She'd chosen the restaurant – central, fairly intimate but usually quite busy – in the hope that a neutral setting would allow the space that she and Nick needed to work out if their relationship was worth saving. Now, waiting for him to appear, Kate knew that she'd overreacted to his comments and that asking him to leave had been an uncharacteristically extreme reaction. She missed him. It was so simple that to consider breaking up seemed ridiculous and totally unnecessary. But she had no idea how Nick felt.

A waiter hovered expectantly, so Kate caved in and ordered a glass of red – she could always put it to one side until Nick arrived. She was good at putting things to one side. Wasn't that what she'd been doing with Nick while she'd been dealing with the Angela Fox case? But now Fox had been charged, Kate felt the need to sort out her personal life.

Wrapping up the details of a case was often as tiring as trying to solve it in the first place. Fox had confessed to four murders; Chris Gilruth, Margaret Wallace, Simon Charlton and

David Wallace. She claimed that she'd been acting of her own volition and hadn't been coerced by anybody.

Nearly everything she told them could be evidenced. She'd attended the reunion and seen Bradley, Grieveson and Rhodes together, and their meeting had tapped into her guilt. She'd witnessed the assaults on Rhodes and Bradley, but she wasn't aware that Grieveson had also been a victim. She had access to hospital records which showed that Margaret Whitaker had had a male child and she'd eventually worked out, through her research into the family, that Margaret had given the baby to her sister.

Her IT skills had also enabled her to use her NHS access to break into the records of the nursing home and change Margaret's next of kin information. She also found it relatively easy to track down Simon Charlton. It all made so much sense. Angela's experience with costume and make-up with her theatre group made disguising herself a simple task.

There were only two things which still niggled in Kate's mind.

Firstly, a thorough search of Fox's premises had failed to reveal any computer equipment. The woman claimed to have done all her research at work using the NHS computer system – and she said she'd then covered her tracks. Kate wasn't convinced. There was a tablet or laptop somewhere with more evidence on it. What Kate didn't understand was why Fox wanted to hide it. She'd confessed to everything.

The second niggle concerned Vicky Rhodes. Angela had named her former classmate as her solicitor. Kate had no idea why Fox thought that a property lawyer who lived in Spain would be a good choice to help her to negotiate the British criminal justice system, but she'd been visibly devastated when Rhodes had refused to help. Sam hadn't been able to place them together at the reunion, but Kate was certain that something had happened between the two women, though both denied it vehemently. Despite Angela's Fox's full confession, Kate felt there was still more digging to be done.

'Hey, you've started without me.'

Kate looked up into Nick's deep brown eyes as he smiled down at her.

'I didn't know what you'd want to drink, sorry.'

'No problem,' he said as he pulled out the chair opposite and sat down. He'd made an effort with his appearance, Kate noted. Jeans and a suit jacket over a pale blue shirt with an open collar – very much the off-duty consultant. And very attractive.

'You're going to stay then?' she asked.

'Yep. I'm starving. No moussaka on the menu?'

Kate's stomach lurched as she remembered the last time she'd seen him, and the awful things she'd said. 'Nick, I'm so sorry I yelled at you. I was so stressed and Das had just kicked me off my own case.'

He stared at the menu, his lips tight.

Kate carried on, 'And I'm sorry that I accused you of having no right to ask me about my past.'

Still no response. This wasn't going as planned.

'Nick, say something. Can we get past this?'

He slowly raised his eyes to hers. 'I don't know. It's not what you said about your past, I get that. And it's not the yelling that hurts.'

He was struggling to keep a smile from his lips – there was a joke coming. Kate's stomach unknotted.

'But you insulted my cooking. You called it,' he lowered his voice, '*fucking* moussaka. It's my speciality. It's a family recipe. How could you dismiss it so easily?'

He was grinning fully. 'Look, I know you get stressed and I probably shouldn't have pushed you. And I accept that you over-reacted, Kate. But there are still things we don't know about each other and some of those might be surprising. If we're going to move forward, we have to acknowledge that and be prepared. And you need to talk to me. I know you've been busy, but a couple of texts isn't really communicating.'

He was right. Kate knew that she was in the wrong – that she was the one to blame – and she felt a wave of gratitude that Nick had turned up.

'Can we start again?' she asked.

Nick nodded. 'We can. Maybe one day I'll even let you taste my moussaka.'

'Are you talking dirty to me in the middle of an Italian restaurant?'

'Not yet. But give it time.'

Kate smiled and picked up her menu. 'I think I'll stick to lasagne this evening. It's probably safer.'

EPILOGUE

Vicky Rhodes took another sip of her drink and lit a cigarette. She never got tired of the view from her balcony; the street below, busy even at this time of night, the stunted palm trees and then the sea. How often had she sat here watching the ships unloading their cargoes of goods and passengers? She loved this city: loved this life. And now, for the first time, she felt truly safe. The scars of her past still lurked in her mind and beneath the long sleeves that covered her arms whatever the weather, but she already felt more able to cope, more centred.

Angela's call had been an annoyance but fully expected and she'd felt no guilt for refusing to help. There was nothing she could do anyway – it wasn't her field of expertise and she hadn't practised law in the UK for years. But Angela hadn't known that and had believed Vicky when she'd promised to help when it was all over. She'd believed so much of what Vicky had said. When they'd met up after the reunion, Angela had been tearful from the start but, when Vicky had shown her scarred arms and explained how awful Lee and Neil's lives were, the woman had been barely consolable. Her state of mind had made for easy manipulation.

A green bus sped along the street below, heading out of town. That's what Vicky wanted to do next. To get out of town for a few days, maybe head for the mountains or the west coast. Somewhere quiet where she could reflect; and celebrate.

Behind her, in the living room, her laptop beeped to indicate that it had completed a factory reset and had reformatted the hard disc. Tomorrow, Vicky would take it apart and destroy the disc drive. She knew that Angela would have done the same – following instructions once again. She'd be willing to bet a large amount of money that Angela's laptop was gently sinking into the mud at the bottom of Tickhill duck pond. It had been a throwaway suggestion but one that she felt sure Angela would have taken to heart.

Vicky picked up the thin pile of papers from where she'd placed them on the table next to the ashtray. They were all that was left. The only evidence. She hadn't been able to resist printing the e-mails out for one last read but now it was time to destroy them. She flicked her lighter and studied the flame as it danced in the gentle breeze that blew in off the Atlantic. The words at the top of the page caught her attention for the last time. Such a chatty tone for such a serious matter.

'Do you know how difficult it is to cut up a body? I had no idea. The drugs were the simple part – I'd just...' The flame caught the bottom of the page and quickly the words were consumed by the fire. Vicky dropped papers to the tiled floor of the balcony and watched until the flames died away.

The mountains. She would definitely go to the mountains.

ACKNOWLEDGEMENTS

As always, thanks to all the Bloodhound team for their continued faith in my writing and for everything they do to help promote my books. Thanks once again to Clare for the edit – especially for spotting the infestation of Alans! I'm also grateful to the other Bloodhound authors for their encouragement and general banter.

A massive thank you to everybody who has bought and read the first three books in the series – it's wonderful to know that Kate has something of a following.

I'd also like to acknowledge all the online book groups and bloggers who do an incredible job in helping to publicise authors.

Writing can be quite a solitary occupation, so I'd also like to thank members of the dog-walking community in Stanwix who always seem to have time for a natter when I need to get out and clear my head for an hour or so.

And thanks to Viv for time, encouragement, support and much-needed coffee breaks.

Printed in Great Britain
by Amazon

37861359R00163